DEAD
INSIDE

Noelle Holten is an award-winning blogger at www.crime-bookjunkie.co.uk. She is the PR & Social Media Manager for Bookouture, a leading digital publisher in the UK, and a regular reviewer on the Two Crime Writers and a Microphone podcast. Noelle worked as a Senior Probation Officer for eighteen years, covering cases of domestic violence and abuse. She has three Hons BA's – Philosophy, Sociology (Crime & Deviance) and Community Justice – and a Masters in Criminology. *Dead Inside* is her debut novel and the start of a new series featuring DC Maggie Jamieson.

 @nholten40
www.crimebookjunkie.co.uk

DEAD INSIDE

noelle holten

KILLER ~~READS~~

A division of HarperCollins*Publishers*
www.harpercollins.co.uk

KillerReads
an imprint of HarperCollins*Publishers* Ltd
1 London Bridge Street
London SE1 9GF

www.harpercollins.co.uk

This paperback edition 2019

First published in Great Britain in ebook format
by HarperCollins*Publishers* 2019

Noelle Holten asserts the moral right to
be identified as the author of this work

A catalogue record for this book
is available from the British Library

ISBN: 978-0-00-833224-2

This novel is entirely a work of fiction.
The names, characters and incidents portrayed in it are
the work of the author's imagination. Any resemblance to
actual persons, living or dead, events or localities is
entirely coincidental.

Set in Minion by
Palimpsest Book Production Limited, Falkirk, Stirlingshire

Printed and bound by CPI Group (UK) Ltd, Croydon, CR0 4YY

MIX
Paper from
responsible sources
FSC
www.fsc.org   FSC® C007454

To Buster (aka #TheBear) – my sounding board, best friend, soul mate and saviour.
Missing you every-single-day.

PROLOGUE

The crash at the bottom of the stairs woke me instantly.

I could see the smallest sliver of light peering underneath the door. The rest of the bedroom was in complete darkness.

I froze.

Should I get up and check on Siobhan? But, I knew if she had woken up, she would tap her fingers on her headboard like she always did, to let us know she was awake.

No tapping.

I didn't want to move. I couldn't, I was paralyzed with fear. I had always accepted the verbal abuse that was thrown at me. I could take that. It was the physical abuse that filled me with shame. I couldn't help but shudder in dread as he stumbled his way up the stairs. I pretended to be asleep, but my heart raced faster with the sound of every footstep. My fear of him weighed me down, suffocated me, and pinned me to the bed.

We had two years of bliss before he proposed to me.

Two years of living normal, happy lives.

What happened?

Six months into the marriage, I realized I'd sealed my fate when I'd said, 'I do'.

Ten years later, and the regrets were mounting.

Who would have thought that two little words would have given me such a long sentence?

Why me? What did I do to deserve this?

The bedroom door creaked open slowly. That's what he did. Let me know he was coming, then built on my terror by taking his time to enter the bedroom.

I could hear his breathing as he stood there, his eyes bearing down on me. I tried to keep as still as possible. I wanted to disappear, sink deep down into the depths of the mattress where it was safe.

The foul stench of alcohol filled the room, stinging my eyes, and threatening to choke me.

Oh God! Please let him just ignore me tonight.

The dull thud from the change in his pocket startled me, as his clothing fell piece by piece to the floor.

I can't take this anymore.

I wanted to shout but couldn't wake up Siobhan.

He crawled in beside me. Hot, smelly breath burned at my neck, making me cringe. I couldn't stand him anywhere near me.

In my mind, I was screaming, *get away please just leave me the fuck alone!* But not a sound escaped my lips.

He put one of his rough, calloused hands under my oversized T-shirt, his fingers icy to the touch. I shivered, not because his hand was cold, but because I knew what would happen if I said no.

He wrapped his arm around my neck, pulled me closer. Tight, uncaring and rough, until he was almost choking me.

'Please … don't.' There was a whimper in my voice.

Sometimes, my weakness made me sick.

'I want you.'

'I have to work in the morning, Patrick. Please … don't.'

He shoved his hand between my legs. Not gentle or loving, but forceful.

Through gritted teeth he snarled, 'I don't care. I. Want. You.'

'Please. Think of Siobhan. You'll wake her.'

I remember tears flowing down my face like a waterfall. Like they'd never stop. I squeezed my eyes shut and tried to think of something else.

Anything else. *Anything would be better than this.*

I was dead inside, numb to it all, even as I tried to remember the happier times.

When I thought he loved me.

When I loved him.

That night was the first time my husband raped me.

The look in his eyes when he finished and cast me aside told me it wouldn't be the last.

CHAPTER ONE

With only a few hours left in his shift, Amit was itching for a break. He saw Beacon Park up ahead and, as the moon reflected brightly off the bonnet of his black cab, he pulled up at the kerb and turned off his engine. It was nearly 4 a.m.

He stretched his arms and the twinge in his leg told him he needed to get out before they cramped up. He opened the door and felt the chill in the air. Reaching over to the passenger seat, he grabbed his jacket and stepped out of his car. It was so quiet. Not a person in sight, but as it wasn't the best area in Markston, he made sure to lock his door before heading to the park entrance.

Amit stood by the gate and debated whether to have a quick walk down the path. The lamps were few and far between, thanks to the bloody council. He pulled the collar of his jacket up to keep his neck warm and started walking. A gust of wind blew a plastic bag in front of him and made him jump. He shook his head, looked over his shoulder. Laughed to himself.

In the distance, he could see something in the middle of the path – a large lump was blocking the way. He took out his mobile phone and searched for the flashlight app. Turning it on, he held the phone in front of him and saw that it was a person, lying flat on their back. *Probably some drunk passed out after a few too many.* Could be a potential fare if he played his cards right.

'Hey! Are you OK?' He waited for a response. Kept waiting. After a minute or so he decided to approach. They may have hit their head when they fell backwards. The clothing indicated that it was probably a man and, as he got closer, he noticed something wet on the ground. *He must have been sick.* The man's arms were splayed out beside him, like he was rejoicing in the glory of his drunkenness.

Amit wasn't prepared for the sight that met his eyes and he could feel the bile rise in his throat. *Oh Christ!*

The man was not sleeping – though Amit wasn't sure if he was alive or dead. He shone the flashlight over his chest and couldn't see it rising. It was then that he spotted the slash across his throat and realized that it wasn't puke oozing beneath the man's head – it was blood. He jumped back. *Shit. Shit. Shhhhhhhit.*

Hands shaking, he ran back along the path. Punched in 999 on his mobile and raised the phone to his ear. Time stood still as he stopped running, heaving in a breath. Heard the phone ring once, twice and finally an answer.

'Uh … hell … hello? Yes, police p-p-please. I've found a body.'

His phone fell from his shaking hands and the contents of his dinner emptied on to the grass.

CHAPTER TWO

Lucy came downstairs and looked at Patrick. He was slumped in the chair with his hand wrapped around a can of lager and – for one appalling moment – Lucy hoped he was dead. She shook the thought from her head in disgust and focused instead on her busy morning. He was supposed to take Siobhan to school. Lucy told him last night that she had an early meeting with one of her offenders. She sighed.

Getting angry at Patrick was a waste of energy – it never achieved anything. With her parents and sister coming to dinner later, Lucy could do without anymore stress. All she wanted was for Patrick to be semi-sober and civil. Not too much to ask, or so she thought.

Seeing Patrick now, Lucy couldn't explain what had drawn her to him in the first place. She supposed it was the usual things – cheeky smile, piercing eyes, and a charismatic personality. But it was what he was like behind closed doors that scared her. As a probation officer, Lucy knew all the signs – the *I'm sorrys, it won't happen again; I love you so much* … the list of excuses was long and never-ending. Despite this, she still found herself unable to leave.

Lucy left the room and walked back upstairs, pushing Siobhan's bedroom door open. She looked over at the bed and paused.

Social services had placed Siobhan in the care of Patrick, giving Lucy temporary special guardianship. The court battles were expensive and emotionally hard to endure, but Lucy wouldn't have changed a thing. She loved Siobhan as her own.

Lucy tiptoed inside and shut the door behind her, looking around at the room. The pink walls and plush carpet were Siobhan's choice, and matched her duvet perfectly. Her eyes fell on a photo of Siobhan's grandparents, standing outside their house.

Ten-year-old Siobhan still had supervised contact with Becky Parks, her mother. She would spend most weekends at her maternal grandparent's house, where Becky could go and visit. Lucy was fortunate to have forged a reasonably good relationship with Becky's parents, Ed and Maria Parks. Although it was initially strained, they seemed to understand why their daughter needed to be kept away from solely raising Siobhan.

Lucy made excuses for herself. Reasons why she stayed, because to believe that she'd allow this to happen to herself was incomprehensible. Taking on Patrick's daughter played a large part in Lucy staying in the relationship. Siobhan was the result of Patrick's toxic past with Becky Parks – an alcoholic and pretty vile creature-of-a-woman, whose voice could send a shiver down your spine. But it wasn't all bad; there were some good days with Patrick, when the house was filled with laughter, and Lucy even felt a little bit of love. She knew that things weren't perfect, but she had made the decision to stay, so now she just had to deal with it.

Lucy crouched down next to the bed and gently pulled back the covers. 'Siobhan, wake up, sleepyhead! Daddy is poorly, so I'm taking you to school today, OK?'

Siobhan rustled in her bed. 'OK.'

Lucy headed back to her own room to get ready for work, knowing Siobhan could get dressed without any fuss. Lucy planned on leaving Patrick a note to remind him about their dinner plans. Picking up her mobile, she texted Sarah Hardy, her friend and colleague at Markston Probation, to let her know she was on her way.

Lucy looked in the mirror and stopped. She nearly cried, something that was becoming a bit of a habit. Once silky, her hair was now a greasy mess – always pulled back in a bun or ponytail. Eyes that previously held a mischievous sparkle, were dull and puffy. Looking herself up and down, she saw an overweight, frumpy woman who chose oversized jumpers and cheap trousers to hide her body and make herself less attractive.

Lucy was finally beginning to realize that she had gradually cocooned herself in a protective shell. Withdrawn from friends, family, and neighbours, she had become someone she no longer recognized – or liked. Although she remained happy and assertive at work, at home – she glanced again in the mirror – she had become *this* person.

Snapping out of self-pity mode, Lucy knew she needed to get a move on, and Sarah would only cover for so long. Lucy had a supervision session booked for 9:00 a.m. and she hated being late – it didn't set a good example for those she supervised, especially when she was constantly reminding them they were breaching the conditions of their order or licence if they didn't show up on time.

After dropping Siobhan off at school, she arrived at the office with twenty minutes to spare. She rushed past Sarah, thanked her, and threw her coat over her chair. She logged into her computer and opened up her emails.

'Everything OK, Lucy?'

She gave Sarah a thumbs up and hoped she wouldn't ask anymore questions. She noticed a red-flagged email identifying a 'Transfer from an Out of Area Probation Office' waiting for a response. It would have to wait a little longer, because her desk phone buzzed to announce the arrival of her first appointment of the day. Lucy gathered her notes, made her way to the printer, and picked up the warning letter she had just printed off for Robert Millard. Taking a deep breath, she headed for reception.

Robert wasn't going to be happy today, in fact, his mood may end up being worse than hers.

CHAPTER THREE

DC Maggie Jamieson woke with a start, drenched in sweat. The nightmares had been happening more frequently now, even though she knew Bill Raven was safely behind bars. Bill Raven, also known as The Chopper thanks to the creativity of the news media, was convicted on his confession alone. Three missing women brutally butchered, their body parts strewn across unknown locations in Staffordshire and the surrounding areas. Maggie shuddered and threw back the covers.

After his confession, forensics used luminol in Raven's flat and had found a huge amount of blood, covering the floor, walls, and bathtub. However, the bleach and other industrial cleaners he'd used had deteriorated the samples so that they couldn't state, with one hundred per cent accuracy, who it had belonged to, whether it was more than one person or if it was even human. The police had had to go by what Raven had told them during interviews and match his statement to those women reported missing at the time. Fortunately for the police The Chopper was so concerned with infamy that he gave them full disclosure of his gruesome crimes.

Raven's roommate, Adrian Harrison, was also questioned during the initial investigation. Both men were as odd as each other in Maggie's opinion but, despite her gut feeling, the evidence had all pointed at Raven and eventually he confessed, leaving Adrian in the clear.

Maggie had learnt recently that Raven had suffered a breakdown following his sentence and was currently on a hospital order until the doctors deemed him fit to return to prison.

She sat up and ran her fingers through her knotted hair. She groaned; it was only 5:30 a.m. and way too early to head in to work. Although she was keen to start her new post with the Domestic Abuse and Homicide Unit – or DAHU – she didn't want to appear overeager or tire herself out before the day had even begun. Maggie still cringed at the use of the word 'homicide'. When she had queried it with her boss, DI Abigail Rutherford, she'd been advised that as homicide covers the offences of murder, manslaughter, and infanticide, the Police and Crime Commissioner, or PCC, was keen to use it to describe the newly formed team.

Hearing the patter of tiny feet across the laminate flooring, Maggie looked down to find Scrappy staring up at her. A big meow made her laugh and she picked him up for a cuddle. Now that Scrappy knew she was awake, there was no way his belly was going to let her get another twenty minutes under the covers.

'OK, cat, let's go get you some brekkie.'

Maggie put Scrappy down, grabbed the sweatshirt she'd thrown on the floor last night, and pulled it over her head. With Scrappy leading the way, she headed into the kitchen and flicked on the kettle.

'Coffee first, Scrappy-boy, or I'm going to be grumpier than usual today!'

Once she'd sorted the cat out, Maggie sat down at the breakfast bar and turned on her iPad to browse the news. She had this fear that Bill Raven would try to gain more notoriety with a story and she'd be pulled back into something that she was desperately trying to forget. The case was officially closed based on his confession, but if more bodies were discovered and linked to him,

Maggie could find herself back with the Major and Organised Crime Department, or murder team as she preferred to call it. Maggie hated labels – keep things simple was her motto. She let Scrappy out and started to get ready. She had enough struggles of her own to worry about without repeatedly going over Raven's case in her head. The best thing about starting with a new team was the chance to move forward and leave the past behind.

After a quick shower, Maggie donned her usual black trouser suit and white blouse, opting for her low-heeled court shoes in case the day entailed any physical activity. She looked at herself in the mirror.

'That's as good as it gets.'

Not really one for a lot of make-up or accessories when it came to work, Maggie pulled her shoulder-length, auburn hair back into a loose ponytail and straightened her collar.

She grabbed her coat from the hook by the door and headed out.

OK, DAHU – let's see what you have in store for me.

CHAPTER FOUR

Robert Millard was what was known in the criminal justice arena as a domestic abuse perpetrator. Each agency used a lot of different acronyms, which Lucy found hard to keep track of at the best of times.

She was currently supervising Robert on a two-year suspended sentence order, after a judge felt his years of sustained abuse against his estranged wife more than warranted the threat of custody if he breached the imposed requirements. Robert's wife, Louise, was also granted an indefinite restraining order – which meant that he could have no contact with her unless it was removed.

Lucy made her way to the reception area and called out for Robert. He looked exhausted and unkempt as he dragged his feet and followed her into the interview room designated for the riskier, more volatile offenders. Pointing at the chair across from her, Lucy asked Robert to sit down.

'Why are we in here? We usually go upstairs.'

She could feel the paranoia and edginess emanating from him as she asked him again to sit down; the last thing she wanted was for Robert to be standing up when she confronted him with the information she now had. She waited as he pulled the chair out and sat down.

'Do you want to tell me what happened the other night, Robert?' Lucy had learnt over the years that if she gave her offenders the opportunity to come clean, they were less likely to lash out when challenged. She had been supervising Robert on and off for three years now and wanted him to be the one to tell her. This would also give her a better idea of where his risk status was at.

Robert's face darkened. He clenched his fists tight and his eyes began to glaze over. Suddenly he snapped.

'Who the fuck do you think you are, you fucking bitch?' The spittle from his lips hit Lucy's face like toxic raindrops. Grabbing a tissue from the drawer, Lucy wiped her face without losing eye contact with Robert. She'd not let him get the better of her.

Lucy raised her hands to her ears to lessen the painful sound of metal screeching as Robert pushed back his chair. He leapt towards the wall and Lucy cringed when she heard the crack of his knuckle as flesh met concrete.

'You're ruining my life! All you bitches are the same.'

Robert obviously wasn't going to be forthcoming about the other night. Her hand hovered over the alarm button beneath the desk. Lucy glanced at the camera in the corner and was grateful that reception would be watching. Punching the wall was meant to intimidate her, but she wasn't impressed. Robert paced the small room then grabbed the back of his chair.

'Now what the fuck is going to happen to me?'

Lucy waited for his breathing to return to normal. 'Are you through then, Robert?' She let the question hang in the air and watched as he calmed down. He nodded his head.

'Then take a seat and I'll explain everything.'

Robert reluctantly sat down again, his eyes blazing. She could tell he wasn't going to trust a word she said, and she prepared herself for another angry outburst.

'Robert, you broke the conditions of your restraining order. That means, you also broke the requirements. What did you think was going to happen?' Somehow she kept her voice icily calm.

'She asked me to come over. Why am I the one getting into trouble?' He almost sounded like a spoiled child.

'You know why, Robert. I told you this. You signed the paperwork and said you understood what you were signing. Let's not kid ourselves here: this is not the first order you've been on.' Lucy cocked her head to the left and raised her eyebrows knowingly. 'I explained to you that even if your ex-partner made contact, you were not to reply. Ignoring those instructions, you went to her house; you were drunk, you got angry, and you smashed a window—'

'Oh, for fuck's sake! She wound me up. She was drunk too. Rubbing it in my face that she has a new boyfriend that treats her better – fucking slag. How did she think I was going to react? I didn't even touch her.'

This wasn't the first time Lucy had heard this story. Day in and day out, it was always the same. Always someone else's fault; always the alcohol or drugs that 'made them' do it. Not one of these men, or women, ever wanted to accept responsibility for their actions.

'Look, I have no choice but to give you a warning. You know that. You've been charged with a further offence. My hands are tied.' She pushed across the envelope with his warning letter inside.

'Are you fucking serious?' The chair flew back as he stood up and towered over her.

There was no way Lucy was going to let this dickhead take control. She pushed her own chair back calmly, stood face to face with him and looked him directly in the eyes.

'Whoa, whoa – you need to calm down, Robert. I don't want to have to push the panic button; there's no need for you to stand over me like that. Can't you see how your behaviour could be viewed as threatening?'

Robert once again grabbed his chair but this time he sat back down almost immediately, and Lucy watched his chest rise and fall as he took deep breaths to control his temper.

'Sorry, miss, but it just seems like every time I'm getting some-where, it gets thrown back in my face and that pisses me off.'

There it was again. That whiny voice. For a moment it was Patrick sitting across from her. She sat back down.

'Robert, it's your actions that've caused all this. We've been here before. You need to stop and think about things first. You have your group programme coming up soon. You'll learn some more techniques that will help you recognize the triggers and avoid reacting violently to situations that anger you. We've also discussed alcohol previously. And before you say that if you were sober, this wouldn't happen – just remember, alcohol doesn't make you do the things you do. You act this way because you choose to. You know you need to keep away from your ex.'

Lucy pointed at the warning letter in the hope that it would encourage Robert to read it. He jammed it into his back pocket unopened.

'Are we done now?' He stood up to leave.

'Do you want to talk anymore about things? Maybe put a plan together in case the situation comes up again?'

'Fuck that! I'm sick of that bitch getting me into trouble! Just give me my next appointment.'

'It's on your warning letter.'

Robert tried to storm out of the room as Lucy smirked behind his back – he needed her to use her swipe card to exit the room. The power was still hers.

'Open the fucking door!'

'Right, Robert! Lose the bloody attitude and calm down!' If she wasn't careful she'd find herself facing a complaint, but she was so fed up with these men and their controlling ways. Lucy swiped her card and let Robert back out into the reception area.

'See you next week, Robert.'

Lucy couldn't help but mutter 'wanker' under her breath. The receptionist briefly glanced up from her computer, and Lucy shrugged her shoulders.

There was no response from Robert, but she hadn't expected one. She knew he was still pretty pissed off, so she made a note to call the domestic abuse team and flag Louise's address. With Robert in this mood, there was no telling what he might do to his ex-wife.

Lucy needed caffeine to calm her nerves. Her job as a probation officer had her supervising some of the area's most violent offenders and today was no different.

'Hey, Lucy. Your hands are shaking, another tough session?' Sarah asked as she made her way to the coffee machine. Sarah was a brilliant probation officer but also a very good friend.

'Nah, just the usual, Sarah.'

It wasn't Robert Millard causing Lucy's nerves to be on end. She knew that after work her parents and sister were coming around and she didn't know what kind of mood Patrick would be in, considering he'd been still drunk before she'd left for work. Lucy wished she had the same confidence to deal with the situation at home as she did at work. Self-loathing crept over her as she put a false smile on her face to carry on with her day.

Sarah looked at her in such a way that Lucy wondered if she knew. She rubbed Lucy's shoulder reassuringly. 'You know where I am if you need me.'

CHAPTER FIVE

Lucy tapped her fingers on her desk as she stared at her computer screen, reading the Crown Prosecution documents for the pre-sentence report she had to complete. She wasn't too keen on interviewing this guy as the offence was brutal in nature. Mr Talbot was late and bail conditions attached indicated that should he fail to attend his interview, a warrant would be issued. She would have to inform the courts. She remembered she needed to stop off at the shop on her way home and picked up her mobile phone to remind Patrick about collecting Siobhan from school.

I know! I got your fucking note

was the text she received back.

Putting her head in her hands, she didn't hear Sarah come up behind her.

'Everything all right, Lucy?'

Lucy jumped. 'Yeah ... sorry, I was in a world of my own there for a minute. Everything's fine, Sarah. I'm just a little distracted. My family is coming for dinner – you know what it's like.' Lucy caught Sarah glancing at her phone screen and quickly turned it over.

'Oh God, yes! Family, eh? The joys!' Laughing awkwardly, Sarah again squeezed Lucy's shoulder. 'Well, let me know if I can do *anything*. You're just looking a little stressed.'

'Thanks, Sarah. I'm fine. Seriously. Just that bloody Robert Millard and now the guy I was interviewing for this court report has failed to show up. Not sure why I agreed to take on the domestic abuse cohort now. Sometimes I just think it would be better if they were all dead! Fucking controlling arseholes.' Lucy wished she could take back the words as soon as they left her mouth. 'You know I don't really mean that, right?'

'Obviously. Take a few deep breaths, inform the courts and grab a cuppa. Do you want me to contact the police about Robert?'

'Oh God. I nearly forgot. See what I mean? Thanks for reminding me. I'll do it now, I need to speak with PC Fielding anyway.'

She watched Sarah walk back to her desk and noted all the tasks she needed to complete for the day. Any excuse to stay a bit longer today at work suited Lucy just fine. The last time her parents visited had been a disaster and she wasn't sure they'd forgiven her, or Patrick, yet. The longer she left it before seeing them, the better.

Lucy smiled as she picked up the phone to call PC Mark Fielding, she could do with hearing a friendly voice.

CHAPTER SIX

Maggie felt a buzz of excitement as she stepped into the room and took in her new surroundings, the open-plan office lined with modern 'pods' on the second floor of a grey building. She thought back to when she had first been called into the DI's office to discuss her move from the murder investigation team. She had been advised that given her recent experience with The Chopper case, her superiors felt that a step away from the team on a temporary basis would do her good, while still allowing her to be involved with the job she'd dedicated her life to. DI Rutherford had said she thought it would help her development.

Maggie walked through the modern office. All the new offices seemed to be set up this way now. The desks were together in groups of two, facing each other. Plain white walls lined with motivational posters preaching the higher up's latest mantras. Although there were eight of the 'pods', only three desks were currently occupied. There was also a small office that looked out over the open-plan area. Maggie suspected it was the detective sergeant's.

'Hi! Are you DC Jamieson?' One of the people in the room called out, a young male of average build. He had a bright smile which immediately made her feel welcome.

'I am indeed. You can call me Maggie in the office though. And you are …?'

'I'm PC Mark Fielding – Mark. The guv said you were starting today. How about I give you a quick tour of the place? No doubt DS Hooper will sort out the formal side of things when he arrives and give you a rundown of the murder case that just came in. Start as you mean to go on and all that.'

'Murder?' She swallowed, then recovered her composure. So much for a break from homicide. 'Thanks, Mark, it would be great if you could show me around.'

With Mark making the introductions, Maggie learnt that PC Kat Everett was a feisty one and suspected that they would get on well. Maggie could smell the cigarette smoke from Kat's clothing and noted her colourful nails. The other officer was PC Pete Reynolds. Pete looked to be in his late thirties or early forties. He barely looked up from his computer screen as he said a strained, 'hello'.

'Don't mind Pete.' Mark laughed. 'He's just joined the team and is fairly new to the police. DS Hooper is making him read all the policies for a test at the end of the week.' He winked, and Maggie understood the implied message – there was no test, his colleagues were just winding him up.

'Ah, right then. I'll leave you to it, Pete.' Maggie gave him a quick nod.

'We can grab a coffee and I can take you through to DI Joseph Calleja if you want?' Mark headed towards what Maggie assumed to be the communal kitchen.

'Hmmm … OK, but maybe that's something DS Hooper will want to do? I don't want to step on any toes, my first day and all.'

'Good point! Right, let's get the brews in. Hooper's in a meeting at the moment. He'll be back for the briefing at 11 a.m. Why don't you take the desk across from me? I've left the details of the other agencies on your desk. We're what they call an *integrated team* and have probation, the Independent Domestic Violence Advocate, Drug and Alcohol services, as well as a few other agencies involved with our team on varying levels. I'm sure the guv will explain more. Sorry, you probably know all this, right?'

Maggie smiled. Having never worked directly with other agencies as part of one team, she wondered if they ever pulled rank or allocated blame on each other when things went wrong. She followed Mark into the kitchen hoping to pick his brains, but before she had the opportunity, a phone rang, and Mark dashed past her to answer it.

'Domestic Abuse Unit, PC Mark Fielding speaking. How can I help you?'

Mark's voice was a welcome sound considering the way today had started, Lucy thought.

'Hi, Mark. You forgot the homicide. It's Lucy Sherwood from Markston Probation. How are you?' Due to the nature of the individuals she worked with, Lucy, like many of her colleagues, used her maiden name for professional purposes.

'Hey, Lucy! Great to hear from you! I know, I know. I still can't get my head around homicide – why can't they just say murder? Though I suppose DAMU is probably not the best acronym for a team like ours, is it?'

Lucy heard him laugh down the phone.

'All's fine here … just the usual – overworked and under-resourced. To what do I owe this pleasure?'

Lucy felt her cheeks get warm and knew she was blushing. She seemed to blush every time she spoke to Mark. He was so kind to her and made her feel like her opinions mattered, the total opposite of Patrick.

'I had an interesting supervision session with Robert Millard.' Lucy heard the groan that Mark tried, unsuccessfully, to hide.

'OK, are you concerned that something is going to kick off?'

23

'A little. I just wondered if you could flag Louise's address and maybe do a safe-and-well check?'

'The address is already flagged, but I'll log this, and note that a safe-and-well check needs to be done. I can't promise it will be today, we're a little short staffed, but it is noted. We have a few new additions to the team, so maybe that will help. For now, though, we have to rely on the field teams to pick these up, depending on the other priorities.'

'Cheers, Mark. That will at least put my mind at ease. I would hate to think he goes around there and something even more serious happens. Louise does have a personal alarm, but we both know she doesn't use it. I'll record all this in his case records and make contact with Sharon Bairden; she's still the victim's advocate in the unit, right? Hard to keep up with all the changes. Mr Talbot also failed to show up for his pre-sentence report and, because he has bail conditions, I informed the court and expect a warrant to be issued soon. Soooo, anyway, spill. Who are the newbies, what are they like, and when will I meet them?'

'We know why Mr Talbot failed to report, I'm afraid. Someone should have contacted you. I can't go into too much detail because it's an ongoing investigation, but needless to say, it's one less report you'll need to write. About the newbie: DC Maggie Jamieson is with us from the Major and Organised Crime Department.'

'Whoa! You can't tell me what's happened to Talbot? And nice to see you keeping it professional. I take it there are other people in the room with you then?' Lucy laughed.

'I'll definitely keep you posted on Talbot, but I don't have too much info myself. You know me, Lucy, I'm always professional.'

She could just imagine Mark glancing around the room to make sure no one of authority was eavesdropping.

'Of course, right, I best get back to work. I should be over at the police station soon for a catch-up. Keep me posted on any developments concerning Robert Millard and thanks for the heads-up on Talbot.'

24

'Yeah, sorry 'bout that. I'll have to find out why probation wasn't contacted. Looking forward to seeing you though. Make sure you bring me a latte, or I'll have you arrested at the enquiry desk.'

Hearing his laugh made her smile. Lucy sighed as she hung up the phone. If only Patrick could be more like Mark.

CHAPTER SEVEN

Maggie's first encounter with her immediate superior did not go as she expected. She found herself sitting with her new colleagues near the back of a large briefing room, listening to the details of the murder her team would be investigating.

'Good morning, everyone.' Her boss, DS Jim Hooper, looked around the room, stopped at Maggie, giving her an uncommitted nod, then carried on outlining details of the gruesome murder.

'This is what we know so far. A taxi driver called 999 at 4 a.m. this morning, to notify us that he stumbled across the victim's lifeless body while he stopped for a break—'

Maggie's take-charge instinct kicked in and she interrupted Hooper mid flow. 'Has the driver been questioned by the responding officers or will we be interviewing the witness?' She immediately regretted her decision.

'If you let me finish,' he glared at her then looked down on the desk at a piece of paper in front of him, 'DC Jamieson, I'll give you all the information you and the rest of your colleagues need.'

Maggie felt her neck burn with embarrassment.

Hooper posted a picture on the investigation board and a

chorus of gasps could be heard around the room. It wasn't a pretty sight and Maggie regretted having that cream cake when she first arrived.

'As I was saying, the victim – Drew Talbot – was found lying on his back blocking the path not far from the entry into Beacon Park. The witness indicated that no one else was around and given the time, it is unlikely that anyone else was about – though we'll still need to confirm that. An empty syringe was sticking out of his neck. His arms were outstretched beside him – palms up – and his hands completely pulverized. You can see from the pictures.' He pointed at the screen. 'It looks as if someone took a hammer or a similar implement and battered both hands to a pulp. A large pool of blood gathered underneath his head, the top portion of his legs and his groin area. Initially it was unclear where the wounds were located, but his jeans had two slices on the upper inside thigh of each leg. The wound across his windpipe was easily identified.'

Maggie tapped her pen on the desk and glimpsed at the pictures that were being passed around the room. She made a note to have a closer look once the briefing was finished. Her fascination with crime scene pictures was well known at her old office, but she didn't want her new team to learn that just yet.

Hooper continued, 'With the arrival of the pathologist, photographs of the male victim were taken and evidence collected. A wallet found in the back pocket of the body determined that the victim's name was Drew Talbot – although a formal ID is yet to be made.

'PC Reynolds, I'd like you to work with the handover team to track down and notify Mr Talbot's family after the briefing. Mr Talbot had recently appeared in court under a charge of grievous bodily harm, and he has a history of violence against partners. I understand that Lucy Sherwood was supposed to be writing a report—'

'I think Mark told her earlier that Mr Talbot would not be

making the appointment, but he didn't go into too much detail.'
Maggie looked at Mark.

'That's right, guv. Lucy called to let me know that her pre-sentence report had not attended for interview. That's when I advised that Talbot wouldn't be making his appointment and, because of an ongoing investigation, I couldn't share anymore information with her yet. Not sure why someone didn't contact probation.'

'As he was one of our nominals, that would have been down to one of you lot. We'll call it crossed wires and move on, shall we? Fiona Blake, the Home Office pathologist, noted that there was an injury to the back of the victim's head. She believed that Mr Talbot was attacked from behind and knocked unconscious. It appears he was then rolled over onto his back, a syringe stuck in his neck – we will have to wait for toxicology to find out what substance he was injected with – his hands were mashed to a pulp and the three cuts were then made. Any one of them could have led to his death. That's where we are at. So, what are your initial thoughts?'

Maggie jumped straight in. 'Do we have the time of death established? And do we know where Mr Talbot's victim was during the relevant times?'

'Talbot's ex-partner is in hospital with a broken cheekbone, broken jaw, broken arm and strangulation marks around her neck. She is barely able to stay awake for more than an hour at a time and is heavily medicated; we don't believe she is directly involved, but we will need to interview her family and friends, in case they decided to seek their own revenge. Estimated time of death is any time between 12 a.m. and 4 a.m. when the body was found. Anyone else?'

'The injuries would suggest to me that this was personal. The injuries on his hands indicate someone was clearly angry with Mr Talbot and took that anger out on his body. Could the killer have been making a statement against Mr Talbot's abuse?' Maggie said. Hooper looked at her and she thought she saw the makings of a smile forming on his face.

'Interesting observation, Jamieson. That's a line of enquiry I would like you to explore further. You and Mark can look at people close to Talbot's ex-partners and see if you can eliminate any of them as persons of interest. Kat? Pete? Mark? Do you have anything you want to add?'

'Fuck sake, guv. I can just about keep my breakfast down at the minute.' Taking a deep breath Kat added, 'Were there any other witnesses or vehicles around the area at the time?'

'Only the taxi driver. Pete can trawl CCTV to see if there were any cars or people acting suspiciously during the times noted and let you know.'

'OK, guv. I can go out and interview anyone we come across,' Kat said.

Pete made note of his task and sighed. He had been hoping to get out in the field more.

'Mark, can you speak to the pathologist and see if she can shed some light on the exact cause of death, and then chase up toxicology?'

'Maggie, you and Kat can interview Wendy Parker; her daughter is the victim of domestic abuse at Talbot's hands,' Hooper said.

Mark gave him a thumbs up and gathered his papers.

'That's it then. You all know what you need to do. Keep me informed of any developments … oh, and Maggie – welcome to the team.'

CHAPTER EIGHT

Patrick had made sure Lucy knew exactly how he felt about her bloody note when he'd texted her back earlier. He wondered if Lucy's sister, Melody, would also be coming over. A bit of eye candy would make it easier to tolerate the whole situation.

Unlike Lucy, Mel looked after herself. She had big tits she liked to put on show and wore short skirts to accentuate her long, toned legs. Even though she was a solicitor, Patrick liked her down-to-earth personality. He often wondered if he had chosen the wrong sister. He made his way to the bathroom, the thought of Mel still stuck in his head.

There were only a couple of hours before he had to collect Siobhan, so he jumped in the shower in an attempt to sober up. Lucy would have a go at him if he was drunk and he couldn't be bothered with the hassle. If the nosy bitches that hung around the school gate smelled alcohol on him, that social worker would start her home visits all over again. He wouldn't put it past any one of those tramps to ring social services. Lucy would go ballistic.

Back downstairs, he picked up the post, sat down in his favourite chair, and went through the envelopes. Bills, bills, and more bills. He threw them on the coffee table for Lucy to deal with when she got home. He thought about looking for a job, but remembered how quickly he had lost the last one. The row with his old colleague that had spiralled out of control. The way people had laughed at him, taken the piss. A good kicking is what they deserved.

Patrick's main concern was his kids – Siobhan and Rory – and anyway there was no need to work if Lucy continued to pay for everything. They were struggling financially, but he wasn't going to just take *any* job. He wanted his kids to be proud of him. He saw the way they looked up to Lucy. Patrick was hoping that Rory would visit again soon, though he knew Rory's mother did her best to poison his son's mind against him.

Another stupid bitch.

It was no secret that Patrick loved his drink, so why did the women in his life always make an issue out of it? They knew what they were getting from the start. Beer was his drink of choice, but, if truth be told, he'd drink anything. It let him see things more clearly, made everything quieter, even if it did sometimes make him angry or sad. *Fuck Lucy – what does she know?*

Today he felt a bit down and Lucy's constant moaning didn't help. Patrick was no fool. He had a rage inside, he'd had it from a very young age. He couldn't help it. It was his parents' fault. After all, witnessing his mother being beaten and getting a few hard slaps at the hands of his father would be hard for anyone. What did people expect? His father wasn't selective though – he beat all his children equally. Fair is fair, he used to say.

Patrick clenched his fists. He used to promise himself he'd never treat a woman the way his father treated his mother. Promises he found hard to keep. He didn't care what anyone said – he wasn't like his father.

31

CHAPTER NINE

Maggie and Kat arrived at Wendy Parker's house after going to the hospital to check on Drew Talbot's ex – Heather Parker. The nurses had confirmed that Heather had been in the hospital for the last three weeks and, with the recent infection she had from her injuries, there was no way she could have left the hospital in her condition and the only person who had visited her since she was admitted was her mother, Wendy.

They knocked and waited for Mrs Parker to answer the door.

'I'm coming,' a frail-sounding voice called out.

The door could use a bit of WD-40, thought Maggie, as it squeaked open. The haggard-looking woman inside had grey hair, tightly piled in a bun on the top of her head, and wore a pair of slacks with a neat blouse.

'If you're selling something, I'll save you the time. I'm not interested.'

Maggie smiled. 'Are you Mrs Parker?'

'I am.'

'My name is DC Jamieson, and this is my colleague, PC Everett. Would it be OK if we came in and had a chat?'

She noticeably relaxed at the sight of their ID. 'Of course.

Please, make yourselves at home. Would you like a cup of tea or coffee?'

'That would be lovely. I'll have a coffee – milk, no sugar – and PC Everett will have a cup of tea if it is not too much trouble. Milk and one sugar.' Kat looked almost surprised that Maggie had remembered how she liked her tea.

'Is this about Drew? Was it him that was attacked? It's been all over the news. I won't be at all upset to hear that someone finally gave him what he deserved.'

Kat piped up, 'Yes, I'm afraid it was Drew. We just have a few questions for you.'

'For me? What in the world would I know about this?'

'Standard procedures, Mrs Parker.' Maggie stood up to help the woman with the tray of tea. She looked like she might fall over.

'Oh. Thank you. I can normally manage, but I've been having dizzy spells lately. Old age, I guess ... and please, call me Wendy.'

'OK, Wendy. Can you tell me where you were on Monday between the hours of midnight and four a.m.?' Maggie watched her eyes.

'Are you having a laugh? Look at me. I'm in bed before nine most nights. I can barely lift a tray of tea. How do you expect me to have inflicted all those injuries that the news reported? And the size of him! I'd need a ladder to hit his head ... pffft.'

'Please just answer the question, Wendy, so we can eliminate you from our enquiries. Did you ask anyone to hurt Mr Talbot? Or do you know of anyone who would want to hurt him?' Maggie asked reluctantly.

'Absolutely not! How dare you even insinuate such a thing. Do you know what HE did to my daughter? Do you?'

Trying to calm the situation, Kat changed the subject. 'We do know, and it was a horrible assault on your daughter. But as I'm sure you understand, we have to ask these questions. Mr Talbot's family need answers too.'

Wendy seemed to soften at the mention of other victims. 'It was awful … just awful what that man did to my girl. I could see the imprint of his hands around her throat in the bruises.'

Maggie handed her a tissue and patted her knee.

'We're so sorry, Wendy. At least he will never be able to hurt anyone again.'

'It's all my fault. *My* fault. I turned her away when she came here. I thought she just wanted money for drugs. Why did I do that?'

Seeing the anguish in Wendy's eyes, Maggie's throat tightened. She could only imagine what Wendy was feeling. If someone had hurt her, both her parents would have the same view. 'We're sure you did what you thought best. How were you to know what was happening?'

'My head knows that. My heart says: a mother should know.'

'This is not your fault, OK?' She smiled and patted the woman's knee again. 'But like my colleague has just said, you must understand how Mr Talbot's family are feeling. We just need to help them get closure too?'

'I understand. But I am still so angry with him. Walking about here when he was out on bail. No shame or remorse. And my daughter, lying battered and bruised in the hospital. It wasn't fair and I wasn't the only one who thought that either.'

Maggie looked at Kat. 'What do you mean you weren't the only one? Could you have said something to someone and maybe they took matters in their own hands?'

'Did you not hear me before? Don't be daft. I don't have many friends and the ones I do have wouldn't hurt a fly. I'm tired now, so if you're not going to arrest me, I'd like you to leave. As far as I'm concerned, the man who hurt my baby got everything he deserved.'

Kat handed Mrs Parker a card. 'Thanks for your time. If you think of anything else, our number is there. You can call at any time.'

'We'll be in touch.'

Kat and Maggie returned to the pool car.

'What did you make of that, Kat?'

'She was angry, but I don't think she had anything to do with Talbot's murder. Way too frail. She's just concerned about her daughter. Do you think she was involved?'

'My gut instinct is no, she wasn't. But can we rule her out completely? I mean, she sure has motive. You saw her daughter. What Talbot did to her was vicious. I don't think we should cross her off the list just yet.'

CHAPTER TEN

Finishing work without any further major incidents, Lucy arrived home tired. When she opened the door, she was met by an excited Siobhan. *Well, at least Patrick remembered to pick her up.*

'Hey, sweetie! Where's your dad?'

Patrick appeared in the doorway. His eyes were slightly glazed, and Lucy sighed.

'What the fuck was that for?'

'Patrick! Please don't swear in front of Siobhan. I'm just tired, OK? That's all. My parents are going to be here soon, and I'm not really in the mood. I guess I'd better start the dinner.' Lucy turned and put the shopping bags on the counter. To avoid confrontation with Patrick, Lucy prepared the dinner.

'Will your sister be coming?' Patrick called. Lucy's shoulders tightened. She didn't have to turn around to know that Patrick was sneering at her.

'I'm not sure. Mel just split up with her husband. She wasn't sure if she could make it.' Melody and Lucy didn't share the best of relationships, though she hoped that would change. Lucy hadn't told Patrick that Mel was single again, because she knew he'd use that to wind her up. She saw the disgusting way Patrick ogled her sister. At one point, Lucy had confronted Mel about

36

the way she flirted with Patrick. Mel had laughed in her face and told her that *flirting was one thing, fucking was another*. Lucy never thought that Mel would ever make her feel the way Patrick did, but with that one sentence, Mel had confirmed how weak she believed Lucy to be. Their relationship was never the same after that.

'Pity. Would be nice to have something pretty to look at.' Patrick purposely knocked into Lucy as he made his way to the fridge for another can of beer.

'How many of those have you had?'

'Don't start,' he warned. 'I'm really not in the mood. Isn't it bad enough I have to sit across from your father and listen to his snide remarks about me?'

Lucy didn't answer. She had seen the look in his eyes.

'So, what's for dinner then? I hope you're going to make something edible for a change.'

Trying a different tack, Lucy put on a cheerful voice. 'Your favourite. I thought I'd make a shepherd's pie.'

'Well at least that's something. Even *you* couldn't fuck that up.' He headed back to the living room.

Lucy's stomach was cramping with nerves. This wasn't going to be an enjoyable evening. *Why didn't I just keep my mouth shut?*

Forty minutes later, with the dinner in the oven and the kitchen tidied, Lucy asked Siobhan to set the table and went to get changed. If Mel was coming, Lucy would feel like a frumpy, old woman. Every one of her nice outfits was now too tight, all she had were her work clothes. She held back her tears, knowing that her father would start asking questions if he saw her red, puffy eyes. Lucy put on a little make-up, black trousers with a sweater, and stared sadly at herself in the mirror.

Mel was a high-paid solicitor in Birmingham. Her soon-to-be ex-husband was also a solicitor, and this always made Lucy feel slightly inferior. At work, Mel would wear power suits and come across as the total professional that she was. Outside of the office, though, it was short skirts, tight tops, and stiletto heels that were her sister's weapons of choice. It never used to bother Lucy, until now – now she'd let herself go. Not caring served a purpose though: it reduced the number of times Patrick could accuse her of cheating. Instead, he would put her down, pointing out that she was lucky he wanted her as no one else would. Lucy sighed and headed back downstairs.

Patrick looked up from the chair. 'Why are you wearing make-up?'

'I just thought I'd make a bit of an effort.'

'Oh, nice, you don't make any effort for me, but you're happy to put a bunch of shit on your face to impress your parents.'

Lucy knew she shouldn't have bothered, but she didn't want her parents wondering why she'd changed so much. Questions would be asked, and she just couldn't cope with the look of disappointment she knew she'd see on her father's face. Taking a tissue out of her pocket, she wiped some of the make-up off and sat anxiously on the edge of the sofa to wait for her parents.

The knock on the door startled her. Siobhan ran to answer it, but Lucy called after her. 'Hang on, sweetie. I'll get it.' She ruffled Siobhan's hair on the way past. Lucy hadn't seen her parents for some time, so wanted to be the first to greet them. They had been very supportive of her – particularly her father – allowing her space to make her own decisions. It broke her heart that she now felt so distant from them. Straightening her sweater, she took a deep breath and pasted on a smile as she opened the door.

'Hi, Mum. Hey, Dad!' She invited them inside and kissed each of them on the cheek as they squeezed by her in the doorway. She was about to close the door when her sister put her hand out.

'Eh! Charming, sis!'

'Oh sorry, Mel. I didn't see you hiding there.' Lucy's hands squeezed into fists as she looked her sister up and down. They were complete opposites. Mel worked out and showed off her toned arms and shapely legs with a tank top and short skirt.

'Aren't you cold? You barely have anything on.'

'Don't be jealous, Luce. It's not an attractive feature.'

Why did I even invite them around? Shrugging her shoulders, Lucy shuffled them all from the kitchen to their seats in the dining room. Lucy cringed when her dad sat at the head of the table. The sooner this was over, the better.

The tension in Lucy's shoulders subsided as dinner and drinks were served; the talk around the table was polite if not semi-strained. Lucy was embarrassed to see Patrick drinking heavily and leering over Mel. She seemed to be loving the attention, giggling like a teenager. The scowl on her father's face said it all. Lucy figured her mother must have asked him to keep his mouth shut, because he barely said two words during the meal. Siobhan, as always, was as good as gold and Lucy smiled at her.

'I'll help you clear the table, Lucy.' She really was a little diamond and Lucy gave her a hug as she gathered the plates.

'Is everyone ready for dessert?' Lucy called from the kitchen. She heard a few moans; the shepherd's pie must have filled them up. But once dessert was served, Lucy knew her father would want to make a quick exit and that suited her just fine. The room was silent except for the awkward sound of cutlery scraping on plates. Someone coughed uneasily. Lucy didn't want to make her parents stay where they were clearly uncomfortable. Her sister was the first to answer.

'None for me, Luce. Can't afford to add any extra pounds, if you know what I mean?'

Lucy held her tongue. She noticed Patrick lean over and whisper something in Mel's ear. Mel giggled and slapped Patrick playfully on the arm.

The flirting between the pair was making Lucy feel physically sick. How could he do that in front of her? In front of her parents and Siobhan? Her hands shook with rage.

Before she could say anything, her father interjected, 'Enough now, Melody. Can we just enjoy dessert without any of this nonsense?' Lucy looked at her dad and thanked him with her eyes. He returned the action with a smile and a nod. Lucy really did miss her father, but she knew that the less contact she had with her parents, the less likely they were to realize what she was going through. She couldn't take the pity looks and she didn't want to hurt her family.

Everyone devoured the dessert in record time. Patrick made it clear the night was over by abruptly standing up and making a move to leave the table. 'Right, time to clear the pipes out! Think that's the first decent meal Lucy's cooked in ages; my body isn't used to it!' He laughed loudly.

'It's late, darling. I think we're going to make a move,' Lucy's dad said.

Patrick didn't acknowledge him but turned to Mel, leaned in, and kissed her on the cheek.

'It was really nice to see you. Don't be a stranger.' At least this time Mel had the courtesy to blush as she saw the look on Lucy's face.

'Take care, Patrick,' Mel said. She reached her hand out to Siobhan. 'Come give your Aunty Mel a hug, sweets.'

Siobhan walked over and gave Mel a big hug as everyone said their goodbyes. Patrick disappeared upstairs as Mel and her mother got into the car. Lucy's dad, however, pulled Lucy aside and they stood in the front garden outside the open door.

'Why do you put up with that, sweetheart? You're so much better than him.'

'Oh, Dad ...' Lucy hugged her father tight. 'He's not always that bad. He's had a tough time lately.' Lucy saw the look of disappointment in her father's face. She could feel the tears welling up, too ashamed to tell him the whole truth.

'It's OK, Lou-lou.' He used to call her that when she was a little girl. 'There is always a place for you at ours, if you ever change your mind.' He wrapped his strong arms around her and gave her a squeeze.

Lucy choked back the tears. 'Thanks, Dad. That means a lot.' She gave him another hug and waved them off, not seeing Patrick as he stepped back from the open bathroom window directly above the front door.

CHAPTER ELEVEN

Across town, at the same time Lucy's parents were saying their goodbyes, field officers were about to carry out the safe-and-well check for Louise. They knew Robert well as he'd been arrested a few times for drunk and disorderly.

As they approached the house, they saw a light in the front room. One of the officers knocked while the other tried to look through the window.

'Who is it? Do you know what fucking time it is? Taking the bloody piss!'

'Police, ma'am. We're here to check that everything is OK.'

'Well it is, so get lost!'

The officers looked at each other.

'Please, ma'am. Do you mind if we come in for a few minutes for a chat?'

Both officers knew that if they left the property without actually seeing Louise, there could be trouble; Robert could be inside coercing Louise to get rid of them.

They heard the chains rattle and multiple bolts being undone. Clearly Louise was concerned for her safety. The door eventually eased open slowly. One chain remained, and Louise poked her head between the gap.

'There! Satisfied?' The officers heard her mumble some not so savoury words underneath her breath.

'Uh, no – sorry, ma'am. Could you please open the door fully?'

'Oh, for fuck's sake …' Louise shot back the final chain and wrenched open the door. 'Happy now?'

'Yes, ma'am. Sorry to have upset you. Can we just come in for a quick chat?'

'Please yourselves.' Stepping out of the way, Louise ushered the two officers into the living room. They could see curtains twitching in the street outside; Louise was clearly keen to get them out of sight.

'When was the last time you saw Robert?' The officer closest to Louise asked while his colleague stood looking around the room.

'The last time I saw that waste of space was when I called you guys. Yesterday I think it was, it could've been the day before. Fucked if I know. There is a restraining order in place but that seems to do jack shit – which is why I never got one before! I mean, what is the point of having it if he can swan over here, do some damage, and *then* the police act?'

'We understand your frustration, Mrs Millard. But it really is the best option. And with the panic alarm and your house being flagged – the police will respond immediately.'

'Yeah, yeah. I get it. Just pisses me off.'

Before leaving, the officers advised her what she should do if Robert turned up at her house again but neither were confident she would heed their advice. They only hoped the next visit wasn't for something more serious.

CHAPTER TWELVE

Patrick stood back from the bathroom window. *Fucking prick should mind his own business.* He gripped the sink and tried to control his breathing. It wouldn't have bothered him so much if he hadn't been drinking that evening. But he had, and he was fuming now. Blaming it on the alcohol made him feel better. He'd often say to Lucy, 'If I'd been sober, that would never have happened,' but Patrick knew the truth. It would have. Patrick hated feeling out of control, hated people treating him like a muppet. It wasn't his fault if people kept winding him up. People like Lucy. People like Lucy's dad. They did it on purpose. Especially when Lucy used her probation speak. *If she's going to treat me like an offender, I may as well behave like one.*

Patrick loved Lucy despite all the arguments … the other women in his life were just a means to an end. A man has needs, and if Lucy didn't want to fulfil them, he knew plenty of other women who would. Maybe he should make a move on Mel, make Lucy really appreciate what she has. He'd never leave her though. There was no way she'd leave him either. He'd make sure of that.

He flushed the toilet when he heard her come back inside and went into Siobhan's room.

Inside the house, Lucy shut the door and leaned against it. Looking around the kitchen, she knew she'd have to clean up before going to bed. She turned on the hot water tap and started to fill the sink. While she waited, she wiped down the counters, and the dining table. Bitterness filled her mouth at the fact that her sister had *reciprocated* Patrick's flirting. Actually enjoyed it. Especially after Lucy had confronted her and told her how she felt. Lucy wiped the table harder, her jaw tight. She thought her sister was better than that.

Lucy could hear Patrick upstairs with Siobhan. Although unusual, she was grateful that he was getting Siobhan ready for bed. She didn't have the energy. It still made her suspicious, though. Patrick never did anything without expecting something in return, even for his own child. She wouldn't let that prey on her mind; instead she wanted to get the kitchen cleaned and get up to bed before Patrick came down, that way, she might avoid any argument.

As she was finishing the last of the dishes she heard him on the stairs. Staring out the window at the overgrown back garden, her heart sank. She'd missed her opportunity. With a sigh, she prepared herself for whatever insulting comments he was about to unleash on her.

'So, what's your dad's problem then?' The accusation in Patrick's voice was undeniable.

'What are you talking about? My dad barely said two words all evening.'

'Ah. OK. Are we playing that game then? I hate when you play dumb, Lucy … really fucking annoys me.' Patrick's lip curled in that sneer that Lucy recognized; she had to think fast, or something bad was going to happen.

'Seriously, Patrick. I have no clue what you're talking about.'

Patrick prodded her shoulder sharply as he accentuated each word spoken. 'Don't. Worry. I. Know. Exactly. What. I. Am. Talking. About.' He then tapped his nose and winked. Making his way to the fridge, he peeked past the open door, staring at Lucy as he took out a can and cracked it open. He knew she hated that sound.

Lucy cringed and turned away. He won. She placed the tea towel on the counter and started to walk off. Patrick's phone pinged indicating he had a text message. Just as Lucy reached the bottom of the stairs, she heard Patrick call out, 'Well, will you looky here! Looks like your sister might fancy a piece of me.' Lucy stopped dead in her tracks. Her head was screaming, *Ignore him. He's just doing this to wind you up.* She clenched her jaw and began to turn around. *What the hell was Mel playing at? When did she start texting MY husband?*

Lucy was on her way back to the kitchen when Patrick came out. 'Oh, you're back. I thought you were slinking off to bed. And not even a goodnight kiss.'

'What did my sister want?'

'Wouldn't you like to know.'

She swallowed down her rage.

'Forget it. I'm going upstairs.'

She made a move to turn around, but Patrick was fast. He grabbed her by her upper arm and pulled her close. He gripped her mouth, his thumb and index finger pinching her face so her lips puckered, and he kissed her. Hard. When she eventually broke free, he leaned into her ear and whispered, 'I wonder if your sister kisses better.'

CHAPTER THIRTEEN

Patrick smirked as he sat down and looked at the text from Lucy's sister.

Hi, Patrick. Great to see you tonight. If you ever fancy a pint, give me a bell. Would be great to see you and Lucy again. X M.

Of course, he didn't tell Lucy about the last bit. He could use it to wind Lucy up. She might even appreciate him more.

Sipping on his beer, Patrick withdrew into his dark place. He knew that alcohol was a bad mix when he was in a mood, but he didn't care. He drank for many reasons, but mainly to stop the demons that haunted him.

As a child, he was abused sexually, and rather than deal with the abuse, his mother ignored the problem. As Patrick's dark thoughts spiralled, he was suddenly fifteen years old standing in his bedroom.

It was dark outside and he was shaking with fear, trying not to think about Uncle Stan ... He looked at the baseball bat wrapped in barbed wire that he had spent weeks making ....

He nearly beat Uncle Stan to death that night before his mother stopped him. The police weren't called, and Uncle Stan was warned if he ever stepped foot in the house or was seen anywhere in the area, his life was over.

Patrick stood up and started pacing the room, trying to walk away his memories. If he ever saw Uncle Stan again, he knew exactly what he would do; he had been planning every single detail for years. Patrick kicked a chair across the room.

People wound him up. He told himself he couldn't help it, but really, he could. He knew exactly where and when he could lash out. Spotting weakness in others a mile off was his biggest talent. He preyed on people's vulnerabilities and had a charm about him that got him into their favour. People could be very stupid sometimes. He drew the line at his kids though. He'd never lay a hand on them and God help anyone else who tried.

Upstairs, Lucy sat up on the bed, listening for Patrick. By the sound of it, he was settling downstairs for the night as she heard another can of lager being opened. After he had forcefully kissed her she had run upstairs, desperate to scrub the taste of him out of her mouth. Lucy hoped he wasn't going into one of his moods: the mood when he'd start his drunken ramblings, his voice getting louder the more he drank, until he was shouting at the walls, the floor, or his own reflection. It wasn't good for Siobhan to hear her dad that way. She was a deep sleeper, like her father, and Lucy only hoped that she slept through it.

The rants did give Lucy insight into Patrick's behaviour as an adult, though. For instance, she'd learnt that he was always getting into trouble as a child. A tearaway teen is how he'd described himself, telling her that he was always in and out of trouble – but never getting nicked. He believed he was too clever for that.

Patrick was estranged from his family, but Lucy had caught him calling his mother a few times, ranting vile words down the phone. Eventually, his mother had changed her number and moved to the Isle of Man without giving Patrick her address.

48

Even his family didn't want to be anywhere near him. Another warning sign Lucy had ignored.

At the start of their relationship, Lucy had blamed his family, but she now understood the truth and only wished she'd seen it sooner.

Although Patrick had never told her directly, it was clear from his rants that he'd been physically abused by his father. Lucy also suspected other abuse, because Patrick had an extreme hatred for someone he called 'Uncle Stan'. When Patrick had been barely coherent through alcohol one night, he'd told Lucy that Stan was never talked about by any of the family members. Although on occasions in the past when they all had met up, little snide remarks were made and Patrick would usually end up storming off. Eventually, he stopped going and the invites dried up. Lucy tried to find out more about Stan but, on one particular night, pushed too far and received a punch in the mouth for her concern.

'Now will you shut the fuck up?'

Lucy got the message loud and clear. When Patrick mentioned Uncle Stan now, Lucy stayed silent.

CHAPTER FOURTEEN

Maggie Jamieson stretched her legs and looked out the window of her office. It was getting dark but she was pleased with how her first day at DAHU had gone, even though she'd had to put in extra hours. The team had the perfect balance of banter and seriousness. Recent cutbacks made specialist teams a rarity, so Maggie knew she was going to get as much out of this experience as possible. Maybe Rutherford *was* right.

After the Talbot briefing and interview with Wendy Parker, Maggie met with DI Joseph Calleja – Maggie guessed he was about five feet nine; he had a slim build and he had a shadow of a beard. The DI came across as a force to be reckoned with but a firm and fair boss. Calleja explained the overall workings of the team, and where each agency fit. The more she learnt, the more impressed she'd been. Calleja informed Maggie that she'd be reporting directly to DS Hooper.

Maggie grimaced. Making her way to the communal kitchen, she reflected on the team so far. Her initial impression, during her first meeting with Hooper, was that he would keep her on her toes. He wasn't a particularly tall man, but he had a certain look about him – stubble adorned his face and despite her colleagues warning her that he could be a right pain in the arse, he had a kindness in his eyes. It was good to know that he always had their back. That's all she could really hope for. There was nothing worse than a boss who was only interested in furthering their own career, often to the detriment of their team.

Maggie turned the tap on and filled up a cloudy glass with cold water. She also learnt that Probation Officer Lucy Sherwood would occasionally come to the police station with Mark, as he was the most experienced in working domestic abuse cases. Although Maggie had yet to meet Lucy, her colleagues had nothing but praise for her. Maggie was still trying to figure Mark out, though. She was curious why he joined this team as he had very strong, negative views about domestic abuse perpetrators and it seemed he wasn't afraid to express them openly. She'd need to keep her eye on that. The last thing Maggie wanted was a black mark on her record because of something a colleague had said or done.

Maggie returned to her desk and cleared a spot to place her glass down. Thinking about the rest of the team, she laughed to herself. Kat Everett, the mouth on that one. Every sentence seemed to have a fuck or a shit in it somewhere. Maggie wondered how Kat managed to get through court cases or deal with the public without a 'fuck' flying out of her mouth.

Maggie was aware that a civilian, Dr Moloney, would also be joining the team soon to share her insight as a criminal psychologist and Calleja clearly admired her work. What really interested Maggie though was the multi-agency approach. She liked that this team had specific individuals from other agencies working directly with their nominals and based within the police station, even if it was just once a week. She'd see how this all worked now with their first murder investigation – how much collaboration really took place.

Working at Markston Police Station would be a challenge, too. Markston was a relatively average size town, but the station was also responsible for covering Littlefield, Barston, and some of the more rural surrounding areas. Domestic abuse was a big problem in Staffordshire as a county, which was why the Police and Crime Commissioner had decided it was a priority offence that needed to be dealt with by a specialized team.

'Any further updates that I need to be aware of before we call it a night, Mark?' Maggie picked up her coffee and walked around to her colleague's desk.

'Well you know that Lucy called earlier today. She wanted to flag up Louise Millard's address as Robert left probation a little pissed off. Robert is one of our *regulars*.'

Maggie shuddered at the thought of what this description entailed.

'Safe-and-well check then, I presume?'

'Yep. All sorted. Two of the field team officers have been tasked with the job. Looks like it has happened, but the system hasn't been updated with the full details yet. We can pick anything up in the morning from the log but, as nothing has been flagged, it must have gone OK. Any emergency will be dealt with by the field team tonight.'

Looking over Mark's shoulder, Maggie noted the long list of call-outs to the address. 'Hmmm … so Robert Millard has recently been bailed for a breach of the harassment order in place?'

'Yeah. Lucy will send me the details of their session today. She emails over any concerns, especially if she isn't going to be at the police station any time soon.'

After scanning the records, Maggie's own experience with domestic abusers told her it wouldn't take much to trigger Robert.

'Do you know if Lucy contacted the victim's support worker? Sorry, I know this is stuff you're all probably aware of and doing, I just need to check, to satisfy myself before I go home. Once I've been here for a few days, I promise the questions will ease up, but only just a bit.' Maggie smiled.

'That's OK. I get it. Lucy said she'd be contacting Sharon – oh, sorry, you won't know who Sharon is. Sharon Bairden is the victim's advocate connected to our team. You'll meet her soon enough as she attends our operational meetings. I sent the details over to her as well. Always good to cover our asses.' Despite being an integrated team, each agency worked on separate computer systems, so information was often duplicated.

'So, although it has been one hell of a long day, it's been a productive one and it really has been great getting to grips with things as much as I can.'

Maggie could tell from Mark's immaculately organized desk that he would have everything in order. She glanced at her own desk – organized chaos – and hoped Mark wasn't OCD. She'd only been in the office one day and already it looked like she'd been there years. Despite this, she got the impression that they would work well together.

Maggie felt her mobile phone buzz in her pocket. Pulling it out and seeing his name on the screen always filled her with dread. *Why now?*

CHAPTER FIFTEEN

Maggie stared at her mobile debating on whether she should answer it. She clicked to answer, putting the phone to her ear.

'What have you done now?'

'Hello to you, too.'

'Cut the bullshit. I'm still at work. What do you want?' Maggie stood up and walked out to the hallway.

Glancing back into the office, she noticed Mark quickly turn and look at his computer screen. Maggie needed to keep calm and lower her voice; she didn't want any awkward questions that she couldn't answer.

A familiar whine reached her ears.

'Sorry, I thought you'd be at home now, it's late. Can I stay at yours? I've been thrown out of my flat.'

'Oh, for fuck's sake. What have you done now?'

'Nothing! I swear. The landlord has it in for me.'

Maggie looked at her watch and sighed.

'I'm done now. Meet me at the café on the corner near my flat. We'll talk.'

'Thanks, Maggie. Really – you have no idea how much this means to me. Should I, uh, bring my stuff with me?'

'You can … but I'm not making any promises. Let's talk first.'

Maggie hung up. She saw Mark looking her way again, but ignored him and headed back to her desk so she could wrap things up for the day and get out of there.

Why the fuck am I the only one he calls?

He was already seated and tearing napkins to shreds when Maggie arrived at the corner café. This was a nervous habit from his childhood that seemed to have carried on into his adult years.

'Do you want a coffee?' Maggie gently tapped his shoulder.

He nearly jumped out of his seat. 'Shit, Maggie! You scared the bloody hell out of me! The waitress will be back in a sec. I already have a coffee on the way. I didn't think you'd be here so soon, or I would have got you one too.'

'Oh, right. How would you have paid for it, if I had changed my mind about coming?'

'Don't be like that, sis. It's good to see you.'

Maggie sat across from her brother and, despite her best efforts, her lip curled slightly into a smile.

'It's good to see you too, Andy. Though why is it you only call or come to see me when you're in trouble?'

The waitress arrived at the table with Andy's coffee and took Maggie's order.

Maggie noticed the waitress had a pretty smile and watched her walk back towards the counter.

'I see you still like the ladies then? Guess it wasn't a phase after all?'

Maggie picked up a coaster and gripped it firmly.

'Oh, I see. You're still in denial? Nothing wrong with being a lesbian these days, you know.'

'Watch your fucking mouth, Andy. I'm not a lesbian. I date men! When have you ever seen me with a woman? Don't bloody label me. Not that it's any of your business anyway.'

'OK. OK. Calm down. So, you're bisexual. What's the big deal?'

55

'I've had just about enough of your shit, Andy. Enough, already. And keep your fucking voice down, will you … What I do in my personal time is none of your business. Can we move on now? We're not here to talk about me.' Maggie glared at her brother.

Holding up his hands, Andy Jamieson admitted defeat. 'Look, I'm sorry. I didn't realize it was a sore subject and I didn't come here to upset you. Is that Chopper case still getting to you? You seem a bit on edge. I've missed you, OK, and I thought if you knew that I understood about the … ladies … well, things could get back to normal with us.'

Maggie waved her hand dismissively. 'So, what is it that you really want, Andy?'

'I told you on the phone. I need a place to stay. My landlord evicted me, and I just need to get my head together and sort out where I go from here.' He was fidgeting and playing with the corner of the tablecloth.

Maggie frowned.

'Who do you owe money to?'

Andy had a gambling problem and their parents had washed their hands of him years before. Maggie had bailed him out a few times but knew this wasn't something she could keep doing. He was her brother though, and she hated to think of what he'd do if things got desperate.

'No one! Why do you always assume the worse of me?'

'Erm … because I know you! Why would you get evicted if you were paying your rent? And why aren't you paying your rent if you have no other debts? You're still working, right?'

'Yes, I'm still working – but I may have missed a few rent payments, OK? Seems my landlord is not the negotiating type.'

'Here's the deal then, Andy, and I mean this. You have four months. You need to be honest with me, but more importantly, with yourself. I'm guessing you're back gambling and that has got to stop; I won't be helping you out again. If you pressure me, you will find yourself out on the streets.' Maggie knew she sounded harsh, but Andy pushed everyone to the limits and he had to know that this would be the last time.

They picked up a pizza on the way back to Maggie's flat and over the next few hours, Andy had told his sister that he owed six-thousand pounds to a loan shark for a gambling debt. Maggie didn't know whether to scream or cry. Every week that he missed a repayment, the debt went up. His job at the factory wouldn't cover the repayments, but he assured Maggie that if she helped him out this one last time, he'd pay her back.

Maggie had eight thousand pounds in her savings and agreed that she'd pay back the debt on the condition that she could go with him to this loan shark. Maggie also stipulated that within the four months that he was staying with her, he was to do all the odd jobs that needed doing in the flat without so much as a moan.

Andy had already depleted their parents of their savings and she wouldn't let him do the same to her without getting something in return. He would earn the money and if he messed up again, she would cut him out of her life completely. It was tough love, but it was the only thing that would get through to him.

CHAPTER SIXTEEN

Robert Millard was sick and tired of having his life controlled by others. A restraining order, a licence, and fucking women. He took another sip of Tennent's Super and licked his lips as the first hit of alcohol took over. It was noon, so he was doing well. The shakes had kicked in not long after he woke up this morning, but he managed to hold off, desperate to prove to himself that alcohol didn't dictate his life.

Robert looked around the cramped bedsit. Black bin bags mixed full of dirty and clean clothes were piled in every available space. He needed to get out of this shithole or he'd go crazy. Picking up his mobile, he scrolled through the numbers until he came across the one he wanted. He pressed call. Let it ring until the answerphone kicked in.

'Hey, it's me. I know you're there. Just pick up the fucking phone!' He hung up and dialled again.

'Quit playing games. I just want to talk. I want my stuff.' He put the phone down. He felt the anger rise in him and grabbed another can. He pressed redial on the phone.

'Fucking bitch! Pick up the phone or I will come round there and then you'll be sorry!'

Robert grabbed his coat and headed to the pub. He wouldn't

let that bitch wind him up anymore. Her new boyfriend could deal with her now. He needed to be around people who understood him. If Louise had called the police, they would go to Robert's bedsit first, so he thought it best to get out of there. If he was going to spend a night in the cells, he may as well be shit-faced first.

The usual suspects were propping up the bar when he walked into his local. He headed to the bar and ordered a pint of Stella Artois. Reaching into his pocket he pulled out a £20 note. The last of his dole money. He hated this. If it wasn't for Louise, he'd still have his job. A job he'd managed to keep for nearly four years. *That bitch will pay one day.* He looked around the room and spotted a familiar face.

'Hey, Vicki. When did you get out?'

Vicki Wilkinson had lived in the area since the beginning of time. Shell Baker, one of Vicki's oldest and closest friends, was also a regular at the pub, though she was nowhere in sight right now. Robert knew that Vicki had a terrible temper in drink and often found herself in and out of prison for short periods for fighting. Recent changes in the law meant that Vicki and other offenders who were given prison sentences under twelve months, now had to report to probation following their release. Robert laughed inwardly – Vicki wasn't going to like that one bit – and the laughter continued when Robert said he was on probation too.

'Who's your PO, then?' The words were slurred, and Robert had to lean in close to understand what Vicki was asking. She'd clearly been drinking since the early morning.

'Some bitch ... Lucy. Thinks she's hard, but I see her hands shaking ... She's probably a fucking alky!' They laughed again.

'Mine is Sarah something or other. She's OK, I guess.' Vicki shrugged. 'You still married?' Vicki tried to focus on Robert's wedding finger to see if he was wearing a ring.

'Nah. That bitch threw me out. Says I beat her when the reality is, she gave as good as she got. What the fuck am I supposed to do when she flies at me? Let her hit me? Fuck that shit!'

'Ah, you're probably better off without her. Gis a drink will ya?' The crooked smile on her lips told Robert that Vicki was still up to her old tricks.

CHAPTER SEVENTEEN

Kate Moloney wasn't your average doctor. In fact, she couldn't be described as average in any way. Her goth appearance really did throw people when she introduced herself as a doctor. She was proud of her PhD in criminal psychology and didn't care that people questioned her credentials based on how she looked. Pettiness or jealousy could rear its ugly head; it didn't bother her.

She looked in the mirror. Her long, shiny, straight black hair glistened as the sun reflected through the window. Pools of blue, her eyes were hidden beneath a dark, grey shadow. Her silver nose ring and deep purple lips made a statement that she wasn't to be messed with. She straightened her perfectly fitted black blazer, wiped down her pencil skirt and slipped on her most comfortable combat boots.

Dr Moloney had moved from her hometown in Galway, Ireland, to London so she could finish her studies. There wasn't much need for a criminal psychologist where she lived and the jobs in Dublin were scarce. She'd made London her home away from home and managed to blend in nicely. But the move to the small market town of Markston, Staffordshire, was a welcome change to the hustle and bustle of life in the Big Smoke.

Even if it wasn't considered as glamourous as some of the

larger neighbouring townships, Dr Moloney knew she'd settle in quickly. It was the type of place where everyone knew each other, and new faces were often made to feel unwelcome. If she let it bother her, she wouldn't last very long. Dr Moloney wouldn't let it get under her skin.

Dr Moloney had also learnt that the neighbouring boroughs were managed by both Markston Probation and the local police station. When she'd googled the area, she hadn't been surprised that this caused controversy with offenders who had to travel some distance to reach their appointments on time.

Substance misuse was a growing concern in Staffordshire. Kate also noted from her research that six pubs were located throughout the town, the most popular of which were The Black Penny and The Smith's Forge, thanks to low prices and seemingly 'friendly' patronage. Many of the offenders who frequented the probation office were often found in The Smith's Forge next to the train station and bus depot.

Kate was happy that, although the town had a retail park with various shops – Asda, Sainsbury's, Boots – if you took a twenty-minute walk, you'd find yourself in a very rural area surrounded by fields and lakes. Yes, she'd settle here just fine.

CHAPTER EIGHTEEN

Lucy's days and weeks often passed in a blur of busy activities. Today was no different. Although nothing untoward had happened, the whole week had flown by, and Lucy didn't know whether to be glad or sad that the weekend had finally arrived.

'See you later, Sarah!' Lucy grabbed her coat and headed for the bus stop. It was her turn to pick up Siobhan from school, even though Patrick wasn't working at the moment. A bone of contention with Lucy but not one that she was willing to pursue. She tried to pick her battles wisely, though not often with success.

Lucy loved seeing Siobhan's face light up as she neared the school gate.

'Lucy, Lucy! Guess what.' Siobhan ran excitedly to the gate.

'Hey, munchkin! What's all the excitement about?'

Lucy picked up Siobhan and gave her a big hug. Putting her down again, Lucy rustled her hair, and reached out for her hand.

'The school is having a dance. Can I go? Can I? Pleeeeeease!'

'Hey, sweetie. You know the rules. We have to ask your father.'

Siobhan's shoulders drooped, and she let out a sigh. 'Aww. He's probably going to say no. He always does.'

63

'When's the dance?'

'Next Friday. Everyone's going.' Siobhan was on the verge of crying.

'Well, there's plenty of time. If you do your chores, we'll catch your dad when he's in a good mood. I'll speak to him, I promise.' Lucy regretted the words as soon as they left her lips. Siobhan's blue eyes lit up again with hope. With Siobhan at her grandparents over the weekend, Lucy would speak with Patrick on Saturday … just in case anything kicked off.

'There's the bus. Shall we make a run for it?'

Lucy glowed with pride as Siobhan raced ahead. These were the moments that she cherished. The smile on Siobhan's face was so big, it pushed her cheeks up and made it look like she was squinting. More often than not, when happiness made her heart swell, Patrick was nowhere to be seen.

Lucy paid the bus fare and sat down, wedged between Siobhan and someone who was in serious need of a shower. She stared aimlessly out the window, wishing her life had been different.

No lights were on as Lucy and Siobhan walked up the path to the front door. Once inside, Lucy looked for a note or anything that would let her know where Patrick was. Although Siobhan didn't say anything, Lucy saw the tears glistening in her eyes. She had wanted to say goodbye to him before her granddad arrived. Lucy suspected Patrick was at the pub or avoiding Becky's parents. She reached into her handbag, digging her mobile out to text Patrick and see if he'd be back in time.

Lucy held Siobhan's hand and they both headed to the living room, waiting for Patrick to answer. Siobhan turned on the television and flicked through the channels. Fifteen minutes had passed and still no response; she had no doubt then that he was at the pub. She turned to Siobhan and placed her hands gently on the child's shoulders.

'Looks like Daddy is at an important meeting, sweetheart, so I doubt he'll be back in time. Let's make you a quick snack and get your things together.' She couldn't bear to see Siobhan's trembling lip and hated lying to her.

As she wiped the crumbs leftover from Siobhan's cake, Lucy heard the familiar chug of Ed's car pulling up in the drive. She waited for the billow of smoke from his exhaust to clear before she opened the door. 'Siobhan, your grandad's here. Grab your stuff and come give me a hug.'

Siobhan raced down the stairs with her weekend bag dragging behind her.

'Love you, little one.'

'Love you too, Lucy.'

Lucy gave Ed a wave and watched as they left.

The house was quiet when Siobhan was away. Patrick's son, Rory, sometimes came around, but they didn't speak much.

Rory had found Patrick online through Facebook. The pair had been reunited six or seven months earlier and had since been making up for lost time. Rory was fifteen years old now and mature for his age. Lucy had occasionally noticed a flash of Rory's temper. Given his age though, that wasn't unusual. She only hoped he didn't end up like his father.

With the house to herself, Lucy struggled with deciding what she wanted to do. She found it difficult to relax when he was out, because she spent the whole time worrying what sort of mood he'd come back in. She almost wished he'd been at home, passed out drunk when she got back today. That way she could sneak past him quietly and make her way upstairs to the spare room, which she'd turned into a mini library.

Lucy loved her little haven. She'd sit on the futon she'd brought when they had first moved in to the house together. Patrick hadn't always been a monster. Life with him had started out pretty good. For the two years of dating, they'd had some amazing times – in fact, when looking back Lucy realized that most of those times

65

he hadn't drank any alcohol, at least not in front of her. Lucy held on to the belief that deep down, Patrick had a good heart.

Of course, the whole *Mr Nice Guy* routine soon changed after they moved in together. At first, he'd have a few cans of lager after work. Nothing wrong with that. After all, he'd spend eight to twelve hours a day on building sites and just wanted to unwind a bit. Then the little sarcastic jibes started, which Lucy initially laughed off – *he didn't mean that,* she thought. *He's obviously had a stressful day.*

It was when Patrick lost his job and couldn't keep any of the other jobs he managed to lie his way into, that the worst of it started. Life, for them, soon went from bad to worse. With Patrick slowly slipping into a depression and alcohol becoming his solace, it quickly became Lucy's worst nightmare.

CHAPTER NINETEEN

Shell Baker could always be found surrounded by men at one of the pubs in Markston. Most people who had grown up on the estates knew Shell. Her beauty made women jealous and her personality attracted men like moths to a flame.

The minute he walked in the door, Shell was intrigued. She had heard of Patrick Quinn and wondered if he really was as bad as everyone made him out to be.

He smiled at her as he made his way towards the bar. 'What are you drinking, love?'

She had to admit, he had a certain charm.

'Don't you think you'd better introduce yourself first, *love*? I don't take drinks from strangers.' He seemed surprised by her straight-talking, but she liked the sound of his laugh.

'Don't get your knickers in a twist, the name's Patrick – you going to share yours now?'

Shell was no fool. This guy was clearly a charmer, but a free drink didn't mean she had to marry him, so why not.

'Shell.' She stuck out her hand. 'Pleased to meet you, Patrick. I'll have a cider and black.'

She'd seen Patrick at the pub before. Although he hadn't grown up in the area, there were only a few pubs in Markston and most people knew the regulars. Shell didn't like much of what everybody said about Patrick, but she always believed in giving people a fair shake.

Of course, Shell was no angel either. If Patrick messed her about, he'd regret it.

Patrick told Shell that he needed a break from home and the banter flowed easily between them.

'So, why are you here talking to me if you have a wife and daughter at home?' Shell said.

'Lucy doesn't get me. She's controlling and always complaining. I can't talk to anyone or go anywhere without getting the third fucking degree.'

Shell wasn't convinced. He didn't strike her as a man who would let someone control him. He oozed confidence and had a slight arrogance about him.

'Why do you put up with that shit, then? I'd be out of there like a shot if anyone tried that with me!'

Patrick didn't answer right away. He looked as if he was thinking carefully.

'Not sure, if I'm honest. Been thinking about leaving her, but I have my kids to worry about too.'

Kids? 'I thought you said you had a daughter. What do you mean by kids? She ain't pregnant, is she?'

'No. No. No. I have a son, he just turned fifteen but lives with his mother. I was with his mother before Becky, Siobhan's mum.'

'Oh, right. I see. Well, if she's like that with you, what's she like with the kids … especially when you're not around?'

'Hmmm. I see your point. I never thought about that.'

'Where's your daughter's mother then? She still in the picture?'

A strange look came over Patrick's face. 'She's probably in a psycho ward! She's a raging alcoholic who fucked anything that gave her the slightest bit of attention.'

Shell wondered if Patrick could sense her surprise at his outburst.

68

'Look. I'm sorry if that came out a bit harsh. Siobhan's mum has problems. She needs help. She's a violent, aggressive drunk, and I worried she'd hurt my little girl. Not sure what happened to her before she met me, but it made her drink herself stupid nearly every day. I couldn't take it anymore, so I just upped and left.'

'You left your daughter with her?' Shell's mouth gaped open and she inched away.

'No. I took Siobhan with me and rang social services. I explained why I took Siobhan; they came, did their assessments, and the courts gave me custody. I would never leave my kid in a situation like that. What do you take me for? Sorry, I guess you don't really know me so that was a fair comment.'

Shell was beginning to warm to this guy. As well as being good-looking, with his cheeky smile, Patrick gave off all the signs of a decent, caring father. Someone with a troubled past who was doing their best. Shell could relate to that. She fidgeted in her seat with embarrassment at jumping to the wrong conclusion. Her hand went to Patrick's and she gave it a squeeze.

'Oh God, that sounds like an awful situation. Thank Christ you had the sense to get your daughter out with you. Not many men would.'

He looked down and shook his head. 'It was awful. I know girls need their mums, but there was just no way I'd put my princess through that.'

Patrick went on to tell Shell about Rory. How he'd last seen him ten years ago and, when Rory made contact via Facebook, Patrick knew they had to meet up. He told Shell that he had needed to explain his side of the story to Rory, because his mother had just left one day without an explanation, taking him with her.

Shell gasped. 'How could she do that?'

Patrick shrugged his shoulders. 'Still don't know. Maybe she was having an affair? Who knows. I don't care anymore, I'm just happy my kid found me.'

They had continued chatting until the pub closed and said their goodbyes outside. Patrick kissed Shell on the hand and suggested they exchange numbers. She reluctantly agreed but made it clear that she wasn't into breaking up families. Patrick had mumbled a comment, but Shell just waved it off and headed home.

CHAPTER TWENTY

Lucy had a meeting with Claire Knight before work that morning. The knots in her stomach were agony, because she dreaded having to make yet another excuse for Patrick's no-show. The loud snores from downstairs reaffirmed that he'd spent Sunday night drinking himself into a stupor and was still sleeping it off.

After getting into an argument with Patrick on Saturday about Siobhan's school dance, Lucy had left him to his own devices for the rest of the weekend. It was best to avoid him when he was in one of his moods.

When Siobhan had come home on Sunday, Lucy was the one left to tell Siobhan Patrick's decision. The little girl's tears broke her heart and once again, Lucy was left to pick up the pieces. Siobhan barely said a word to them that evening and Lucy was furious. She could only hope that Siobhan would sleep off the disappointment as only kids could do.

Lucy took Siobhan to school and waved goodbye to her at the gates. She headed to the nearby Costa, grabbed a coffee, and rushed to Claire's office. She hated these meetings. Hated lying. But if she wanted to keep Siobhan safe from her mum and from Patrick, she knew she had to play the game.

Lucy gave her name at the reception desk and sat down to wait. Within minutes, Claire came out and called her through.

'Hi, Lucy. How are you? It's been awhile hasn't it?'

'Hi, Claire, yeah, it has. Maybe three months?'

'Wow! Well hopefully we can withdraw our involvement completely if everything keeps going as well as it has. Where's Patrick today?' Claire had a funny look on her face and Lucy knew that her excuses were probably being questioned.

'He has a job interview.' Lucy smiled and couldn't believe how easily the lie rolled off her tongue.

'Hey, that's great. I hope something comes of this one. It has been quite some time since he lost his job, right?' Claire probably guessed there was more to the story of Patrick's unemployment. But Lucy was a strong, protective factor in Siobhan's life; Claire wouldn't want to upset that.

Lucy hated the look of pity on Claire's face. 'Yeah, it feels like forever, though. Can be a struggle supporting four people on my wage alone.'

Claire coughed and looked up from the notes she'd been writing. 'Four?'

Oh shit! Patrick is going to kill me!

'Um. Well, not always four … What I mean is, Patrick's son recently made contact and stays over some weekends.' Before Lucy had the chance to change the subject, Claire pounced.

'Really? I didn't know Patrick had a son. How old is he and can I get some more details off you?' Claire began writing furiously in her notepad, and Lucy bit her lip angrily. Just when social services were finally looking to get out of their lives.

Shit! Shit! Shit!

'Of course.' Lucy gave Claire as much detail about Rory as she knew offhand and told her she'd have to email later with the rest.

As he was only fifteen years old, social care would have to do some further checks on Rory and speak to his mother. Although this would not affect the case with Siobhan, who knows what

Patrick's ex would say to Claire? Lucy could just kick herself. Patrick had made it clear to her, on more than one occasion, that this was all her fault because she'd called the police once when Patrick came home drunk and kicked off.

Siobhan was already known to social care because her school had contacted them when Becky arrived drunk and caused a scene. She had told social care that Patrick's abuse made her drink and, although there was no evidence recorded, any child that came to spend time overnight with Patrick had to have an assessment.

Lucy didn't know much about Rory's mother or why she left Patrick – he'd always clam up or get angry when she asked questions – but she had a pretty good idea what had happened. If she was right, and Claire went digging further, Lucy was expecting all hell to break loose.

CHAPTER TWENTY-ONE

Shell couldn't seem to get Patrick out of her head as she worked. She pushed the vacuum across the floor of the office, careful to avoid the plant pots as her thoughts returned to him once again. *Who was this guy?* She was reluctant to get involved with him, even as friend, but she had to admit there was something about him.

Shell's own experience of a violent father made her portray herself as hard and overly cautious. But Patrick seemed really genuine when talking about his children, and Shell knew that some women were bitter when relationships ended. Maybe things had been blown out of proportion.

The anger she felt towards her father, who was currently serving time at Her Majesty's pleasure, often invaded her thoughts. She couldn't believe that nearly seventeen years had passed; even though she was now thirty years old, it only seemed like yesterday.

Shell knew what happened to her mother wasn't her fault, but there were days when guilt still ate away at her. She'd only been thirteen years old – what could she have done?

The nights when Shell managed to get some sleep were filled with nightmares. Her mother screaming as Shell hid in her room, hoping she hadn't been heard, wanting to run down and stop her father. The glass table shattering. The million pieces of ice-like shards rotating through the air and scattering across the floor. Her life had been changed forever the moment she had gone downstairs and seen her mother's battered body, barely breathing, in a heap on the living room floor.

She shuddered when she recalled the smirk on her father's face. Him standing in the doorway watching her. Shell running towards him, him shoving her back so hard she hit her head on the corner of the broken table.

'Get the fuck away from me, you little bitch. Just like your mum.' The memories after that still only came to Shell in brief flashes. Hazy. According to the police reports and pictures from the night, Shell sustained a head injury that affected her memory.

Shell had drifted in and out of consciousness that night in the hospital, but she'd never forget the look of pure hatred and disgust in her father's eyes. How he had kicked her mother, grabbed his coat, and walked out the door.

Shell felt a cold chill up her spine as she bent over to switch the vacuum off. At the time, she'd spent a few nights in hospital and now, as she subconsciously rubbed her head, it was only the psychological scars that remained. It didn't take the police long to find her father, though. He was arrested a few days later, pissed up in a pub a few miles away, and charged with the attempted murder of her mother.

Her father had initially pleaded not guilty – which meant Shell had had to give evidence in court, thankfully via video link– but it was all part of his desire to exert power and control over the women in his life.

He argued publicly with his solicitor during the trial. But continued the mind games after the damage had already been done to Shell's fragile emotional state by eventually changing his plea. He was convicted of attempted murder against her mother and GBH against her. Due to the brutality of the offence – he'd beat Shell's mother so bad that nearly all her bones were broken – he received the maximum sentence: life.

The thought of what she and her mother had had to endure all those years ago was still too much to bear. Shell hated when the post arrived; she was crippled by the constant fear that she'd find out he was eligible for parole.

Her mother's diary had been produced as evidence. It detailed the years of abuse, both sexual and physical, that she'd endured at the hands of Shell's father. Shell had kept this diary and it made for a very dark read. Her mother had survived the brutal attack, but something had died inside her that day. Shell had been taken into care as her mother turned to alcohol and drugs to escape the memories, and eventually prostitution, to pay for her mind-numbing addiction. She overdosed a few years later and Shell would never forgive her father for that.

Shell snapped out of the painful stroll down memory lane and carried on with the job at hand. She picked up her cloth and cleaner before she leaned against the window and looked down at the traffic rushing past in the street below. Never forgotten, she knew this abyss would rear its ugly head again. She was just grateful that she was able to push the dark thoughts aside and focus on the positive things in her life. She had made something of herself and wouldn't let her father get the last laugh. She had to admit though, sometimes it was hard to keep her anger in check and she feared what that could lead to. Would she turn out like him?

CHAPTER TWENTY-TWO

Lucy had spent Tuesday and Wednesday at work making sure her cases were up to date and her appointments were covered. She had the Thursday off to deal with personal matters.

The family courts were busy on Thursdays. Patrick and Lucy had met with their solicitor and handed over the paperwork that Lucy had spent weeks preparing. They were going for permanent custody of Siobhan, since it looked like social care were going to withdraw their involvement with the Quinns shortly. Although Lucy had been concerned after she had let slip about Rory spending weekends, she had been assured by Claire that the case with Siobhan and her custody would be dealt with on its own merits. Their solicitor and Cafcass also believed that there would be no issues; Rory was not a permanent resident, the agencies just wanted to ensure that there would be no further disruption to Siobhan's home life.

Becky Parks was sitting at the other side of the waiting area and kept shooting daggers at Lucy. She looked drunk.

As a married couple, and with Lucy's job, social care and their solicitor felt they had a strong case of securing permanent special guardianship and residency.

While Patrick and Becky were in the courtroom, Lucy rang Sarah to keep her updated.

'Are you sure you are doing the right thing, Lucy? You could be bringing more problems into your life. You'll be tied to Patrick then and find it harder if you want to make … changes.'

'I hear what you're saying, Sarah, but I know what I'm doing.' Lucy stubbornly ended the call. She made so many excuses for Patrick that she almost believed them herself.

He was having a bad day.

He was tired.

He's under a lot of stress.

He can't cope with his feelings.

So many excuses. Instead of facing the fact that maybe he was just an abusive, controlling asshole.

A few hours later, Patrick came out of the court room with a big smile on his face.

'Do I even have to ask?'

Patrick grabbed her and hugged her close. 'The judge gave me the residency order. Siobhan will be coming home with me tonight!' He kissed her. 'I think a drink is in order!'

Lucy rolled her eyes.

'What? Just a few drinks.' He gave her an innocent look.

'But Siobhan will be with us. She's been taken away from her mother due to Becky's drinking. How is it going to look if we go out to the pub and then pick her up drunk?'

'So what? I'm not getting pissed. For fuck's sake, Lucy, why do you have to turn a happy day into a bloody argument every. single. time?' Patrick headed for the lift, a cold glint in his eye. 'Well, are you coming?'

Lucy grabbed her bag and tried to lighten the mood. 'OK. I guess one drink won't hurt.' She wanted to smooth things over, to avoid confrontation. It didn't always work though, and she wondered why she bothered.

'Forget it.'

As they headed for the bus, Patrick's phone rang.

'Hello? Right, OK. Well when can I pick her up? Right. OK. See ya.'

'Who was that?'

'That social worker, Claire. Siobhan is going to stay at her grandparents' tonight. I have to pick her up in the morning and take her to school. I'm going to the pub. You coming or what?'

CHAPTER TWENTY-THREE

Maggie looked at all the crime scene photos and material collected in the Talbot case. No fingerprints were found on the syringe and no DNA evidence was collected. CCTV footage showed a white van in the area, which PC Reynolds was tasked with tracing. There were no other witnesses.

Holding up one of the photos, Maggie looked closely at the injuries. Hands mutilated – was the killer sending a message? Maggie felt there was something personal to this crime. For Maggie, a crime scene photo was like a film in her head: she could picture the crime as it happened.

She looked across her desk at Mark. 'What do you think occurred?'

'Sorry, what?'

'These images. I can see, almost step by step, what I think the killer did. They knew where Talbot would be – it was carefully planned – and they had everything they needed with them. They followed him and, when they believed they wouldn't be seen, snuck up and hit him from behind. The pathologist's report suggests that the killer searched his pockets and found the empty syringe. They wanted to inject him with an air bubble to kill him.'

'I was still trying to work things out but what you've said is interesting. I was wondering about the syringe – that obviously didn't work. What else do the pictures tell you?'

'I think when the needle failed, they turned him over. It looks like all three wounds to the body were done around the same time – so let's say throat first, and then the legs – just to be sure. The killer used a hammer or heavy-duty meat tenderizer to bash the shit out of Talbot's hands … why? A statement maybe? He'll never hit a woman again?' Maggie ran her fingers through her hair.

'Sounds plausible. So it was revenge?'

'Perhaps … Though after speaking to Wendy Parker, I don't think it was her. Too frail. And her daughter was in hospital, it couldn't have been her. So, who? Drew was an only child, and his parents are devastated. They claim he has no enemies but, given his lifestyle, I find that unusual. Perhaps he screwed someone over? Maybe this has nothing to do with domestic violence.'

'Let's see if anything comes from that white van trace. Reynolds should have something soon enough. Who is interviewing Talbot's erm … associates?' Mark started typing something on his computer. 'Looks like Kat is on the case. We'll see if she can shed any light on that front.'

'Sounds good.' Maggie tapped the photos on her desk with her pen. 'Maybe you could give Lucy a bell and see if she has anything on this guy. He's a repeat offender, so he must be known to probation.'

'Will do, Maggie.'

Maggie's gut told her that they were missing something. A piece to the jigsaw that would point them in the right direction. If only the dead could speak …

CHAPTER TWENTY-FOUR

Most people lived for the weekends, but not Lucy. Ed and Maria had plans on the Friday, so it was agreed that they would collect Siobhan early Saturday morning instead.

With another weekend of being alone with Patrick looming, Lucy feared how he'd behave. Guilt overwhelmed her when she selfishly wished Siobhan could miss out on a weekend with her grandparents and stay at home. The poor kid shouldn't be used as a metaphorical shield. Patrick's moods were unpredictable. This is what worried Lucy the most. What made Patrick dangerous? He had control over his behaviour and would only make snide remarks when Siobhan or Rory were in the house. His excuses for the violence were another manipulative technique to exert control over her.

Patrick was still asleep. He couldn't even be bothered to drag his ass out of bed and say goodbye to his daughter. Rory was coming around later, and Lucy hoped she wouldn't have to make more excuses for his father. She could see the look of disappointment in Rory's eyes every time she had to explain where Patrick was, or why he wasn't ready.

Being older than Siobhan, Rory had more of an understanding of Patrick's moods and had learnt to tailor his own behaviour accordingly. That killed Lucy. She had no fear that Patrick would hurt his children, at least not while she was in the picture, but there had been times when angry outbursts and insults were aimed at Rory. When Rory would storm out of the house and weeks would pass before he came around again. When Lucy would be walking on eggshells, concerned that if Rory said anything to his mother, social services would be all over them again.

Why don't I just leave?

Any time something had happened with his father, Lucy had felt some overwhelming responsibility to smooth things over. She'd message Rory on Facebook to find out if he was OK. Lucy shamefully admitted to herself that part of her genuine concern for his well-being was a selfish desire to make sure he wasn't telling his mother anything. Like his father, Rory seemed to bottle things up inside and she at least wanted to give him the opportunity to get it out. She almost felt like she owed him that. Guilt lay heavy at Lucy's door, for she had no one she could share all her feelings with, in case it exposed the reality of her situation.

There was a stirring upstairs followed by a loud groan. *He's up.* Lucy grabbed the laundry basket and put the kettle on. Patrick did his usual stomp down the stairs, then sidled up behind her as she was bent over, loading the washing machine. He wrapped his arms around her waist and pulled her in to him.

'Perfect position. Fancy a quickie?'

Before she could answer, there was a knock at the door. *Thank God.* Lucy slipped out of Patrick's grasp and made her way to the door. It was Rory. Lucy gave him a hug and offered him a cup of tea, gesturing him inside.

'Only if you're making one. I don't want to put you out.'

Lucy adored his politeness. Very unlike his dad.

'Of course, she is! You need to learn a woman's place, son. Go on and have a seat.' He turned towards Lucy with a sneer on his face. 'I'll have a coffee, and make sure it isn't your usual strong shit.'

Lucy was pleased to stay out of their way in the kitchen, letting them catch up. Before long she heard the roar of race cars from the television and knew they would be immersed on the PlayStation for hours. Lucy poured the tea, losing herself as she stirred in the milk. Once she handed the boys their drinks, she returned to the kitchen to make a start on her weekend routine of cleaning, laundry, and anything else that Patrick had not done throughout the week. So pretty much everything.

Things were calm over the weekend despite the initial blip and they enjoyed Sunday evening watching films. It was times like this when Lucy remembered why she fell in love with Patrick. Seeing him enjoy himself, laughing and being kind to her. He even made her a drink before bed.

Maybe it will be OK after all.

CHAPTER TWENTY-FIVE

Lucy woke up in complete darkness. The red numbers on the alarm clock flashed 4:30 a.m. Her head was banging. Unable to recall much of the events of the night before, she felt as if she'd been drugged. Patrick had often joked that he could easily slip GHB into her drinks and do what he wanted to her. As much as she feared this, Lucy could never bring herself to believe that he would actually go that far. Between her legs, the pain was excruciating. Like fire. Red raw. Everything was hazy in her mind. Reaching up to her head, she ran her fingers through her hair.

She felt so stupid. She should never have trusted Patrick when he offered to make her a drink, but they'd had such a good weekend with Rory that she had let her guard down. Sunday night was spent watching a movie with Siobhan when she came home. It had been a good evening.

Has he drugged me? No. No. Even he wouldn't stoop that low, would he? Her head pounded as a series of flashbacks ran through her mind like a flicker of film clips.

Patrick's hand around her throat. Squeezing tightly. The other covering her mouth as she tried to scream. The glazed, evil eyes.

Oh, my god!

Fear and panic set in. She sat up and frantically looked around the bedroom. *Where was he?* She threw the blankets off, pulled on her leggings and T-shirt, wincing as the pain seared through her. Hoping she couldn't be heard, Lucy tiptoed out of the bedroom, checking the landing before she went any further. She could hear snoring from the spare bedroom. Lucy didn't want to wake Patrick. As quietly as she could, stifling a whimper as another shot of pain sliced through her, Lucy went downstairs, sat on the couch, and began rocking herself, hugging her knees close as she cried silent tears.

Time ticked by, and two hours later the drugs – or whatever Patrick had given her – was still in her system, her head fuzzy with tiredness. There was movement upstairs. Fear gripped her. What should she do? It was only six-thirty in the morning, but she messaged Sarah anyway.

Are you free before work? x Lucy

Hey, Luce! You're up early! Yes, I'm free, Why? Everything OK? xx Sarah

No. I need to get out. Sick of this. Can you meet me? Costa? xx

Get out? What do you mean? Never mind, tell me when we meet. What time?

Looking at the clock on the wall, Lucy texted back.

Would an hour be OK? x

That would make it just after 7.30 a.m. and plenty of time to be ready and out of the house. Patrick would have to make sure

Siobhan got to school or be the one to explain why she was missing – Lucy couldn't think straight and didn't care what the consequences might be.

OK, Luce. See you soon. xx

She went through the laundry basket left in the dining room and dressed as quickly as she could. Retrieved her shoes and was just about to sit down when Patrick walked in the room. She fumbled with her phone and quickly deleted the messages from Sarah. Turned it on silent and hid it in her pocket. He'd question her relentlessly if he heard a message come through and accuse her of cheating, even when she showed him the messages.

Why was he up so early?

Patrick looked sheepish.

'Morning.'

It was as if nothing had happened last night, as if they were just a normal couple. But she didn't want an argument, so she put on her brave face and asked him if he wanted coffee.

From the kitchen, she shouted out to him, 'I'm going into work early to catch up on a few reports. You'll have to drop Siobhan at school. Have you got anything planned for the day?' Determined not to let him win this time, Lucy struggled to keep her voice steady.

'What is this? The Spanish Inquisition?' He laughed, but Lucy knew the tone behind it. Her silence went unnoticed.

'I'm just going to call Steve, probably go around his later this afternoon. He said he may have a few days' work for me. I'll drop Siobhan off, but won't be able to get her this afternoon.'

Lucy was curious about this 'Steve'. Patrick had only started mentioning him recently and she'd never met him. But if it meant she was left alone, and not questioned about going into work early, she was happy enough to leave him to it.

'OK.' Lucy grimaced in pain. She put his coffee on the table, kissed his cheek, grabbed her coat, and walked as fast as she could to the bus stop, each step more excruciating than the last.

When she arrived at Costa, Sarah wasn't there so she ordered herself a strong coffee and chose a table as far away from everyone else as possible.

'Hey, Lucy.' Sarah smiled as she waved and walked towards her. Before Sarah could even sit down, the tears flowed. Sarah wrapped her arms around her and whispered 'Hey. Hey, sweetheart. What's wrong? I know things at home haven't been great. Is that what this is about? Enough is enough, Lucy. You need to tell me.'

Sarah listened as Lucy relayed what she could remember from the night before. Then the dam broke. She was crying and talking through her sobs, reliving years of abuse and telling Sarah about everything she had experienced. Lucy felt worthless but having Sarah to confide in helped.

'Oh, my god, Lucy. You don't deserve this. Can't you see that? I knew something was going on. Damn … what kind of friend am I? I should've been there for you.'

'It's not your fault, Sarah. I would have denied it all anyway. I know I should know better. I think of work, the people we deal with … I see Patrick in them … all of them. Every day. I wish he was dead. It scares me. He scares me. If I leave though, what will happen to Siobhan and Rory?'

'Without sounding awful, Lucy, they're *his* kids. You can tell that social worker, Claire. She'll help you.'

'What if I get in trouble? I lied, Sarah. Over and over again. I don't think I can risk it. What if they tell work? I could face a disciplinary or worse. God, I sound so fucking selfish!'

'Lucy, what would you tell someone you were working with? You'd tell them they're putting themselves, and the kids, in danger.

You would tell them they need to protect the children. Speak to Claire. Please, promise me?'

'OK. OK. I will.'

But Lucy had no intention of keeping that promise.

CHAPTER TWENTY-SIX

Patrick waited for about twenty minutes after Lucy left for work, before he got dressed and texted Shell, or 'Steve' as he had her number stored under on his phone. Lucy never checked his phone, but it would be just his luck that Shell would call, and Lucy would see the screen. Shell confirmed she'd be free that afternoon and looked forward to seeing him.

When he woke Siobhan, he laughed at the sleepy, confused face she pulled. 'Hey, princess! Up and at 'em – we need to get you fed and dressed and off to school!'

'Where's Lucy? She usually takes me.'

Patrick paused and took a deep breath before he answered. Why should *his* kids look to Lucy before him? 'Well, today is your lucky day as Daddy is going to take you! And guess what?'

Siobhan rubbed her eyes and shrugged her shoulders. 'Dunno, what?'

'You can have whatever you want for breakfast. I won't tell if you won't?' Patrick tickled his daughter and drank in her laughter.

'Stop, Daddy! I'm going to wet the bed!'

Patrick laughed as he left Siobhan to get dressed. The school run went without a hitch and Patrick ignored any looks from the mums at the gate. He didn't want to cause a scene but he would love to wipe the smug smiles off their faces.

Patrick stopped in the corner shop and bought a newspaper on his way to the café. He didn't want to have to go back home after dropping Siobhan off, so he wasted the time reading the paper, pretending to look for work in case Lucy harassed him later. He circled a few adverts, making it appear genuine. A quick bet at the bookies had Patrick pleased with himself a few hours later. With the extra twenty pounds he had won in his pocket, he jumped in his car and made the journey to Shell's maisonette in record time. Knocking on the door, Patrick licked his lips in the hopes that today might be the day that she finally gave in to him.

Patrick and Shell had been talking to each other regularly, meeting up when possible and he wanted to move things forward. He had done everything he was supposed to do and was confident that she would crack soon. Shell answered with a big smile on her face and he eagerly walked inside. Promising. It was the first time he'd been to her home, and that in itself was a good sign. He followed her through the hallway and into her living room. He was expecting something loud and garish given her personality, but was pleasantly surprised to see the wood flooring, cream walls, and two leather couches. The room had a homelike feel to it. Something he always felt was missing with Lucy. There was a small fireplace, with a flat-screen TV mounted above it in the centre of the room.

'Nice place.'

'Thanks, hun. I bet you were expecting something loud and tacky, right?' she laughed.

Patrick could feel his face flush. 'Well, yeah – if I'm honest.' He took a seat and patted the spot next to him.

'Do you want a drink? Is it too early for alcohol? I have lager, cider, or wine. What's your poison, darling?'

'A girl after my own heart. I'm driving so can't have too many, but a lager please, love. Then park that beautiful backside down next to me.'

Shell giggled as she made her way to the kitchen to get the drinks. Patrick smiled. Any rumours she'd heard would soon be forgotten. If he treated her right for a bit, she'd soon be wrapped around his finger.

Patrick had made himself comfortable when Shell returned and handed him his lager.

'So, what have you been up to, love?' Shell turned to Patrick, giving him her full attention.

Patrick relayed his day in short succession. Less talk meant more time for action as far as he was concerned. As soon as she sat down beside him and rested her hand on his knee with a delicate smile, he knew she was his for the taking. Patrick opened up to Shell, feeding her the lines he knew she wanted to hear. They spent hours talking, kissing, and eventually, one thing led to another.

Patrick woke with a start. 'Babe, what time is it?' He rubbed her back as she leaned over to look at the clock on her mobile phone.

'Two, in the morning, why?'

'Shit! I have to go! Lucy is going to kill me!'

'What do you care? I thought you said you were going to leave her? Or have you been messing me about? Maybe you should tell her. I can come with you tomorrow, if you want?'

'No fucking way.' Patrick snapped. He realized too late how sharp his response was.

Sitting up, Shell let loose. 'You what? What are you shouting at me for? Who the fuck do you think you're talking to?'

Patrick hesitated then smiled carefully, looking her in the eyes. 'Uh, sorry, babe. I'm still half asleep. I didn't mean it the way it sounded.'

He pulled her close and nuzzled her neck. 'I do plan on leaving her. I will leave her. I just need to get the timing right and make sure the kids are sorted. Soon, I promise.'

Looking at his watch, he knew he had to make a move. He sat at the edge of the bed with his back to Shell and got dressed.

'I hope you're not fucking me about, Patrick. Trust me: you don't want to do that.'

'Babe, I'm not. I've really fallen for you.' Patrick had to hide the smirk forming on his face.

Shell reached over and wrapped her arms around him from behind. 'OK. I trust you.' That was Shell's first mistake.

'I'll ring you later. After Lucy goes to work, OK?'

'OK, love.' Giving him a kiss, she waved as she watched him leave.

Never in a million years did she think she'd fall for someone again. When she asked around, no one had any evidence that Patrick hurt women. All hearsay. His wife was a probation officer, she would never put up with that. After being messed about so many times, Shell had virtually given up on men. Instead, she enjoyed taking what she wanted, when she wanted, and then cast them aside, the way they used to cast her aside. She was in control. She pulled the blanket tight around her and sighed. *Things would definitely be different this time around.*

Believing that was Shell's second mistake.

93

CHAPTER TWENTY-SEVEN

Lucy couldn't sleep. Patrick hadn't come home yet, and the house seemed eerily quiet even with Siobhan asleep in the other room. Lucy threw the blankets off her and headed to the bathroom for a glass of water. On her way back, she noticed the box room door slightly ajar. It had always been her escape. She pushed the door open and turned the dimmer to low. A soft glow encompassed the room. A faint scent of Patrick wafted in the air, so Lucy turned on the air freshener.

The walls were plain, but Lucy had put up a few shelves to hold the books and little trinkets she'd collected throughout her lifetime. Deep maroon curtains added a cosy feel and the cream carpet was so plush that Lucy would often take off her shoes and run her bare feet through it. There were a few pictures in this room, one of Siobhan, laughing and enjoying herself on a beach holiday that the three of them had taken before they were married. Some pictures of Lucy and Patrick from happier times. Those days seemed few and far between. Lucy sighed.

Although Rory often used the small room when he visited, Lucy had made sure it stayed as a small haven for when she needed time alone. Patrick didn't understand the day-to-day stresses that Lucy had to contend with as a probation officer.

She settled into her favourite chair – an old rocking chair she'd seen at a boot sale and refurbished – and wrapped the woollen blanket around her legs. Putting her headphones on, she pressed play on the CD player and listened to The Killers, allowing her favourite songs to take her away from misery. She knew it was risky, because she might not hear Patrick when he finally got home, but she really needed to relax.

The cushion behind her jutted uncomfortably into her back. Lucy knew exactly what it was and gently stroked the bump. Inside the cushion was a bag of various pills that Patrick either no longer took or that she'd stolen and stashed away. They were like a security blanket to her. When things became too much she'd visualize swallowing the pills. One by one, washing them down with vodka and going to sleep – forever. There had been times when her suicidal thoughts pulled at her, tempting her to end it all. She had come very close once, but a faint 'tap tap tap' on the door and Siobhan's big blue eyes staring at her had shaken her out of that fantasy fast. As if Siobhan had known. Lucy would never leave her.

Lucy had wanted to speak to her GP, but she couldn't face disclosing her feelings and the reasons behind her low moods.

She hugged her knees close and rocked gently back and forth. The music soothed her only temporarily. Closing her eyes, Lucy continued to rock until sleep took over.

In her dreams, Lucy was strong, confident, and fierce: the way she used to be before she married Patrick. Lucy used to pride herself on being a good judge of character. She assessed people daily and rarely got it wrong. What really astounded her was the fact that her specialism was domestic abuse. She knew what to look for: manipulative, controlling behaviour with a need for complete power and control over someone. Even when these things cropped up briefly in Rory's behaviour, Lucy made the very excuses that other victims of domestic abuse made.

Dark thoughts sometimes took over. They made her feel good.

A particular recurring dream gave her an overwhelming sense of euphoria.

In the dream she was standing in the kitchen chopping vegetables. The knife gripped tightly in her hand was big and extremely sharp. Patrick came through the back door that led directly into the kitchen. Angry, as usual, about something Lucy had no control over. It could be his failure to keep a job, or some knob cut him off on his way home – it could be anything. He was shouting in her face, the spit flying, showering her cheeks. He put his forehead against hers. Hard. Unyielding. Making sure she knew who was in control. Patrick reminded her that in his mind she was scum. A slag. Unwanted. She gripped the knife tighter. Patrick took no notice, he never did, unless he was getting something out of it.

Her knuckles were pure white from holding the knife so tight. The rage inside her building. Inside her head she was screaming, everything she wanted to say aloud, while Patrick screamed in her face. And then, as if it had a life of its own, her arm began to rise in slow motion, like a film. Patrick remained oblivious, too busy shouting obscenities in her face. One deep plunge in his shoulder first. Him stumbling backwards, away from her. Stunned.

Lucy gathered all her rage, held the knife out in front of her and ran towards him, plunging the blade deep into his chest and holding it there. Looking straight into his eyes as the shock hit him. Watching the anger turn to fear in his eyes. Pulling the knife out and stabbing him again, and again. Screaming. *You fucking prick. I hope you die. Everyone would be better off without you!* Patrick dropped to the ground and lay there, on the kitchen floor, in a pool of blood. Blood everywhere. His face confused as his life drained from his eyes. Lucy just stared. Dripping knife still in her hands. And then she laughed. A manic laugh that scared even her. And why? Why the crazy laughter? Because even though she was now free of Patrick, Lucy knew he'd still won – still ruined her life. She would end up spending the rest of her life in prison for killing him. This is the point when she woke up crying because, even in death, he still controlled her.

She heard the front door slam downstairs, bringing her once again back to reality.

A whispered shout called out to her. 'Lucy! Lucy! Are you home?'

Lucy looked at her watch. It was three-thirty in the morning. She'd slept longer than she'd wanted. She stayed silent and turned off the CD player. A mobile phone ring. It was faint; she breathed a sigh of relief that it wasn't hers. Maybe Patrick wouldn't know she was awake. She needed to get back into their bedroom while he was on the phone. She only made out parts of the conversation.

'OK ... will try but ... Lucy doing ... speak soon, babe.'

That woke her up. She opened the door slowly, careful to avoid the creaking floorboard that she'd discovered after a previous attempt to avoid Patrick.

'Why didn't you answer?'

'Shit, Patrick! You frightened the life out of me. I couldn't sleep. I was on the rocking chair in the small room ... where I obviously *did* fall asleep.' She laughed nervously, hoping she sounded convincing.

'Ah. Sleeping, were you?'

Patrick sounded like he was accusing her rather than asking a straight question. She hated when he did that. Always made her feel guilty, even when there was no reason to be. An image from her dream flashed before her eyes: him dead in a pool of blood on the floor. She swallowed.

'Yes, I just told you that.'

Patrick slowly walked up the stairs towards her.

Oh God! He knows I'm lying. She cowered on the landing.

'What's the matter, love? Guilty conscience? I only want to use the toilet.'

Lucy's shoulders slumped in relief.

'Sorry, I must still be half asleep.'

She let Patrick pass and, as he closed the door, he squinted his eyes and pointed his finger at her.

'I hope you're not keeping anything from me, Lucy. You know I hate liars.'

Lucy shook her head.

'What would I be keeping from you?' She turned and headed back to their bedroom.

That's rich. Me a liar? Look in the mirror, Patrick – who the fuck were you calling, babe?

CHAPTER TWENTY-EIGHT

Shell had been up since six that morning working at one of the smaller jobs she had on her books because one of her employees had called in sick. She had a handful of casual workers in her company, but the problem was they felt no remorse when they let her down. Her mind wandered and the curiosity she had about Patrick's wife niggled at her. She wondered why he had no choice but to stay with Lucy.

She began to form a plan. Vicki was still on probation and was always pestering her for a lift. Perhaps she'd offer to take her to her next appointment. That way, there was the off-chance that she might catch a glimpse of Lucy.

After dropping her car off at home, Shell changed quickly, and walked towards the local pub. Even though it was only 11.00 a.m., she knew it was dole day for Vicki, and that the money would be spent as soon as it hit her bank account.

Vicki was alone at a table in the corner when Shell walked into the pub. She already looked well out of it, so Shell would need to move quickly, before Vicki reached the point of no return. Shell approached the table, removed her coat and hung it on the back of the chair. Vicki glanced up, bleary-eyed.

'Hey, Vicki. Long time, no see. Can I get you a drink?'

Vicki looked at Shell warily. Then a big smile of recognition erupted on her face.

'Well, fuck me! Shell Baker, how the hell are you? I'll have a *large* pint of cider if you're buying?'

Shell smiled to herself. *This might be easier than I thought.* Although they were still good friends, Shell and Vicki had had their ups and downs over the years, due to Vicki's drinking and choice in men. Shell had become tired of bailing Vicki out of one bad situation or another She had hoped that once Vicki hit rock bottom, she would start sorting herself out. So far, that hadn't happened.

Shell smiled sadly at Vicki, made her way up to the bar and ordered a large Coke for herself, wanting to keep her wits about her. She asked the barman, Kevin, to hold a £20 note behind the bar for Vicki. When Shell returned to the table and sat down, she began quizzing Vicki about her recent release from prison, working her way slowly to the question that had been burning in her mind ever since she arrived: 'So who's your probation officer?'

'Ah, fuck, now you're asking.' The words were slurred, and Vicki began digging around in the pockets of the oversized coat she was wearing. She pulled out a piece of paper and threw it towards Shell.

'It's on there.'

Shell picked it up. *Damn!* 'Sarah Hardy' was written on the appointment slip.

'Do you always see this Sarah lady? What's she like?'

'OK. Bit bossy, but guess she has to be. Sometimes I see another one. Lucy, I think her name is or it could be Lacy. I've also seen a bloke – but can't remember his name.'

'Well,' Shell smiled, 'if you ever need a lift or want someone with you, for support, or anything – let me know, OK? I'd hate to see anyone take advantage of ya.'

Another big, crooked smile lit up Vicki's face. 'You're a fucking star, Shell – I'm on my way there in a bit. It's only down the road, but I could do with the company.'

CHAPTER TWENTY-NINE

The following day, Shell paced up and down the kitchen anxiously, thinking about the text she had received from Patrick:

We have to talk.

She wondered if he'd found out that she'd 'met' his wife. He'd made it quite clear that he wanted Shell to stay away. It wasn't a big deal. She'd just sat in the room with Vicki at her appointment. Lucy had come across as a bit bossy, but Shell had managed to keep her mouth shut; she hadn't wanted Lucy to remember her and tell Patrick about her when she got home.

Shell took out the mop and sloshed in some hot water, scrubbing her floor with vigour – cleaning was a slight obsession. Satisfied with the job she had done, she looked around and noticed some dust on the TV above the fireplace. She wiped the sweat from her brow and moved swiftly across the room, duster in hand.

The knock at the door made her jump. 'Will be with you in two minutes,' she shouted. She scrubbed the counter for the third time, her heart racing, hoping that it was Patrick on the other side of the door. Shell splashed her face with cold water and washed her hands, drying them on the tea towel that lay by the sink. With one final look in the small mirror on the windowsill, she made her way to the door and opened it with a big smile on her face.

'Oh …' She frowned. 'It's you. I thought you were someone else.'

'Charmin', cuz,' Louise said as she pushed her way past Shell.

'Don't make yourself too comfortable, Louise, I'm expecting someone.' Shell watched as she plonked herself down on the couch.

'Oooooooh. Do tell. We haven't had a proper chat in ages.' She put her feet up on the coffee table and Shell glared at her.

'How about I meet you at the pub tomorrow and we catch up then? I seriously need to finish and get myself sorted. This place is a mess!' She tapped Louise's feet.

Louise looked around the room and rolled her eyes. 'Are you crazy? This room … this house, is *pristine*, Ms OCD. Don't worry, I get you're a bit highly strung right now, so I'll see you at the pub tomorrow eve. Seven-ish OK?'

'Yep. Great … now go, please.' Shell practically pushed her cousin out the door and slammed the door behind her. Thank God for that. Shell went back into the kitchen, did another quick wipe of the surfaces and popped the kettle on. The floorboard creaked behind her.

'I hope it's me you're thinking about.'

'Oh, my god, Patrick! You scared the shit out of me!' Shell was shaking as Patrick stepped across the room and put his arms around her.

'Calm down, babe. It was just a joke.'

'Wait. How did you get in?' Shell was sure she'd secured the door after Louise left.

'The door was open. How do you think? I ain't bloody magic and haven't mastered the art of picking locks yet.' He laughed.

'Oh … OK. Weird … oh well! It's amazing to see you, love.' She planted a long, passionate kiss on Patrick's eager lips.

'Feel the same, babe. If you're making a cuppa …' he looked at the boiling kettle, 'then I wouldn't mind a brew.'

Patting Shell's bottom, Patrick made his way to the living room and sat down. Shell felt so lucky to have him and couldn't understand why his wife was such a bitch. She was glad that Lucy didn't treat Patrick the way he deserved. Otherwise he wouldn't be sat in her living room right now. She handed him his tea and sat down next to him.

'So … what did you want to talk about?' A nervous croak escaped her lips.

'Well. I have this chance for a job, you see.' There was a glint of excitement in his eyes and Shell smiled. 'But my car needs some new brakes and tyres. I won't be able to get there if I don't get those things sorted.' He sighed and looked sadly into Shell's eyes. 'Lucy's moaning about money, even though this would *help* our situation and – I'm embarrassed to ask – but I was wondering …'

Before Patrick could even finish his sentence, Shell grabbed her wallet and started leafing through the notes. 'How much do you need?'

'Ah, Shell. This is why I love ya. Are you sure you can afford it?'

'Yes. Now tell me, how much?'

Did he just say he loved me?

'It's going to be a couple of hundred.' Shell's cheek flickered slightly. 'It's too much, right? Look – sorry. Forget it. I shouldn't have asked you. I'll just have to look for another job or figure something else out.' Patrick put his tea down on the table and made a move to get off the couch.

Shell rested her hand on his leg, pushing him down.

'Don't be silly. I just don't have that much in my wallet. Let me grab my coat and we can go to the cashpoint … yeah?'

'If you're sure.' Patrick smiled.

Patrick was still smiling as he walked to the pub, Shell's cash in his pocket. For someone who thought she was so clever, he marvelled at how dumb Shell could be. She didn't even bat an eye at his excuse for getting into her house. He had found her spare key when he'd been waiting for her to get ready one day, took it, and made a copy. The next time he was around, he put the spare back. It was actually tagged *spare key*, and Patrick just couldn't resist. He'd thought how easy it would be to sneak in and steal some of her possessions when he she was at work.

Patrick could get a fair whack for some of her things. Shame there were so many people around the area who would tell Shell if they saw him going into the house. He couldn't risk that – not yet anyway. He wondered how much money he could get off her before she started asking questions.

That's what he loved about women like Shell – desperate to be loved, they would believe, and put up with, any shit. Sad cow. He walked into the pub and ordered a pint of Stella. It wasn't the classiest of places, worn carpets and chipped paint on the walls, but it was comfortable and cheap.

'What's with the big smile on your face?' Kevin queried.

'Just a happy man, Kev. A happy man.' Patrick saw Robert Millard sitting in the corner looking a bit forlorn and shouted over, 'You OK, Rob? Would a pint cheer you up?'

Raising his head, Robert nodded and said, 'Cider, mate … and thanks.'

Patrick carried the drinks over to the table. 'So, what's up? Woman troubles again?'

'Sort of. Don't know if you heard but Louise and I split. Again. Bitch called the coppers after a stupid row and now I'm on fucking probation. One foot wrong and I could go to fucking prison.'

Patrick's curiosity got the better of him. 'Oh yeah. Who's your probation officer?'

Unsure whether Robert Millard had put two and two together, because Lucy used her maiden name for work, Patrick waited for the answer.

'Lucy – bloody bitch she is.'

A swell of anger bubbled inside. Patrick's jaw clenched. He knew it was ironic that other people insulting his wife infuriated him when he did it on a daily basis. 'What's her last name?'

'Not a clue, mate. Not that interested to be honest. Don't get me wrong,' he gave Patrick a wink, 'she's a bit of all right, but I think she's going out with a copper.'

Patrick sat upright in his seat.

'And why would you think that?' His jaw tensed as he choked on his anger.

'I see them together all the time. At the probation office, the group, and a few times in the coffee shop before the group starts … hey, man, why do you look like your head is going to explode?'

Realizing that he could use this information to his advantage, Patrick took a deep breath to calm down.

'I'm OK, mate. Just felt a little funny there. Can I get you another cider?'

CHAPTER THIRTY

Maggie looked across the room and smiled at Pete. She opened her bag and took out her laptop, ready to hook it up to the main police computer on her desk. She had heard from some of the others in the team that DI Calleja had been worried when he'd been asked to head the DAHU. She could understand his misgivings after watching the Violent and Sexual Offender Management Team struggling with resources, trying to deal with the most serious sexual and violent offenders. Apparently the DI was concerned that the good record he held in terms of conviction rates would start to plummet.

Although she had been with the team only for a short while, she was more than confident that they would get the desired results to keep the higher-ups off their case. When the DI had told Maggie about the civilian joining the team, she'd been looking forward to observing Dr Kate Moloney's work with both the victims and perpetrators of domestic abuse. Kate came highly recommended, having played a massive role in developing the domestic abuse programme that many of the charity organizations currently used to reduce reconviction rates for domestic abuse perpetrators. Maggie had settled quite quickly into the team, so she had no fear about Dr Moloney doing the same. Her qualifications as a criminal psychologist would be an asset to the DAHU.

The team had been told that Dr Moloney would be popping in to meet them all today, and Maggie was startled out of her thoughts when she heard the phone ringing in DI Calleja's office. Moloney had arrived. When the front office receptionist walked in ten minutes later with a young, goth female, Maggie could see the look of confusion on her colleagues' faces. The young lady was escorted to their office and introduced as Dr Moloney. Maggie raised her hand and covered her mouth as she tried to hide her smile. DI Calleja did less well to cover his surprise.

'You need some help closing that mouth of yours?' Dr Moloney joked.

Maggie thought she detected a faint Irish accent. Maggie couldn't help blushing; with her raven hair, dark and distinctive make-up, she was curious how someone so young could have all the accreditations behind her. For some reason, she was reminded of the conversation she had in the café with her brother and shifted uncomfortably in her chair.

'Am I not what you were expecting, Detective Inspector?' Directing her response to the DI, Dr Moloney leaned over and looked at the ID badge hanging around his neck. 'Calleja? I can assure you that I'm old enough – and clever enough – to take on this job.'

It seemed Maggie wasn't the only one staring.

'Uh … OK … you caught me.' The DI put his hands up in the air. 'I guess I wasn't expecting someone who … erm … looks like you, to be a criminal psychologist.' Everyone in the room laughed as his neck reddened. 'My apologies, Dr Moloney. Would you like to see your office and then come back and properly meet the team?'

'There's no need for formalities. Yes, if I could leave my things in my office and meet everyone, that would be grand.'

The team watched as DI Calleja and Dr Moloney made their

way to the box-sized room with dull grey walls, a desk, chair, filing cabinet, and bookcase, which was just off the open-plan area.

'This is perfect.' Kate touched the walls and bookcase and smiled. She seemed to be taking note of where she'd put her pictures, charts, and reference materials.

'Great!' the DI said. 'I know it's kind of small but when they set up this unit, the cutbacks meant we had limited space and bodies. To be honest, I was a little shocked when they agreed to second you to my team!'

'Well, with the rise of murders within the context of domestic abuse, and Staffordshire having such a high volume recorded, I think they'd have a lot to answer for if they didn't.'

No one could argue with that. Maggie liked Kate's enthusiasm and attitude immediately. She hoped that her energy wouldn't be dulled by DS Hooper, who had a knack for putting people's noses out of joint.

'Right then. I'm looking forward to meeting the team ... lead the way.'

CHAPTER THIRTY-ONE

When Mark had suggested meeting up for coffee before the evening's offender group started, Lucy felt a few butterflies in her stomach. *Mark knows you're married. He's just being nice!* But that didn't stop her from daydreaming. She knew he wanted to ask her about Drew Talbot, but she also hoped he was using that as an excuse to see her. Looking up from her computer screen, she caught Sarah's eye.

'OK. I give in. What's with the big goofy grin? And why do you keep looking at the clock?'

'Don't be ridiculous. I'm just happy the day is nearly over.'

'You have a group tonight, so that can't be the reason.'

Lucy shuffled some papers on her desk. 'I know. I'm meeting up with Mar— PC Fielding for coffee before the group starts. So, it's a bit of a break.'

'Oooooooh, Mark now, is it? Oh, my god, you should see the colour of your face! Ha ha! Beetroot suits you.'

Lucy looked around the room to see who was within earshot and made her way over to Sarah's desk.

'Ssshhhhh. OK, OK. I have to admit, I do think he is quite good-looking. It's just a silly crush, all right. Not even that. Mark's a nice guy. Besides, he knows I'm married, and more importantly, *I* know I'm married.' Lucy smacked Sarah's arm playfully.

'I was just teasing, Lucy. Haven't seen you smile like that in a while, though. I won't tease you about it … much.' They both laughed. Sarah picked up her mug and headed towards the kitchen.

'Have fun on your date.' Sarah then laughed, and it was clear to Lucy she wasn't waiting around for a reply.

Lucy met Mark at the café just across the road from probation before the facilitators were due to go over the group practice. She felt so at ease with him and, although he was good-looking, Lucy would never cheat on Patrick – it wasn't in her nature. Mark pinged question after question at her, but Lucy had nothing new to add. She only knew Talbot because of the pre-sentence report, and his previous officer had nothing of significance to say either. They soon changed the topic, because the group would be draining and they would need something light to focus on. The conversation was so engrossing and it felt so good to laugh and relax that Lucy didn't notice Patrick staring at her through the window.

Back in the probation office after their coffee, Lucy read through the list of attendees and rolled her eyes at the names of the 'regulars'. Serial perpetrators, never likely to change. Lucy did notice a few new, unfamiliar names and made a note to investigate them.

Lucy and her colleagues would be running the group alongside a police officer. The first in the country to pilot this way of working, probation were keen to get involved. There was every chance that an offence may be disclosed within the group, but in order that the group felt 'safe' in discussing their offending behaviour and history, any individual who disclosed an offence couldn't be arrested until after they left probation property. She had been thrilled when she learnt that Mark would be one of the officers involved. Although she knew Mark had a strong dislike for domestic abuse offenders, he was good at what he did and left his personal feelings aside when it came to the job at hand.

Sitting at her desk as she prepped for the group, Lucy couldn't believe she'd had to show Patrick a letter from her boss, outlining her role as programme facilitator and also advising she'd get paid £50 per session, just to prove why she'd be working later some nights. In the end, Patrick seemed to warm to the idea – no doubt because of the extra money she'd be earning.

Lucy loathed having to explain herself to Patrick. Sitting at her desk she clenched her fists and once again found herself fantasizing about beating Patrick to a pulp. It was wrong, especially given her job – but Patrick brought out those feelings in her. She could kill him some days, and most other days, she just wished him dead.

Shaking away those thoughts, Lucy focused on the task in hand. The meeting was about to start. She sipped her coffee and quietly ran through the briefing on the new programme that she and Sarah would be delivering. Sharon Bairden, who worked closely with the victims, probation, and the police, would be acting as a mediator between the offenders on the group and their victims.

Lucy and Sharon got on well. Sharon was a feisty Scottish woman who held her own in the most difficult situations. Lucy admired Sharon's assertiveness and often wished she could be more like her. Having worked for a number of years with victims of domestic abuse, there wasn't much Sharon hadn't come across. So many times, Lucy had wanted to reach out to her, but she worried what Sharon would do with the information. The irony was, Lucy knew what she needed to do – she just couldn't find the courage to do it.

CHAPTER THIRTY-TWO

Lucy watched as the men filed into the room and took their seats. It was a small enough group, but the tension was palpable. These men did not want to be here, and most wouldn't last. A group that started with twelve individuals often ended with only six or eight. Lucy sometimes questioned whether these groups even made a difference. It wasn't the right way to think, but her own personal experiences sometimes overshadowed her professional objectivity.

Scanning their faces as they took their seats, Lucy was struck by how 'normal' they all looked. But she knew there was nothing normal about these men. Rape, constant beatings, threats, emotional torture – that only touched on some of the things their victims suffered daily. While these men sat around, joking, making derogatory comments about the 'bitches' in their lives, their victims were sitting at home, alone and terrified, wondering what would trigger the next episode of abuse. Not all women stayed in these relationships; some found the strength and courage to stand up to their abusers.

If only ...

'Hey, earth to Lucy!' Mark's distinctive voice bellowed across the room.

Lucy reddened as he approached.

'Sorry, I was miles away. Thinking about how I wish I could be anywhere but here on a Thursday night.'

One of the men overheard her comment and shouted back, 'You and me both, love! This is bullshit!'

Mark glared and reminded him that Lucy had a name and another unwelcome comment would end with him being escorted off the premises. Lucy didn't recognize him, but something about him put her on edge. He was in his late fifties, with a chiselled and worn face, and judging by the telltale bright veins littering his nose, he liked a drink. This is what the job did to you – Lucy imagined the police were the same – everyone you come across becomes an instant assessment. What label or box do they fit in to? Do they abuse substances? Are they violent? Should you keep your kids away from them?

Mark playfully nudged Lucy's arm.

'There you go again. Off with the fairies. You OK?'

Lucy laughed. 'Of course, it's been a long day. Right, should we get started?'

The session seemed to go well, if you could describe a group of men talking about the different ways they abuse women in their lives as 'well'. There were the usual challenges – the jokers, those who talked over others, those who made snide remarks – but nothing Mark and Lucy couldn't handle.

During the break, Lucy scanned the attendance sheet and felt the blood drain from her. She was sure she'd read about this guy – Michael O'Dowd – in the newspaper a few years ago.

'What's wrong? You OK? You've gone as white as a ghost,' Mark said.

'Do you know anything about him?' Lucy pointed at the last name on the sheet.

'Off the top of my head, no – but I can find out for you. Why?'

Years of experience and a gut feeling made her uneasy. 'I just want to make sure all our assessments are right, because he seems

114

to have come from another area, and my spidey sense is on high alert.'

Mark looked at her but didn't press the matter further. The break was over and people were filing back into the room.

After a few more heated discussions, the group finished on time. Lucy watched the men leave and grabbed her bag.

'Fancy a coffee, Lucy?' Mark smiled at her.

Knowing that Patrick would only harass her if she was late, she declined but suggested a rain check. It would be better to meet with Mark before the next group started, like they had done today. Less likely that any questions would be asked if they were seen together. Not that there was anything going on, but Lucy just had to be careful.

'Well at least let me drop you off somewhere.' Mark had a look of concern on his face.

Lucy felt bad for having to turn him down, but Patrick would flip if he saw her get out of a man's car. Knowing her neighbours, even if she got dropped off down the road, someone was bound to tell him.

Lucy locked up the office and said her goodbyes. She could see Mark still hovering around to make sure she got to the bus safely. As the bus arrived, she waved in his direction and smiled. It was nice to have someone looking out for her.

CHAPTER THIRTY-THREE

Michael O'Dowd, or Mick as he preferred to be called, left the group frustrated and gagging for a pint. *That was the biggest load of shit.* As far as he was concerned, there was nothing wrong with giving a woman a slap if it meant she did as she was told. He learnt that at an early age, from his own father, a man who never got in trouble with the law. Mick felt there was a double standard when it came to women and men who hit each other. All his ex-partners gave as good as they got. *Fuck 'em all.* He did like that probation officer, though – Lucy. *Almost makes the group worth going to.*

Mick was new to the area but had found a pub near his hostel. His licence conditions meant he had a curfew and he didn't want a bollocking so shortly after release. He walked into The Smith's Forge and had a quick look around. The décor was as bland as the customers that occupied the space – the stools had tears in their padding, the carpet was worn and the pictures showed Markston pre-1950. On the plus side, it was quiet, so he could enjoy his pint in peace. He had to admit, he was slightly disappointed at the lack of female company in the place. But as he couldn't take anyone back to his hostel, he shrugged his shoulders, and headed towards the bar.

'Can I have a pint of Stella, mate?'

The barman gave Mick a nod, grabbed a glass and pulled the pint. Mick wasn't in the mood for small talk anyway, so this suited him just fine. There was nothing worse than a barman who felt obliged to ask twenty questions when a new face appeared. Mick yanked out the remainder of the change from his pocket, placed it on the bar and made his way to the corner booth. From there Mick could keep an eye on the door and spot any trouble before it started. Not that he wanted any trouble; it just always seemed to find him.

Not even five minutes had passed and in it stumbled. A petite woman, looking a little worse for wear.

'Oi, Kevin! Can I have a pint on tic, mate?' Her hair was tied tightly in a bun resting on the top of her head. Her clothing virtually hung off her. She had trouble written all over her.

'Come on now, Vicki, you know I can't do that.'

'Aw please, love. I get my dole money tomorrow. Just the one, I promise.' From where Mick was sitting, her appearance indicated that one more drink would be enough.

'Right, just the one. Any sign of trouble and you're out, OK?' Flashing a lopsided smile, Vicki thanked him. From the look on his face, Mick suspected that Kevin knew the woman didn't get her dole on Fridays, but he still pulled the pint and placed it on the bar in front of her.

Mick noticed that Vicki was using the bar to balance herself. He looked away when he saw her scanning the room and hoped she hadn't clocked him. He guessed she was a regular and probably knew most if not everyone in the area. Glancing back, he watched her squinting at a boisterous woman standing with a crowd of men around her. Mick groaned as Vicki's sights finally found him and she headed towards his table. She seemed to be concentrating more on not spilling her pint, probably out of fear that the barman would not be so generous with the offer of another. He glanced at his phone in the hope that she would move on, but she just waited for him to finish.

'Well helloooooo. Haven't seen you here before; new to the area?'

Mick wondered if she knew how much she was slurring her words.

'Look, fuck off, will you? I just want a quiet pint before I head out. I'm not in the mood for your kind of company.'

'Well, aren't you the fucking charmer?'

Unfortunately for Mick, the boisterous female had overheard the conversation and she didn't seem impressed. She turned and gave him a look that screamed, *watch yourself*. When Mick icily stared back, she made it her business to step in.

'Hey! There's no need to talk to her that way. She was just trying to introduce herself. Be friendly, you know what *friendly* means, right?'

'Leave it out, Shell.' Vicki swayed on her feet.

'Are you her fucking mother? I didn't ask her to come over. I didn't even glance her way. The fact that I'm sitting in a booth, keeping to myself – how much more of a hint do you both need?'

Mick's lip twitched and his neck throbbed. Shell didn't seem to be bothered by the fact that she was pissing him off. Eventually this Shell woman looked away and mumbled something in Vicki's ear. Mick overheard the word 'licence'. Given the state she was in, her friend was probably warning her to behave. The boisterous one tugged Vicki's arm gently and steered her away from Mick's table.

Looking over her shoulder she mouthed, 'Watch yourself, mate.'

'Yeah, whatever.'

Mick couldn't be arsed with any grief and downed the remainder of his pint. He left the pub, ready to walk the short distance back to the hostel.

Mick gagged as he entered the building and took in the stale smell of the people who stayed there. He focused on getting to his room without being pulled into any conversations with the other residents. As he passed the communal living room, he noticed one or two people sitting around, blank faced, watching the television. *Fucking druggies.* Mick planned on moving on as soon as possible. He still wasn't sure whether a return to London was on the cards, or whether he should just stay around and see what this area had for him.

He needed something else to focus on and decided to log in to his Facebook account, scrolling through the endless feed of nonsense that people seemed to post about themselves. He didn't keep in contact with many of his old associates or friends but still had been curious to see how some of them, including his estranged children, were getting on with their lives. He may not have been the best father in the world but nobody is perfect. Mick would find his children again one day, he'd show them what a great father he was and what their mother was really like.

CHAPTER THIRTY-FOUR

After making sure Lucy got on the bus safely, Mark left the probation office and walked the short distance to where his car was parked. The lighting was poor in the parking lot, but it was fairly empty at this time of night. He unlocked the door and sat down, throwing his jacket in the back seat before he started his car and headed home. He couldn't shake the feeling that something was up with Lucy. She was acting strange at the end of the night and he didn't know why she was so adamant to take the bus home. He waited around to watch her go, in case any of the group members lagged behind to harass her. He hated the way the men in the group eyeballed her. In fact, he just hated the men in the group. Mark was brought up to respect women.

Bloody arseholes should get a taste of their own medicine.

The drive home was uneventful. He pulled up outside his flat, sat for a moment and then gathered his things, before making his way inside. Dropping his keys in the bowl by the doorway, Mark sat down and reflected on the evening. Lucy had been creeped out by one of the group members and mumbled something about seeing him on the news. Mark made a mental note to follow it up in the morning. He knew it was none of his business but he had a soft spot for Lucy. Had she not been married, he may have eventually asked her out. He shook his head. Mark felt tired and his vision blurred. He realized that his blood sugar levels were probably high. It had been a while since he'd checked, and his mind was otherwise occupied. He went to the bathroom and took out his kit and tested himself. He was hyperglycaemic, probably distracted with all that was happening at work. He immediately injected himself with insulin, relaxing as he felt the effects almost immediately. He needed to keep on top of it in future, as he couldn't risk any side effects while on the job.

Mark hated that he had to monitor his injections. He threw the used needle in the sharps bin and made his way to the kitchen to put the kettle on. He was lucky that the police no longer forced people with conditions like his to strict desk duties. He'd have ended up choosing a career he hated otherwise. He took his mug of tea and the newspaper and sat down on his lumpy couch to relax.

LONDON WOMAN BEATEN TO DEATH
BY JEALOUS EX-HUSBAND

was the headline that greeted him on the front page. Mark threw the paper on the floor in anger. He had wanted to chill out but instead found himself thinking about Drew Talbot's murder. The crime scene photos turned his stomach but he wasn't sorry to see that Talbot was dead. He rubbed his neck; he needed to escape from the case for tonight at least. Sticking in a DVD, he lay back and closed his eyes for a moment. Sleep came quickly.

CHAPTER THIRTY-FIVE

After watching the prick that Vicki had been trying to talk to leave the pub, Shell walked over to the bar and asked Kevin whether he knew anything about the nameless arsehole who had insulted her friend.

Kevin shook his head. 'He just asked for a pint of Stella, Shell. I've no idea who he is, and I'm not really interested. As long as he pays for his drinks and doesn't cause any trouble I'm happy to leave him to it.'

That wasn't the answer Shell had been looking for. She didn't take too kindly to unknowns coming in and playing the big I am. Especially a man. She'd leave it for now, though. The pub would soon be closing for the night. Finishing her drink, Shell grabbed her coat deciding it was best to head home. Patrick would be calling later.

'You ready to leave, Vicki? I'll walk with you.'

Holding up her pint glass, Vicki looked at Shell sheepishly. 'Ah, I just have a bit left, go on if you want to.'

'Suit yourself. But stay out of trouble, OK?' Reaching into her pocket, Shell handed Vicki a £5 note and asked her to take a taxi home.

Shell was always looking out for people – especially those less fortunate. Vicki had led a troubled life and it was no wonder that alcohol had become her only friend. Abused, forced into prostitution, and beaten by one boyfriend or another, it was no surprise that Vicki just accepted what life threw at her. It angered Shell that Vicki still put herself in compromising situations when she wanted a drink. But Shell understood that having been told she was worthless over the years, Vicki had begun to believe that sex in exchange for money was all she was good for.

Shell made her way outside into the chill night and pulled her collar up tightly around her neck. Not too far to walk and she enjoyed the fresh air. She wanted a clear head when she spoke to Patrick. Living within a decent walking distance of the pub, if she cut through the park, gave Shell the freedom to have an active social life and not have to worry about transport. If she could, she avoided the park because of the hostel nearby. She had nothing against offenders – hell, half the people she knew got into one form of trouble or another with the law – but she'd seen a few people come and go from there recently that sent shivers down her spine. It was the quickest way home, though, and all Shell wanted was a cuppa while she waited for Patrick to call.

Shell picked up the pace as she made her way along the leaf-covered path, shivering in the cold. The dark trees surrounded her and fear hit her like icy water. A twig snapped behind her and she stiffened. Turning slowly, she looked behind her, being careful not to slip on the wet path. Her heart was racing but soon calmed when she realized there was nothing there. The hostel was coming up soon and she kept an eye on it as she walked by. Someone was standing in the top left window, a dark shadow staring onto the park grounds. She instantly recognized that face. It was the dickhead from the pub, an ugly smirk across his face. He spotted Shell staring and gave her a wave. She quickly turned away and sped up.

She didn't see Mick O'Dowd laughing as he watched her run.

When she arrived home, she took off her coat, hanging it on the hook by the door. Placing her handbag on the side table, she dug around in her bag for her mobile phone. She was pissed off when she noticed the black screen and realized that the battery had died. *Shit!* Shell headed to the living room in search of her charger. If she missed Patrick's call, her night would be ruined. She quickly plugged in her phone and switched it on. It immediately buzzed and dinged as eight missed calls and a voicemail flashed up on her screen. She called the voicemail service and listened.

'Where are you? Thought you'd be waiting for my call but I guess I'm not as important as you make out. I had to sneak out of the house especially for this. It's not on, Shell. But what can I expect from a woman – you all screw me over.'

The call ended abruptly. Shell didn't like the harsh sarcasm in Patrick's voice. She wondered if she should ring him back but, looking at the time, she decided the best thing to do would be to text him in the morning when his wife had left for work. Maybe he'd had a bad day. Too wired to sleep, Shell read the message her cousin Louise had sent her, and her blood boiled:

Shell, help. Rob is at my house.

CHAPTER THIRTY-SIX

Robert Millard wasn't impressed at being woken up by the loud banging on his door.

'I'm coming, for fuck's sake.'

Robert yanked the door open and stared at the officers in front of him. 'What the fuck do you pair want?'

'Now, now, Mr Millard … that's no way to greet people.' The sarcasm dripped from Maggie's lips.

'What lies did that bitch say now? I haven't been anywhere near her.'

'If by *that bitch* you're referring to Louise, I'm going to have to ask you to rephrase your question. If on the other hand you're referring to that female dog we passed down the hall from your room … I can assure you, she has not made any complaints … yet.' Maggie wanted to let Robert know that he wasn't going to intimidate her either.

Robert turned to PC Reynolds. 'How can you put up with that shit? You in charge here? I'd rather talk to you.'

'DC Jamieson is my superior, and I suggest you look at her and answer her questions.' PC Reynolds struggled to maintain his professionalism when it came to dealing with this kind of vermin. The domestic abuse cohort just happened to be full of them.

'PC Reynolds is right, Mr Millard. The longer you play these childish games, the longer we're going to stand out here and the more of your neighbours are going to hear our conversation. Is that what you want?'

Robert sneered at Maggie and stepped aside. 'Come in then. But it's only a bedsit, so if you're expecting a seat you're in for a surprise.'

Maggie and PC Reynolds pushed past Robert and stood in the cramped room. Maggie noticed the bin overflowing with Special Brew cans, and the stale smell of beer from the worn-out carpet burned her nostrils.

'We're just doing a routine stop and check to go over the conditions of your restraining order. You know, that order that you recently breached. Remember that? We're also here to offer you any additional support that you may need. Has your probation officer discussed our involvement with you yet?'

'Ha! Are you kidding me? Another useless bi—'

PC Reynolds cleared his throat loudly as a warning to Millard.

'Woman. Lucy does nothing for me. Look at this place. This is where she sticks me even though I was paying the rent on the house. Then I lose my job because of Louise, so I have no choice but to live out of black bin bags in this shithole. So, to answer your question … Lucy has told me jack shit. And coming around at this time to discuss my licence? What do you take me for?'

Maggie decided to take on another tactic.

'OK. Well, let's just say we can do this the easy way or the hard way, Millard, so why don't you calm down before I have to make you.' She touched her baton and smirked as he gave in.

CHAPTER THIRTY-SEVEN

The police had left and Robert had only just begun to drift off, when he was woken by another knock on the door. *What the fuck?* He had nodded in the right places just to get them out the door quicker. Looking at the clock, he saw it was just after one-thirty in the morning. Now he was really pissed off. *If this is those fucking coppers again I swear to God!* He yanked the door open, ready to shout *What?* in their faces, but it wasn't the coppers.

'Who the fuck are you? Do you know what time it is?' He began to shut the door, but a swift movement caught Robert's eye. By the time he realized that a needle had been plunged into his neck, it was too late. He felt the sting of the injection, the burn of liquid flooding into his veins. He stumbled and almost fell. Tried to reach up and touch the spot on his neck where the needle had entered, but his limbs were like lead and he slipped down to his knees in the hallway. He heard the front door close but he couldn't move. His eyes stared straight ahead and a mist clouded his vision as he collapsed onto the floor. A strange sensation took over, an aching and burning that twisted through his neck and down into his back. Looking up at the ceiling, Robert realized that nearly every muscle in his body was paralyzed. His blood ran cold.

What the fuck is happening?

He was fully awake and in his head he was screaming – but no sound escaped his lips. Robert felt his pulse rising as panic took hold. Swallowing and breathing became more difficult. It was then Robert realized the truth.

Oh, my god, I'm going to die.

The person stepped over him and pulled his arms up over his head, dragging him back into the tiny bedsit. Robert stared helplessly at the ceiling as he was left to lie between his bed and the black bin bags lined up against the cupboards. A noise made him look in the direction of the person and he saw more syringes being pulled from their pocket. He could still feel everything, time seemed to have slowed, and Robert was terrified.

The first hit to his face caught him off-guard.

He was too preoccupied with the fact that he was completely helpless to notice the small wooden bat coming towards his face. A pool of urine lay beneath him, his tracksuit bottoms felt damp. A combat-style boot kicked him in his ribs and then landed right on his stomach, winding him.

Why is this happening?

Robert thought he'd endured as much pain as humanly possible, until he saw the knife and heard the laughter.

'Ooooh, pissy pants. Let's see how you like this.' The voice was muffled, barely recognizable, and then Robert felt the edge of the cold blade prodding at his neck.

'You like to rape and beat women. Don't think that will be happening anymore now, do you?'

The blade sliced across his windpipe and a cold, wet sensation tickled his neck as the blood pooled beside him.

'Lights out now, Robbie-boy. I'm sure your wife won't even shed a tear when she finds out.'

Another kick to his side jarred him as the person walked out, closing the door behind them.

Robert Millard lay on the floor struggling to breathe. He felt a tingling sensation in his lower region. He began to cry as the blackness descended; and his final wish was that hell wasn't as bad as they made it out to be.

CHAPTER THIRTY-EIGHT

The list of prolific domestic abuse perpetrators seemed to be growing on a daily basis and Mark was becoming increasingly concerned as he saw the carnage – both physical and psychological – that was left behind. With no leads on the Talbot investigation so far, he also didn't want another murder on his caseload, especially after his visit with Millard a few nights ago which reminded him how volatile these offenders can be. The whole team had shared some concerns about the likelihood that some of the offenders would go on to commit more serious offences. They knew how this would impact not only the resources the team had, but also those who were left behind.

Mark wanted to discuss his concerns with Dr Moloney after learning that she also specialized in criminal profiling. He proceeded to Kate's office and tapped gently on her door.

'PC Fielding. Nice to see you. What can I do for you today?' Dr Moloney had a way of making everyone feel at ease. It could have been the soft lilt in her accent, the way words seemed to flow poetically off her tongue.

'Hi, Dr Moloney. Just wondered if I could pick your brain for a minute?'

'Of course, what do you need?'

'DI Calleja told us that you have experience in criminal profiling, and I wondered if that extended to predicting the likelihood of someone going on to murder? I'm also curious whether you've had a chance to look at the Talbot murder, and whether you had any ideas about who we should be focussing our attention on?'

'I do indeed. Profiling is my secret passion, but it's been some time since I've been asked to use that skill on a real case.' Dr Moloney reached across to the bookcase next to her desk and pulled out what looked like some kind of manual. 'Now that I'm here and settled, it's as good a time as any to brush up on those skills.'

'I can't say that I am sorry that Talbot is dead, but the scum we deal with need to be stopped before we end up with another murder on our caseloads, and this time a victim.' Mark paused and Dr Moloney raised an eyebrow. 'Sorry. I just don't understand why a man, why anyone for that matter, would prey on those they know can't or won't defend themselves.' Mark lowered his eyes to the floor and tried to control his anger. He didn't want her wondering why someone who felt so strongly would choose to work with these individuals.

Dr Moloney shrugged. The look she gave him conveyed that, although she may agree with his point of view, she felt that personal views shouldn't be allowed to cloud professional boundaries. Mark knew that, regardless of his opinion, in order to protect the victims teams such as this specialized unit needed to work with offenders.

'Right then. I'll look over the list of nominals. I have plans to meet up with your probation colleagues soon. Probation's risk assessments may help me form a more valid overall picture of what the team ... or rather *who* the team need to focus on. I will also ask DS Hooper for the case information on Talbot's murder and see if I can start generating a profile. How does that sound?'

'OK, great and thanks for that, Dr Moloney. Is there anything you need me to do?'

'Hmmm … not particularly – but if I think of something, I'll be sure to ask.'

Mark left Kate's office feeling slightly deflated. He'd thought Kate would be able to add more immediate insight on specific triggers he needed to be aware of, but inwardly agreed that speaking with probation was probably the right thing to do. The team were working around the clock, checking CCTV and canvassing the area for any further witnesses in the Talbot case. He hoped they would catch a break soon. He scanned the list of nominals, looking for the highest risk cases. He wasn't surprised by the names that raised the most concerns: Robert Millard, Greg Stanton, the now-deceased Drew Talbot, and that fellow that'd had Lucy on edge, Mick O'Dowd. They needed more information on his transfer from London. Mark noted that this would be one of his priority tasks to complete.

CHAPTER THIRTY-NINE

Lucy wasn't surprised when Robert Millard failed to attend his appointment, in fact she was secretly pleased not to see him. After breaching his harassment order and being fined yet again, she figured he'd be off somewhere getting drunk and winding himself up. She got the warning letter prepared and started drafting her breach report. No doubt the suspended sentence would now be activated, and Lucy would have the displeasure of supervising Robert once again on release. Lucy hated that anyone serving a sentence of under twelve months would automatically have to report to probation for a period equalling twelve months after their release. It used to be the case that if a person was sentenced to six months custody, there would be no probation involvement on release. A waste of time and taxpayers' money as far as Lucy was concerned.

She had to inform her police colleagues of Robert's further failure, so she picked up the phone and dialled the unit.

'PC Mark Fielding. Domestic Abuse and Homicide Unit. How can I help?'

'Hi, Mark, it's Lucy. How are you?'

'All good here, Lucy. What can I do for you today?'

Lucy explained to Mark about Robert and suggested that a visit by the police offender managers might be the best course of action, hinting that the police could hand deliver the warning letter. Lucy told him she believed Robert had been struggling to engage in supervision and he may be internalizing his anger. This, of course, raised the alarm about Louise and anyone Robert would ultimately blame for his situation.

'Gotcha. Not sounding too good, is it? Well, we have Dr Moloney here now, so maybe once the breach is dealt with, we'll have her come along for a prison visit. She also specializes in offender profiling, so she might be able to assist with your risk assessments. Not that you don't do a great job as is, Lucy.'

'That sounds on point. Any chance of some of us coming over and meeting her? I think there will be quite a few of us who would love to pick her brains.' Lucy also wouldn't mind seeing Mark, but she didn't say that out loud.

'I don't see why not. She said she wanted to arrange a meeting with probation, so leave it with me and I'll get back to you ASAP.'

Lucy hung up the phone and could feel the goofy grin forming on her face.

'Was that hubby on the phone, Lucy? I don't think I've seen a smile that big before.'

Lucy blushed as Andy Bourne, her line manager, walked by.

'Uh … yeah. You know what it's like when you're in love.' Lucy nearly gagged as the words came out of her mouth. She could see Sarah giving her a funny look from across the room. It was hard to have a private conversation in an open-plan office.

Her email pinged. It was Mark.

Dr Moloney is free today after the operational meeting until about 6.00 p.m. for anyone who wants to come over and meet her to discuss the cohort. Can you ask your colleagues and drop me a line with the names of anyone who will be attending?

Thanks,

Mark

134

Although it was short notice, Lucy hurried around the room asking her colleagues whether any of them were free to attend later today; she grinned as she sent off a reply to Mark.

Hi Mark,

Looks like you're stuck with me only, if I can get away. Everyone else is busy or out, so I've been tasked with gathering the information and feeding back to the team. Hope that's OK?

Lucy

Before she even had time to move on to her next task, Mark had responded to say it was fine and that they all looked forward to her visit. Now Lucy just had to convince Patrick that she needed to stay a bit later today, without starting an argument.

CHAPTER FORTY

Maggie looked at the agenda for the operational meeting and noted that Sharon Bairden would be giving an update. She had just been to visit Louise Millard, and a few of the other women she worked with. The tone of Sharon's email suggested she was fuming that the victims' partners had repeatedly breached the harassment orders and she'd been left in the dark. Maggie was surprised, because this wasn't how she envisaged multi-agency work. Sharon's email inferred that there was a silo mentality and, had Sharon known this, she wouldn't have agreed to be a part of it. Maggie admired Sharon's fire and could see she wouldn't be one to sit back and wait. Looking up from her desk after hearing a slight commotion, Maggie wasn't surprised to see Sharon storm into the office and nearly knock Dr Moloney off her feet.

'Where is Mark or Joseph?'

'Do you mean PC Fielding and DI Calleja?'

Maggie wasn't sure who would win a fight between Sharon and Kate.

'Sorry, do I know you?' Sharon hissed.

'Dr Kate Moloney. And you are …?' Maggie waited to see if Sharon would shake the hand that was extended.

'The name's Sharon. OK, Kate, now that the pleasantries are done with – I need to speak with Mark or Joseph about what's happening with the restraining orders. Seems they mean nothing, and I want some answers. I have women who believe there is no point in protecting themselves, and the police can't be bothered to do anything. So, where can I find them?'

Maggie wondered if Kate would stand her ground and was surprised to see her raise one eyebrow and point in the direction of the meeting room. 'They'll all be in there. By the way, nice to meet you, Sharon. I'm getting the coffee/tea organized. Would you like one?'

Sharon brushed past her without saying a word.

Maggie got up and followed, seeing all heads turn when Sharon stormed into the meeting room. Maggie tried to catch the DI's attention, but he stood up and began speaking.

'Well hello, Sharon! I didn't know you'd been invited to this meeting. Dr Moloney is just—'

'Never mind about that! Can you tell me what is being done about Robert Millard and the rest of the nominals with their continued breach of restraining orders?' She stood in the middle of the room, hands on hips. 'I had these women in tears, angry, and scared. Fearful that these arseholes can breach their orders without any consequences. What the hell is that about?' Sharon raised a wad of papers, presumably victim statements, and waved them in the air.

Maggie saw Calleja and Mark exchange glances, before the DI responded, 'Sharon. Do you want to have a seat and calm down?'

'No, I bloody well do not!'

'Well, until you calm down, there is nothing I'm going to say to you. Maybe we should take this outside, where it will be a little … erm … more private?' The DI gestured towards the door.

Sharon left the room in a huff and stood outside tapping her foot furiously as she waited for Calleja. Maggie inched her way closer to the door. To her credit, Sharon listened as Calleja assured her he would get to the bottom of her concerns and would do what he could to make sure any issues were brought up and actioned in the meeting. Maggie casually pushed her chair back to its original place as she watched them return to the meeting room. Dr Moloney followed them both in with a tray of hot drinks, which she placed carefully on the table.

'OK, everyone, Sharon's going to join us for this meeting. She has some important information to share,' Calleja said as he took his seat.

Mark turned towards his boss 'What about Probation? Aren't we going to wait?'

'Oh sorry. I forgot. I just had a message from Lucy. She apologizes for not being able to attend – she was looking forward to meeting Dr Moloney – but she can't get away from the office. Instead, she emailed me an update. Can I rely on you, Mark, to liaise any actions from today's meeting with Lucy?'

Mark blushed.

Oooh. Something is going on here.

Maggie couldn't have been the only one to notice the smile formed on Mark's face, 'Yes, guv. Not a problem,' he said.

The meeting lasted about an hour, with all agencies around the table sharing updates on the current nominals. Mick O'Dowd was mentioned and Maggie noted the name down. Maybe it was a person of interest in the Talbot case. She would check it out and then speak to Mark.

Dr Moloney took the floor, opened a folder and read out: '"Mick O'Dowd, also known as Michael to professionals, is a transfer in from London. He was released to a bail hostel in this area from prison after a seven-year sentence for grievous bodily harm on the victim, his ex-partner, Moira. He has racked up numerous offences, ranging from drunk and disorderly to criminal damage, as well as a few common assaults, all of which appear to have a link to domestic abuse. He is a serial abuser against multiple partners – he has two estranged children – and his first wife remains in hiding, following a particularly nasty attack, for which she never pressed charges … so this is someone we need to watch."

'Mark, can you liaise with probation about Mr O'Dowd and find out who his officer is?'

Before Mark could answer, Maggie jumped in with a question. 'Do we have to take him on if there are significant risks like those you have highlighted?'

'Sorry, I'm not sure about police or probation processes. Perhaps DI Calleja can find out, or even Mark when he speaks with probation?' Kate suggested.

Maggie guessed from his previous behaviour that Mark was more than happy to pick this up with probation.

When it came to Sharon's turn, Maggie listened as Calleja asked everyone to pay close attention.

'First, I apologize for the way I barged in here earlier, but I'd just come from meeting some of the women who are part of the survivors' support group. All of them expressed their frustration that, despite going through the trauma of a court case and getting a restraining order in place, every time their abuser breached the order, nothing appears to happen as a consequence.' There were a few murmurs and nods of acknowledgement in the room.

'A bigger concern for me, though, is that they expressed a reluctance to call the police. This is a major warning sign and something we need to act on. But what really scared me was the fact that Louise Millard disclosed she is pregnant. This places her in the high-risk band and, with Robert continually breaking the restraining order, I'm extremely concerned for her safety.' Maggie watched Sharon clasp her hands together, lean forward and look at everyone in the room. 'So, ladies and gentlemen … what the hell are we going to do?'

CHAPTER FORTY-ONE

DS Hooper was called into Calleja's office after the meeting. When he arrived, the DI glanced at him, his eyes tight with worry.

'All OK, guv?'

'Not exactly, Hooper. I just had a call from downstairs. One of the residents of the bedsit where Robert Millard lives says there is a bad smell coming from his room. Two PCs have been sent around to check it out. When was the last time anyone saw Millard?'

'I don't know, but I can find out for you.' Hooper radioed across and learnt from Mark that Millard had been seen by Maggie and Reynolds at least a week or so prior to his missed probation appointment. Mark and Maggie were booked to see him in the morning.

'Did you catch that, guv?'

'Yeah. Right. Let's hope the bad smell was nothing other than sour milk.'

DS Hooper returned to the DAHU office and called everyone around.

'Right, folks, we may have a problem.' After explaining the situation, DS Hooper pulled DC Jamieson aside.

'Can you and PC Everett make your way over to Millard's?

If this does turn out to be nothing, at least we can cover our asses.'

With a curious look, DC Jamieson asked why Fielding wouldn't be coming with her.

'I want him to follow-up on the actions from the meeting. Given this new information, it's vital that we get on top of things now. Also, if something has happened to Millard then I want Fielding available to attend Louise's house. We may need to question her.'

'Right, boss, I'm on it. Everett, grab your coat, you're coming with me.'

Maggie and Everett left the room, and Hooper walked over to PC Fielding, looking over his shoulder at the computer screen. 'Any luck then on finding out more about that Mick O'Dowd?' Fielding jumped when he realized his boss was hanging over his shoulder.

'Judging by his previous convictions, he's a nasty bastard. I'm shocked and annoyed that we weren't told about him. You know how they said his ex-wife is in hiding with the kids?'

'Yeah.'

'Well, the report states that Mick used a metal cosh to beat her around the legs and incapacitate her. He broke her jaw and her left cheekbone and then attempted to set the couch on fire. The kids weren't in the property at the time, but when questioned, he said he had no idea if they were upstairs. He did nothing, just walked out and watched the flames take hold of the bottom floor. A vigilant neighbour saw some smoke coming through an open window. They shouted out, but Mick didn't answer. The neighbour thought he was in shock. The fire brigade was called and when the police arrived, Mick was arrested. He was too drunk to be interviewed at the time.'

'For fuck's sake.' DS Hooper felt his hand start to shake.

'His wife suffered from smoke inhalation as well as from the beating. Luckily, nothing worse happened in terms of the fire, thanks to the quick action of the neighbour. There wasn't enough evidence to prove he'd deliberately set the couch alight; both of them were smokers and there was no proof that an accelerant had been used.'

'Right. Update probation with this information and then contact the police force in the transfer area to find out why the fuck we weren't notified.'

'On it, boss.'

Hooper's radio beeped. He took a deep breath and answered, moving into his office. He slumped in his chair when he heard the information being detailed across the radio: Robert Millard had been found dead in his room and it didn't look like natural causes.

'Ah fuuuuuck …'

Hooper gathered the remainder of his unit in the briefing room. 'OK, folks. We have a serious problem. Millard has been found dead … murdered by the looks of it … and we need answers.'

'How do they know it's murder? Could it have been suicide or natural? He was a heavy drinker after all.' PC Reynolds's enthusiasm was hard to miss.

'They found his windpipe slit. Looks like he bled to death, but we won't know for sure until after the post-mortem.'

'Do they know how long he'd been lying there?' Fielding asked.

'Everett and Jamieson are heading out to the scene, so we should know more soon. Right now, what I need you both to do is trace his last movements. When was he last seen? Who did he speak to? What time did he get back home? Check CCTV at the property. Is there a link to the Talbot case? See if they knew each other.'

Dr Moloney seemed to be calmly absorbing all the information. From her mannerism, Hooper wondered if a little part of her was excited at the prospect of a real life murder investigation.

'What would you like me to do, DS Hooper?' she said when she caught his eye.

Hooper looked at her blankly. 'Apologies, Dr Moloney. In all honesty, I'm not sure at the moment. Until we know more, look over the information we have and see what insight you'd be able to offer in terms of profiling, can we expect more, and all that other … erm … stuff you do.' He hoped his confusion was not too obvious.

'Sure, that would be grand … I'll get started and would appreciate being briefed as new information comes in.'

With a look of relief, Hooper took a deep breath. 'Fielding, make sure you share whatever information we have. We need to solve these as quickly as possible. Two murders on our books already – let's make sure this unit isn't shut down before it starts.' Hooper left the briefing room with his back stooped, as if a new weight had been left on his shoulders, and headed for DI Calleja's office. He knew the DI wasn't going to be happy.

He knocked on the door of his boss's office.

'Yes? Come in!' he heard the DI shout. *Guess he knows already.*

'Ah, Hooper! I wondered when you were going to show your face.' Calleja pointed to a chair. Hooper always felt uncomfortable in his boss's office. Everything was pristine – not a piece of paper out of place. Sitting down, Hooper waited for his boss to speak.

'So, what do you have for me?'

'Well, sir. Another of our nominals, Robert Millard, has been found dead … well, murdered actually, in his bedsit. At least it's looking that way. I don't have the particulars, but Jamieson and Everett are at the scene.'

'Christ.' Calleja stood up. 'For fuck's sake … this is not going to look good for our stats.' He paced the room, his hands clenched behind his back, mumbling to himself and not making much sense.

To Hooper, sitting watching his progress, it felt like he was sitting in a raft and Calleja was about to push him out to sea. But it had been set up to deal with murders linked to domestic abuse. With Millard as a nominal, DI Calleja wasn't going to be able to pass it off.

Doesn't he have confidence in our team? In me?

'Why are you still here, Hooper?'

Hooper blinked.

'Find out everything you can and then call a briefing for later today. I hope you have some more information for me then.'

Hooper made a quick exit and hoped that his officers could fill in some blanks before the briefing this evening.

CHAPTER FORTY-TWO

Standing outside the property, the stench was unbearable. Maggie looked across at PC Everett, who had gone deathly pale. A small window was cracked open, releasing the stench into the air.

'Holy shit, Maggie! How the hell did the residents put up with this for so long?'

Maggie had to cover her mouth so Kat couldn't see her laugh.

Everett tried unsuccessfully to mask the smell by pulling her shirt up over her nose and mouth.

Maggie handed her a tissue. 'Here, use this, it's mentholated. I have no idea how the residents stood the smell for so long, Kat. There are some strange folk. We might want to contact the council and see if any complaints were made about the smell and when. It might help us form a timeline.'

Everett noted down Maggie's instructions in her log book.

'Who is the SIO? My guess is your previous team will be taking over the case soon?' Kat asked.

Maggie nodded. The area had been cordoned off, but residents and neighbours were milling about trying to find out what was happening. Maggie looked in the crowd and saw a group of officers but she couldn't spot her old boss, DI Abbie Rutherford, who would run the investigation, unless it could be linked to the domestic abuse team's nominals. She scanned the area a second time, to see if she could spot Rutherford before she spotted Maggie. She felt a tap on her left shoulder.

'You looking for me, Jamieson?' Maggie turned slowly to come face to face with the DI.

'Hello, ma'am. Yes, I was. Figured you'd be here and wondered what you could tell us?'

'Why would I be telling you anything?'

'Well, ma'am. Robert Millard, the dead man – though I realize a formal identification is yet to be made – is one of our nominals in the DAHU.'

'I get it. So how did you get called in then?'

'Robert Millard failed to attend his probation appointments. Not exactly unusual for him, but he generally makes contact a few days after a failure. It has been well over a week, so we were asked to come out and check on him. It's part of the process. Then we heard that someone reported an unusual smell emanating from his bedsit, two PCs from our office were dispatched, and we were on our way to meet them. When we arrived, the area had already been cordoned off with officers at the scene and we heard about the body.'

'Well, stick around for a bit. Or better yet, until we get a formal ID; can you take a look and let us know if this is your man?'

Jamieson couldn't hide her pleasure. The murder team was where she really wanted to be. Despite only being out for a short time, she was eager to be involved.

'Yes, ma'am! I'll suit up and be there in two secs.' Maggie went to the boot of her car and put on the protective clothing she had stored in her kit bag, before heading towards Robert's flat. Despite the police cordons, she had to push herself through crowds of people milling about outside. Squeezing into Robert's tiny bedsit with two or three people trying not to contaminate the scene was a task in itself.

'Excuse me, I'm DC Jamieson, and was asked by DI Rutherford to see if I could informally ID the body.'

A scrawny, pimpled faced Forensic Investigation Officer looked up at Maggie and smiled a toothy grin. 'Be my guest.'

The body was battered and bruised. His throat slit along the windpipe and, despite the bloated features and severe bruising to his face, DC Jamieson was in no doubt that this was Robert Millard. She nodded to the scrawny officer and he carried on. Maggie spotted Fiona Blake, the forensic pathologist, and gave a wave of acknowledgement.

'Any idea of time or cause of death?'

'Seriously, Maggie? I can barely scratch my ass in here, let alone have a good look at this guy. Once Charlie finishes collecting what he can, we'll get the body to the morgue and carry out a more detailed examination. I thought you left the murder investigation team?'

Maggie nodded. 'I did. This guy was one of our nominals, so whether Rutherford likes it or not, I suspect we'll be involved in the case.'

Maggie left the room and made her way back to PC Everett. Kat still looked like she was struggling with the smell and Maggie laughed to herself. *Gotta love a newbie.*

'You OK, Everett? I think we have all we're going to get from here. Let me confirm with Rutherford that the body is indeed Robert Millard's and then we'll head back to the station and plan our next move. You OK to drive?'

PC Everett shook her head.

'All right then, give me the keys. Just promise me you won't puke in the car.'

147

CHAPTER FORTY-THREE

Lucy looked up at the clock on the wall in front of her and realized that Mick O'Dowd was due in shortly for his probation appointment. He made Lucy uncomfortable. His mannerisms were a lot like Patrick's and, every time she looked at him, she had an overwhelming urge to punch him in the face. Mick's condescending attitude when Lucy had first called him Michael put her nose out of joint. Lucy planned to spend the next two supervision sessions looking at Mick's past offending behaviour, in the hope that she'd be able to form a better risk assessment. The transferring area provided her with a flimsy overview, citing 'lack of resources' as the reason for their incomplete assessment.

Mick arrived for his appointment on time and Lucy directed him to an interview room.

'Have a seat, Mick. As you're new to the area, I'm just going to review what we have discussed so far. I know you'll have done the induction with another officer on release, but bear with me, OK?'

Mick grunted and stared out the window. They went through the basic information and Mick signed where required. Lucy wasn't even completely sure that he'd listened to the conversation, but at this point, she didn't really care. What she wanted to do

148

was look at his previous convictions, but she had to tread carefully. The last thing she wanted to do was trigger him and place a female or anyone at risk.

'Thanks for completing the paperwork. I'll add it to your file and inform the transfer area of its completion. As part of your licence supervision, we need to be looking at your previous convictions, your current conviction, and why these have now placed you on the police domestic abuse nominal list.'

'Yeah, I wanted to ask you about that. How come no one has told me why I'm on the list?'

'In normal circumstances, they would have. The police and myself, or another probation officer, would have come to visit you prior to your release. However, we were informed at the last minute of your transfer and release to one of our bail hostels. All this should have been explained to you by your previous probation officer. Is there any reason you chose our area when you were asked?'

Mick looked a bit shifty but quickly responded. 'No. I just chose three of the places I recognized, and this is where they sent me.' He stared out the window again.

'OK. So, let's look at a bit of background. Is that all right? You're not married at the moment. Are you in a relationship?'

'No, and why the fuck is that your business?'

'Had you been listening, Mick, one of your licence conditions is to inform us of any intimate relationship you may form. It is in fact, in your best interest to be as forthcoming with us as possible so that we don't have to recall you.'

'Fuck's sake. That's what it's always about with you lot. Recall. Send you back to prison. Do as you're fucking well told. Blah. Blah. Blah. Well you want some honesty, bitch? I'd love to bend you over this table right now and give you a good seeing to. How is *that* for fucking honesty?'

Lucy sighed. 'Was that supposed to intimidate or shock me, *Michael*?' She knew it was childish, but she purposely used his

149

full name. Lucy moved in close and looked him straight in the eyes. 'Let me tell you something, I've heard worse from worse so-called men than you – but if you want to carry on, please do. That will definitely lead to recall. As you're new to me, I'll give you another chance.' Lucy leaned back in her chair and crossed her arms. 'But make no mistake, if you ever speak to me like that again I will recall your sad arse back to custody so fast you won't even see it coming. We clear?'

Lucy had to compose herself when a familiar-looking sneer crossed his face.

'Oh, we – are – clear.' Mick took out a packet of tobacco and started to make a roll-up.

Knowing that she wasn't going to get anymore information from him, and being slightly freaked out at the resemblance in mannerisms to Patrick, Lucy escorted Mick out of the building once he'd finished rolling his cigarette. She wondered whether she should just speak to her line manager about transferring his case back to London. With Mick's high-risk status and the fact he'd not disclosed any links to the area, she could probably convince her manager to reject the case. There was just something that didn't sit right, something that sent shivers down Lucy's spine every time she saw him. That rarely happened. Lucy feared Mick had a very high risk of serious violence and it would only be a matter of time before she was facing a serious further offence.

Noticing the time, she typed up her remaining notes and packed up for the day. There was nothing more to do. Her phone rang as she reached the door leading into reception. She hesitated for a moment, wondering if she should answer. Whoever it was could wait until Monday.

CHAPTER FORTY-FOUR

Lucy smiled. A rarity it seemed these days. Siobhan was excited, more excited than usual as her half-brother Rory was coming to spend the weekend. Lucy was always curious about why Patrick had left Amy Swift. He was so devoted to his daughter, but had hardly mentioned Rory when they first got together.

When Lucy had been more assertive and confident, she had asked Patrick, but got the usual cold shoulder. Patrick was a closed book on most subjects when sober. But after a few drinks, he'd drone on and on about his past – the same things again and again. How his father beat his mother. How his mother treated him like a black sheep. He'd shout at the walls, the ceiling, and at Lucy if she ever made the mistake of staying in the room. When he first started opening up in his drunken stupors, Lucy was always understanding. Hugging him as he cried. Pointing out how he wasn't a failure or unloved. These days, however, she'd sit and stare at the wall, hoping that he'd fall asleep and not direct his anger towards her. She couldn't even leave the room anymore to get away from it, because Patrick would follow her or shout so loud she could hear it any way.

Watching Siobhan dance around the room, a moment of sadness overwhelmed Lucy. Clutching her hands to her heart, she silently prayed that Siobhan would grow up to find a loving, loyal, and normal partner. As much as she tried to shield her from her father's behaviour, there were times when Siobhan had overheard arguments and screaming matches. What if Lucy's worst fear became a reality? What if Siobhan grew up to see this as normal? She'd learn from Lucy's behaviour to just shut up and take it. *It's so wrong; this needs to stop.*

She didn't notice that Siobhan had stopped her little dance and was staring at her. 'What's wrong, Lucy?'

'Nothing sweetheart, why?'

'Because you're crying.'

Lucy reached up and touched her face. Wiping the tears away, she answered, 'Must be my allergies, silly billy! I'm fine.' Lucy swallowed and asked, 'So what are you planning on doing with your brother today?'

Siobhan's eyes lit up. 'Daddy said he's taking us to a Wacky Warehouse.'

A pub! What's he thinking? 'Wow. That sounds like fun. Can you make yourself a bowl of cereal, Siobhan, and then get dressed?'

'OK.' Siobhan seemed pleased with herself, being able to get her own breakfast. Grabbing a bowl from the cupboard, she poured her cereal, drowned it in milk and sugar, making sure not to spill anything as she made her way over to the table.

Lucy was in two minds whether or not to say anything to Patrick. She definitely didn't want to anger him and ruin the kids' day. She hated things like this, walking on eggshells when she should be able to have a normal conversation with her husband.

Lucy took a deep breath and headed upstairs to wake him.

Patrick was still snoring and the stale smell of his booze from the night before hit her in the face as she entered the room. She walked around to his side of the bed and gently shook him. 'Patrick ... Patrick ... it's time to get up. Siobhan is having her breakfast and will be getting ready in a minute. Rory will be here in an hour or so.'

He groaned. 'Fuck off and gimme ten minutes.'

'I can't. I need to get ready and go soon. I'm going out with Sarah today. Remember? She'll be here soon.'

'All right! For fuck's sake. No need to bloody go on. I'm up. I'm up.'

Lucy gathered a towel from the clean laundry and went for her shower. She hoped he'd be downstairs by the time she finished, because otherwise she'd have to put up with his leering comments and groping hands as she got dressed.

After her shower, Lucy crept back into the bedroom and breathed a sigh of relief. Patrick was downstairs talking to Siobhan. Throwing on a sweater and a pair of jeans she quickly put on some foundation and towel-dried her hair. Placing her blusher, mascara, and lip gloss in her bag secretly, she decided to put the rest of her make-up on in Sarah's car.

As Lucy brought the wet towel downstairs to put it in the washing basket, Siobhan ran past her on the stairs. 'Slow down, missy! Don't forget to brush your teeth.'

'I know. Can I bring my little purse?'

Reaching into her pocket Lucy pulled out two £1 coins, and gave them to Siobhan. 'Sure, sweetie. Here's a little something to fill it up.'

Siobhan thanked her and raced off to find her purse.

I hope she doesn't tell Patrick or he'll take that money for himself.

Looking at her watch, Lucy saw she had about half an hour before Sarah was due to arrive. She had been looking forward to today. There was a book event in the town centre and they'd decided to make a girly day of it with lunch, window shopping … the works. She still had time for a quick cuppa so headed to the kitchen.

Patrick was standing by the sink, looking out into the garden. He ignored her as she walked in and flicked the kettle on.

'Do you want a coffee?'

Silence. He turned and looked her over, 'Why are you so dressed up? Thought you were only going out with Sarah?'

'I am. I'm just wearing jeans and a sweater, how is that dressed up?'

'Well considering you only wear leggings and baggy jumpers around here … that *is* fucking dressed up. Answer me. Who are you really going to meet?' He walked over and stood in front of her, pinning her against the kitchen counter.

'I told you, I'm meeting Sarah; in fact she will be here soon, and you can see for yourself!' Lucy leaned back slightly.

'If you're lying to me, I swear to God I will kill you. Do you understand?'

The knock on the door caught them both off guard and Lucy tried to get past him to answer it, but he remained firmly in front of her.

'I asked you a question, bitch.' His teeth were clenched, and Lucy knew better than to ignore him.

'I understand, OK. Can I please go and get the door? She'll be wondering what's taking so long and I don't want to lie to her, OK? Please, Patrick.'

He stepped out of the way, allowing her to get past. Lucy went into the hall and opened the door, hoping that her friend had not overheard anything.

'Hey, girly! You ready for what the day has in store?' Sarah had a big smile on her face.

'Uh, yes. I'll just grab my coat, bag, and say goodbye to Siobhan. Do you want to come in … or maybe it's best you just wait in the car?'

'Nah, I'll come in, if you're not going to be long.'

Lucy was hoping she wouldn't say that. The quicker she grabbed her things and said goodbye to Siobhan, the less time Patrick would have to grill Sarah or make her feel uncomfortable.

Lucy walked back into the living room and glanced over at

Sarah, who was sitting down on the edge of the chair. Sarah nearly jumped when she noticed Patrick in the doorway staring at her. Lucy hoped he wouldn't be an arsehole, but saw him smile strangely at Sarah, cock his head, and ask, 'So where are you two ladies off to?'

'Didn't Lucy say what we're doing today?' Sarah asked and looked at Lucy.

Lucy shrugged.

'She did, but I'm asking you.'

Lucy's hands balled into fists as she watched Sarah shifting uncomfortably on the chair.

'Well, we're going to do a bit of shopping – or window shopping as payday is miles away.' Sarah smiled weakly. 'Then lunch and then a book event at Waterstones. A few authors we're fans of will be there signing their books.'

Patrick didn't say a word; instead he just turned around and went back to the kitchen.

CHAPTER FORTY-FIVE

Patrick waited for Rory to arrive. He purposely didn't tell Lucy where they were going, because she'd just nag and nag about not drinking when he took the kids out. *Does she think she's my fucking mother? Two pints is the legal limit for fuck's sake.* He suspected that Siobhan must have told her anyway because of the look she gave him before she left with her friend.

Patrick wasn't keen on Sarah. Lucy said she was married, but the way the pair of them had tarted themselves up for a 'book event' made it obvious they had other things on their mind. He clenched his jaw and tried to control his breathing. Didn't want to be angry when he took the kids out. If he stayed in this mood, Lucy would be sorry when he next saw her. *Fucking sorry.*

Rory walked into the house without Patrick even noticing.

'Hey, Dad!' Rory walked over and gave his father a hug.

'Hey there, buddy! It's great to see you. Siobhan is really excited about today.'

'Are you all right? You seem tense,' Rory asked.

Just then, as if on cue, squeals of excitement were heard as Siobhan came racing down the stairs. 'Rory! Rory! Is that you?'

Patrick looked on as Rory laughed.

'It sure is. How's my favourite sister?'

Siobhan giggled and gave her brother a hug.

Patrick smiled and felt himself relaxing. Both his kids together and getting along. It was something he'd always hoped for. His heart burst with pride every time he saw his children together.

'Right, you pair, are you ready for … the Wacky Warehouse?' Patrick wasn't surprised to see Rory roll his eyes, he was probably a little too old for the Wacky Warehouse, but Patrick saw understanding in Rory's face when he watched how excited his sister was. He was proud of his son, and truth be told, Siobhan's giggles could be infectious at times. Locking the door behind him, Patrick hurried the kids into the car and headed out.

The pub was pretty full, but Patrick left the kids to play while he went and sorted out the drinks. He knew they would be safe enough in the play area with all the mums and dads keeping an eye out. Patrick pulled out the money Lucy had left him. *Forty fucking quid. I'll barely be able to get two pints plus the lunches, so I'm not sure what she was moaning about.*

He shouted over to Rory, 'I'll be outside on the patio, so when you've both had your fill, come over.' He gathered the drinks, and sat outside.

Patrick liked to people-watch. He hadn't been sitting longer than five minutes when he spotted Shell Baker and smiled. Patrick took out his mobile and sent her a cheeky text to smooth things over – he wasn't ready to let go of Shell just yet.

Are you following me? Turn around x P

He watched Shell look around before setting her eyes on him. He waved her over. 'What are you doing here, babe?'

'My cousin's kid – it's his birthday – and a bunch of the family and some friends are here for the party. It's a fucking nightmare.' Shell laughed loudly and started to point out some of the people she was with. 'That fellow in the cap is my uncle, Jack, and sitting beside him is a family friend, Wendy. I do some cleaning around her place once a week to help her out. Those two women are my cousins – but I'm guessing you're not interested in my family history.' Shell laughed and Patrick noticed her looking at the table with the two soft drinks.

'So, where are your kids then?' She glanced towards the play area behind him.

'Rory's keeping an eye on Siobhan in there. They'll be tired soon enough, though, and want some lunch.'

'So, no Lucy then?'

Patrick saw his opportunity.

'Nah, she said she had more important things to do.' He pretended to look gutted. 'I mean, what could be more important than your family, right?'

'Oh, babe! I'm so sorry. She really is a right one, isn't she?'

Patrick nodded in agreement. Sometimes he couldn't believe how gullible women were. He was surprised by Shell. Thought she'd be harder to convince.

'I really enjoy our chats … all this. Fancy doing it again soon?' Patrick gave Shell his best smile.

'Absolutely. I feel the same and I'm so glad you said it, because I was beginning to wonder where this was going.'

He saw her looking around to make sure no one was watching. Then she brushed her hand over his.

'Look, I don't want to put you in an awkward position. I know you feel uncomfortable and you've really been patient. But my marriage has been over for some time. Lucy won't come near me, doesn't talk to me and doesn't even bother with family days.' He paused to gaze into Shell's eyes

'That's bloody awful. You know I fancy you. I ain't no home-wrecker though, so you'll have to sort that soon.' Shell looked away briefly.

'I know. I'm trying my best, babe. Do you think I like this?

158

You know I want to be with you. Haven't I made that clear?' He grinned and knew he had her hook, line, and sinker.

'Cool. I will give you a shout soon.' She squeezed his hand.

They both turned towards her party when her name was called.

'Shell! Are you coming for the photos?'

She rolled her eyes.

'Sorry, gotta go. I'm free next weekend, just so you know.'

Patrick looked around and pulled Shell in close for a quick kiss. He watched as she flashed him a smile and walked back to her family and friends.

Patrick laughed and took a sip of his pint. *Too easy.* Rory and Siobhan joined him shortly after and he asked them what they wanted for lunch. Mindful of the money in his pocket, he planted the seed that they should just get a snack – they would be having a large dinner back at the house – and Lucy wouldn't be happy if they couldn't eat it all. They ordered a plate of chips each and Patrick had another pint. He really did love spending time with his kids and wondered if Shell did too. If Lucy ever found out about Shell, he may just need somewhere else to stay. He was clever like that. Always one step ahead of everyone else. Always looking out for number one … himself.

'Who was that lady, Dad?' Rory asked casually.

'Don't know what you're talking about, son. What lady?'

Rory pointed in the direction of Shell. 'That one over there. I saw you … talking to her.'

Patrick rubbed his neck. 'Oh, Shell? She's a friend, why … what do you think you saw?'

'Erm … Nothing. Like I said, I saw you talking to her and was just curious.'

Patrick glared. Had Rory seen something he shouldn't have?

Once Patrick had finished his second pint, he got bored people watching. The kids were looking bored too, so they called it a day and headed for the car. On the drive home, Patrick couldn't get Shell out of his head. He wasn't lying when he said that he and Lucy weren't close anymore; though they still had sex, Lucy didn't seem to enjoy it and she never initiated it. Not his problem though. As his wife, she was obligated, in his opinion, and if she wouldn't willingly give it, he'd take it. Fair is fair.

When Shell returned to her party, she was bombarded with twenty questions.

'Who was that?'

'Are you seeing him?'

'Whose kids were they?'

Shell laughed at the nosiness of her family, but couldn't blame them because she'd be exactly the same.

Uncle Jack spoke up for her. 'Whoa, leave the poor girl alone. Can't she have a chat with a fella without people making all these assumptions?' he winked at Shell. 'You can tell me all about him later.'

Shell had a soft spot for Uncle Jack. When she got older and started her cleaning business, her uncle offered her the first official cleaning job. As her company grew, Shell never let her employees clean his office. Her uncle trusted only her, and she promised him she'd always do the job herself.

'I'll tell you all about him one day, Jack. At the moment, we're taking things slowly. It's a bit … complicated. I promise to let you know if it goes any further. OK?'

'Sounds good to me. Just be careful. Complicated is never good. You know that.'

'I know. I'm smarter than I look.' She nudged him playfully.

At least I hope I am.

CHAPTER FORTY-SIX

Sarah and Lucy had a great time over lunch. They chatted about anything and everything and it felt good to Lucy to have someone she could just be herself with.

'So, what was up with Patrick and all the questions earlier?' Lucy had shared some of what was happening at home, but Sarah believed Lucy, like most victims, was still hiding the level of abuse and what she knew only scratched the surface. They were having such a good time though, Sarah didn't want to ruin it.

'Oh, you know what men are like. He was just being nosy. I'm sure he didn't mean anything by it. Anyway … are you excited about the book event? I've been waiting ages for today.'

Sarah pretended she didn't notice the change of subject, fearing that if she pushed Lucy too hard, too soon, then Lucy would shut her out.

'I can't wait. So many brilliant authors. I've saved up enough to make sure I can get all the books I want signed. How about you?' Sarah noticed Lucy blush with embarrassment.

'I've put aside a little money, but with Patrick not working and having to live off my wage … well, it can get a bit tight by the end of the month.' Lucy wouldn't look Sarah in the eye.

Sarah tapped Lucy's leg gently. 'Well never mind, if there is a signed book that you want, and you can't get it, I'll buy it for you. Think of it as an early birthday present.'

'Oh, Sarah, I couldn't ask you to do that.'

'Why not? Look, you know how stubborn I can be. I won't take no for an answer!' Sarah saw the worry that clouded Lucy's face. She guessed it had to do with explaining to her husband how she could afford the books, rather than the fact that Sarah was being nice to her.

'I really couldn't. Patrick will just start asking questions. That's so nice of you, but I'd rather avoid any confrontation if I can. I have money for one or two books; I'll just sneak them in and pretend I always had them.'

Sarah shrugged her shoulders, 'OK. But the offer is there if you want it.' Sarah could tell by the reddening of Lucy's face that she was too embarrassed and humiliated to explain the real reasons. Clearly Patrick had a strong hold over Lucy and that level of control was concerning.

The rest of the day was spent enjoying the book event, getting signed copies of some of their favourite authors' books. They were like kids in a sweet shop. Authors really were their rock stars, but Sarah was sad that Lucy wouldn't let her take any photos for her on her phone. She guessed that Patrick would probably flip, if he saw Lucy in photos with other men with their arms around her, no matter how innocent. As it came close to going home, Sarah noticed a change in her friend's demeanour. She was wringing her hands and frown lines adorned her forehead.

Sarah dropped her off and declined the offer of coffee. 'I need to get back to Justin. I promised him we'd catch a film later on.'

'OK. Thanks so much for today. I had a brilliant time.' Lucy waved as Sarah reversed in the cul-de-sac and drove away.

CHAPTER FORTY-SEVEN

DI Calleja received the pathologist's report about Robert Millard and pored over it for what seemed like hours. He was stumped. Millard had been beaten extensively, suffering blunt force trauma injuries. Although not identical, there were enough similarities to link this to the Talbot case. The pathologist couldn't specify the weapon used, except to say that they didn't believe it wasn't a hammer or a knife. It could have been something hard, like a baton, or a bat, possibly even fists. Robert had also been kicked a few times, causing broken ribs, and a tiny part of Calleja couldn't help but think the man had got what he deserved.

According to the report, the slash wound across the throat was done with a thin blade – like a Stanley knife or something similar – and ultimately this is what led to his death. The pathologist noted, however, that on the right side of the neck, the original cut branched off, as if there had been two cuts. What couldn't be explained was the lack of any defensive wounds. Unlike Talbot, there was no evidence to suggest that he'd been knocked unconscious, no head wounds or trauma to the brain. Further down the report, was a reference to a small puncture wound on the right side of the neck – possibly made by a syringe. Toxicology could find no drugs in his system, but this was inconclusive. The time lapse between the murder and the body being found could explain the lack of any substances in his system. Joseph made a note to ask the team whether Millard had a history of Class A substance misuse. He didn't want to waste precious time only to find that the needle mark came from injecting heroin.

The report ended with the conclusion that the cause of death was the wound to his neck, across his windpipe, leading Millard to 'drown in his own blood'. He had died anywhere between six to twelve days before the body was discovered. It was vital that the team find out the last reported sighting of Robert Millard, if they were going to move forward on this case. For some, this would be their first murder case and the experience they lacked would be more than evident. However, he was confident that his team were all skilled enough to grasp this case with both hands and get a quick result.

Calleja advised the team there would be a briefing to discuss the Talbot/Millard murders. Kat and Maggie were out doing door-to-door enquiries, while Mark and Pete liaised with probation and collated a list of the victim's associates.

A knock on the door jolted him from his thoughts. Looking up from the case file, he greeted Dr Moloney. 'Have a seat. What's up?'

'Sorry to disturb you, but I wondered if you knew anything more about the cases that I can include in my profile.'

'I've just received the pathologist and toxicology reports for Millard and called a briefing to discuss the findings. Didn't you get the message?' It was then that Calleja realized that, as a civilian, Dr Moloney didn't have a police radio. Red-faced he noted his error and apologized.

'Ah, I understand. No need to worry. So, should I just wait until the briefing or can you tell me anything now? Maybe I'll be able to go away and update my profile.'

Calleja talked her through the highlights of the report.

'Are we any way forward in terms of witnesses or his last movements? Do we have any suspects?' she asked.

'I'm afraid not. Not unless Maggie or Kat have more info when they return to the office.' Without giving Dr Moloney an opportunity to respond, he looked at his watch and informed her that it shouldn't be too long before he had more information to share. 'Once they brief me, do you want me to send them down to you or can you wait?'

'I doubt I would be able to add anything in such a short time, so I'll wait, and assess the information afterwards.'

Kate had some of her own thoughts but she wasn't sure the team was ready to hear her theories just yet.

CHAPTER FORTY-EIGHT

Vicki collected her dole money and headed straight for the pub. She was shaking already, desperate for a drink. Once her money had dried out, she'd have to latch on to someone and hope they would buy the drinks in exchange for something else. The pub was quiet, but it was only noon. She placed herself at the bar, strategically angled so she could spot a likely target if needed.

'The usual, Vicki?'

'Yes, love.' She hugged the pint glass close to her, like it was her only friend, and the minute the sweet cider dripped onto her tongue she felt like she was in heaven.

Nearly four hours had passed before anyone of interest entered the pub, but then she saw him. Vicki hadn't been impressed the first time they'd met. She'd heard through the grapevine that he was originally from London and just out of prison. That he was a wife beater. He didn't look that strong, and Vicky reckoned she could take him down if need be. She laughed to herself and took a swig of her drink.

The man walked up to the bar and ordered a pint of Stella. She was hoping that he would be alone so she could worm her way into his affections; her drink, and her money, wouldn't last much longer. He glanced her way and cocked his head to the left, as if he was trying to place her.

'Hello, darlin', can I get you a drink?'

A smile formed on Vicki's face. 'I'll have a cider, love, if you're buying?'

'Can I get a cider for the lady.'

When the pint was poured, the man handed Vicki her cider and sat down on the stool beside her. He didn't seem to recognize her, or if he did, he didn't seem to care about their first encounter.

'I remember you in here before. Though I didn't catch your name.'

So, he *did* remember her.

'I'm Vicki. Nice to meet you. And what do I call you?'

'Anything you want, babe. But my name is Mick.' He reached out; pulling her hand close, he kissed it.

Vicki felt herself blush. 'Aren't you the gentleman?' She began to relax.

As they continued to chat she forgot all about their first meeting and, while Mick continued to order the drinks, Vicki continued to consume them.

CHAPTER FORTY-NINE

'Do you live around here?' Mick put on all the charm. It seemed to be working, because she hadn't noticed him checking the clock behind her. She was in a right state, but it had been a while since he had been in the company of a woman and he didn't want her to pass out before he had the chance to test her out.

Slurring her words, Vicki just about managed to get out a, 'Yessss, round corner …' pointing in what Mick could only assume was the direction of her flat. Though if Mick had followed her directions, he'd have ended up in the pub toilets for all her swaying about.

'Well, I'm thinking that you're too pretty to be going home alone this evening, and I would hate to see anything happen to you, so why don't we take this party back to your place? We can stop at the shops and grab a few cans if you'd like?' Mick thought it was a smile he saw, or it could've been gas from the way she was downing those ciders.

He looped his arm in hers and propped her up, as they walked out the bar. Despite the state of her, she was confident where she was going. That was the sign of a seasoned alcoholic. After stopping at the shops and grabbing four cans of cider, it took only a further fifteen minutes to arrive at a dingy block of flats. Mick was beginning to realize just how small Markston was; his own place was probably a fifteen-minute walk from Vicki's. Handy if he needed to make a quick exit.

As they walked into the building, the smell of piss hit Mick in the face and he nearly retched up his lunch. The stench didn't seem to bother Vicki at all. The lift was no better and needles adorned the floor. *Fucking dirty bastards.* Mick was careful where he stood and tried to steer Vicki clear of the sharpies. They got off on the third floor and Vicki rummaged through her bag for her keys.

'Would you like some help, darling?' He rubbed her back. Vicki eventually found her keys and once the door was open, she pulled Mick eagerly inside. *That was easy.* She tasted of cider, but Mick didn't care. He shoved her towards the couch, wasn't in the mood for foreplay. Vicki squirmed but didn't put up too much of a struggle. She was definitely up for it.

When finished, Mick got dressed, and cracked open one of the cans.

'Boy did I need that.' He turned to look at Vicki, but she'd fallen asleep. *Fucking slag.* He'd keep her sweet though; she was handy for a shag. At least until something better came along. Mick wanted to make a quick getaway before Vicki woke up. It was one thing to stare at the back of her head and get his rocks off drunk; he wasn't sure he could stomach looking at her face in the cold light of day. Finishing off his can, he walked quietly around the living room, to see if she had anything worth taking. Given her drink habit, he suspected that any valuables were long gone by now. The carpet was stained with what could only be alcohol and cigarette ash and the walls had the dull hue of yellow that came from years of smoking. Taking the remainder of the cans with him, he made his way to the door and snuck out before Vicki noticed.

Mick arrived back at his flat and picked up his post before going inside. Opening the letter, Mick crumpled the paper up in frustration.

Fucking probation! Do this. Do that! I'm sick of this shit … Knowing he still had quite a while left on his licence, he'd play the game carefully for now. It was getting more difficult though. He was too old for prison and he finally had a decent flat of his own. He thought about his kids and wished it hadn't gone as far as it had with their mother. But if she had just kept her gob shut, they might still be a family today, or at least he'd have some sort of relationship with his kids. If he ever saw her again … He opened another can of cider and took a long hard swig. There was only so long that Mick could keep things bottled up inside, and he pitied whoever was in front of him when that volcano erupted.

CHAPTER FIFTY

The police were no further ahead with the Talbot or Millard cases. Door-to-door enquiries were still being carried out to determine both of the men's movements. Robert was known to frequent the local pub, The Smith's Forge, so Maggie and Kat were on their way there. When they arrived, Maggie noted the drab pub was empty and they were greeted by Kevin, the manager.

'Morning, sir. Are you Graham Smith?' Kat looked at the heavyset, middle-aged man behind the bar.

'Sorry, lass, Mr Smith is rarely here. He has pubs all across the UK, so leaves me to manage this one. The name is Kevin. Kevin Pearson. Is there something I can help with?'

'First off, the name is PC Everett, not *lass* …' Maggie had to stifle a laugh as the manager turned a crimson colour and apologized for his mistake.

Kat gave him an evil grin and continued, 'and yes, we're wondering if you could tell us a bit about Robert Millard? You may have heard that Mr Millard was murdered and we understand from some of his neighbours that he was a regular here. One of my colleagues might also have attended and asked you questions about the death of Drew Talbot. Did he also come into the pub?'

'Ah, yes. I know Robert, but I've never heard of Talbot. I did see the story on the news about him – sounded pretty gruesome. Robert generally spends ... or should I say spent ... three or four days a week here. When he was working, I think it was only the weekends he'd drop in. When he split with his bird, Louise, I saw him more often. Had a bit of a temper and liked to mouth off, but never caused any trouble I couldn't handle. So, he was murdered too, was he? Was it his wife who did it?'

'Why would you ask that?' Maggie stepped forward.

'She was here the other week, that Louise. Chatting to Shell Baker, and a few other people. Louise was bloody angry. Overheard her shouting that she "wished the fucker was dead" – I think those were her words, something like that anyway. Robert used to beat the shit out of her, I hear. He was on probation or something. Shell tried to calm Louise down, but she was having none of it. I had to ask her to leave.'

Maggie processed this information before asking her next question.

'You seem to know a lot about the people who frequent this pub. Did Louise go quietly then? And do you know where we can find Shell Baker?'

'Yeah. Well people tend to tell me things or talk loud enough so I can hear them. Must be my kind face. I had no problem with Louise leaving. A few choice swear words, she was pretty pissed. Shell owns a cleaning company. They clean the pub and Shell's girls are usually here from 5.00 a.m. to 7.00 a.m. on Tuesdays and Thursdays. Sometimes Shell's with them, guess it depends on how busy she is. Not sure I should be really saying all this or be giving you her address without permission. I'll speak to Graham, my boss, and see what he says – gimme five.'

'Hang on.'

The barman stopped, turned, and looked at Maggie.

'Why are the cleaners here so early?'

'We have a twenty-four-hour liquor licence, so we open at 9.00 a.m. We need the place clean before then.'

Maggie looked at the surroundings: the barstools needed replacing, the uncomfortable-looking chairs lumpy with the stuffing coming out of them, the carpet so worn you could see the tatty, wood floor beneath it.

'Thanks. You can make that call now.'

He took a mobile out of his pocket and went into the back room.

Maggie and Kat waited, trying to look as patient as possible.

Ten minutes later, he returned. 'Yeah, no problem with giving you the address. Cragley Court Estate, number five. Just don't say I gave it to you; she has a gob on her and I don't fancy getting an earful.' He laughed nervously, and Maggie just smiled in response.

'Thanks for your help. Can't make any promises, but we'll do our best to keep your name out of it.'

The officers left. Maggie got the impression that Kevin didn't want to point any fingers, but the way he went on about Louise, he seemed to think she'd be capable of anything. Or to want them to think that.

'So, what do you think, Maggie?'

Maggie turned to Kat and they stopped on the side of the road. 'To be honest, I get that Louise Millard probably had a lot of pent-up anger, but given that she put up with all that abuse from Robert, I can't see why she'd seek out revenge now. I mean, there hasn't been any real catalyst. If she was going to do it, there would have been plenty of opportunities.'

'That's exactly what I was thinking. But who knows when a person reaches that point? Maybe she just finally exploded. Should I run a check on Shell Baker? I take it we're heading there now?'

'Good idea. If she has form, we may help direct our questioning.'

Maggie focused on the road as Kat radioed through the checks. She muttered down the line and killed the radio. 'Fuck all, just a public order offence in her teens.' So their questioning would be fairly straightforward.

According to the details they were given, Shell didn't live too far from the pub and the officers arrived just in time to see someone leaving the property. Maggie strained her eyes and noticed cleaning supplies in the woman's hand. It was her. They jumped out.

'Excuse me, Miss! Can we have a word?' Maggie shouted.

Shell stopped in her tracks. 'And who the hell are you?'

'Sorry. My name is DC Maggie Jamieson, and this is my colleague, PC Kat Everett. We wondered if you could spare a few minutes of your time to help with our enquires?' By the look on her face, Maggie could see that Shell's interest was piqued.

'What enquiries? I've done nowt, you know.'

'We know, Mrs ... or is it Ms Baker?'

'Miss, actually, but you can call me Shell.'

'Thanks, Shell. Do you want to step back inside? This is kind of a sensitive topic.' Maggie pointed at the door.

Shell saw some of her neighbours' curtains twitching and she waved her middle finger towards them. 'Fucking nosy bastards. Sorry, but the majority of people around here do my head in. Come inside – but I only have a few minutes. I'm off to one of my priority jobs. It needs to be done before he opens later today.'

'It shouldn't take long.'

Maggie followed Shell inside, with Kat hot on her heels. The flat was tidy and felt quite homely to Maggie, whose own house was a bombshell in comparison. A quick scan around the place suggested Shell lived alone, although she noticed a man's sweater thrown over a chair in the dining area.

'Is your partner home?' Maggie glanced in the direction of the chair.

'Partner?' Shell looked nervously towards the sweater over the chair. 'Oh, because of the sweater? Nah, that's my … erm … cousin's sweater. He was round the other night for a bit of a natter.'

'Oh right. OK. Do you mind if we have a seat?' They followed her into the living room and Shell plonked herself down directly opposite them.

'So, what is this about then?'

'We're questioning people who might have known or come across Robert Millard. His decomposed body was found the other night and it seems that he may have been dead for some time.' Maggie was always curious about people's reaction to this sort of information, and she wasn't surprised by Shell's response, given their greeting earlier.

'So? What has this got to do with me? What did he die of? A heart attack or something?'

'No. He was murdered. It's been on the news.'

Shell covered her mouth. 'Oh, my god. Really? I don't watch the news. In fact, I rarely watch the telly. Too busy.'

Maggie cleared her throat and continued, 'As I said, we can't share specific details, but the circumstances surrounding his death are definitely suspicious. We have been led to believe that you're friends with, or know of, his estranged wife, Louise Millard?' Maggie noticed that Shell stiffened when Louise's name was mentioned.

'That's right. And what of it?' The pitch of Shell's voice had gone up a notch and Maggie instantly caught it.

Maggie looked at Kat, who grinned, each as curious as the other. 'Why so defensive, Shell?'

'Defensive? I'm just pissed off that you're questioning me about a low-life prick who gets his jollies from kicking the shit out of women. If you ask me, he deserves whatever he got, and I hope it was as painful as possible. Was he shot? Stabbed? Had the shit kicked out of him? However he died, it was probably too good for him.'

'We can understand your anger. But we really need you to answer our questions as best you can, Shell. How do you know Louise Millard?'

'Markston is not the biggest of places, is it? If you're not family, you probably grew up with the person. I knew all about what that prick did to Louise. But I have no clue what happened to him.'

Maggie caught Shell looking at her watch.

'Look, I really have to go otherwise I won't get my cleaning job done in time.'

'That's fine, but we may need to speak to you at a later time. Can you jot down some details of the places you work? Here's my card, and last thing: do you know someone by the name of Drew Talbot?' As Maggie passed her details to Shell she thought she saw a flash of recognition in her eyes.

Shell wrote out her work information and handed the paper to Kat.

'Drew who? Sorry, doesn't sound familiar. Hmmm ... Drew Talbot.' Shell shook her head.

'OK, well if you think of anything, call us.'

'Yeah, I will, but I don't know what else I can tell you.' Shell pocketed the card and showed them out. Maggie followed Shell's movements and watched her pick up the cleaning supplies, jump in her car, and head in the direction of the town centre.

'Well, she couldn't wait to get rid of us, could she? And Kevin was right – what a fucking gob on her.' Kat started the car. Maggie raised an eyebrow at her.

'Why are you looking at me like that?'

'No reason.' Maggie hid a smile, 'You're right, she does have a gob on her. Is it just me or did something seem off? I don't know for sure, but I'm pretty sure she was hiding something. She didn't seem keen to share her work details with us. Maybe everything is not above board on that front. We'll have to check it out at some point. Anyway, let's go and speak with Louise. See if we can shed any further light on this. The guv isn't going to be happy if we come back with nothing.'

CHAPTER FIFTY-ONE

Kat let out a loud groan as they reached Louise Millard's house.

'What was that for?' Maggie asked.

'Christ, have you ever met this woman? She gobs off at the police even when they're trying to *help* her. Every second word out of her mouth is fucking this or bastard that ... Couldn't we have left this for someone else to do? We could just pass it over and head back to the station.'

Maggie stared at her.

'What?'

'It's a bit rich that you of all people are talking first about Shell having a gob on her and now Mrs Millard – you can be very much the same!' The conversation felt like déjà vu to Maggie.

'Hey, I know when to be professional! Besides, if someone was helping me, I would be grateful for that.'

'You have to remember what Louise has been through. And her experience with most police officers has probably been none too helpful or positive, especially years ago when the police did fuck all about domestic abuse.'

Kat looked embarrassed then. 'OK. Point taken.'

Maggie and Kat locked the car and approached the house. Just as Maggie was about to knock, the door opened.

'I saw you two sitting there laughing away in your car. You think this is all funny? Well ... *do you*!?'

The officers apologized simultaneously and Maggie felt her face redden. She was aware that if she tried to explain it was a misunderstanding, it would probably anger Louise even more, so she left it.

'Mrs Millard. My name is DC Maggie Jamieson, and this is my colleague, PC Kat Everett. We're sorry about showing up unexpectedly, but we wondered whether we could speak to you about your ex-husband? We're trying to piece together his last movements and gather details about anyone with a grudge against him.'

'Ha! Are you serious? Hope you have a big fucking notepad. There are plenty of people who wanted Robert dead ... including me!' Louise Millard turned swiftly on her heel and walked towards the living room. Looking over her shoulder she shouted, 'Well, what are you waiting for? Fucking neighbours will be gawping out their windows if you stand there any longer. Shut the door behind you.'

Maggie and Kat followed Louise into her living room and settled onto the sofa, both spotting the empty bottle of vodka partially hidden by the chair. Louise followed their eyes.

'And what? It helps me sleep.'

Feeling slightly embarrassed at being judgemental after having a go at Kat outside for the exact same thing, Maggie passed Louise a card. 'That is the Family Liaison Officer's details if you need some help or support. Right now, we're just going to ask you a few questions. Do you want a cup of tea or anything?' She nudged Kat.

'Uh, yeah – I can make us all a cuppa if you'd like, Louise?'

'Like hell you will. Rummaging around my kitchen. Forget that shit! I'm fine, I'm not drunk if that's what you're thinking and if you wanted a cuppa, you should've stopped at the café first. Now, can we just get on with this? I only just found out he

179

was dead and you're already here pestering me. Pity you couldn't be as quick when he was kicking the shit out of me.'

'We're so sorry, Louise. Shall we just start with the basic stuff? The sooner we get this done, the sooner we can leave you in peace.' Looking over her notes, Maggie carried on, 'I know you said a lot of people wanted him dead, but can you think of anyone who would actually kill him? Did he get into any arguments recently or disagreements with anyone that you're aware of?'

'Are you on crack? I had a restraining order out against Robert. Not that it did much good … but I stayed well away from him. The only thing we still had in common was The Smith's Forge – the local pub. I avoided the place on the days when he'd be going there. He was a creature of habit, so it wasn't too difficult.'

'Did you hear anything unusual at the pub?'

'Look. I just told you, I did everything I could to get that piece of shit out of my life. When I went to the pub, it was to catch up with my friends. To escape this shit, the bad memories, you know.' She paused and shifted her position on the chair. 'We may have chatted about Robert and, I'll be honest, after the last kicking I got, I did mouth off. I wished he was dead – but those were just words. You get that, right?' Tugging at her sleeves, Louise continued, 'Ask Sharon Bairden; I met up with her for one of our sessions before I went over to the pub. Probably why I was all wound up. Sharon knows what I'm like, I was only messing about and even she jumped in saying she'd like to give him a good kicking, too. A lot of people didn't like him.' Louise leaned over and grabbed a tissue from the box on the table. 'I hated Rob for what he did to me over the years. Fucking *hated* him. But we'd been married a long time. And there were some good times too, you know. And then … well, the baby.' She stopped and grabbed for a tissue. Blew her nose angrily. 'But that's not a problem anymore … I had a miscarriage. So, I'm finding it hard whether to be happy or sad about this whole fucking mess.'

Maggie nodded. 'We're so sorry for your loss and we understand, Louise. I'm sorry to sound insensitive, but can you tell me specifically who you were speaking with, or who you met, at the pub?'

'Hang on. Am I a fucking suspect here?' Louise shifted again in her seat and half-reached automatically for the empty bottle of vodka.

'No, we're not saying that. We have to question everyone. Right now, we know very little about Robert's movements and we're trying to piece them together to establish when he died. We just need to be sure we have all the information.'

Kat had been noting down everything that Maggie and Louise were saying, and before Maggie could stop her, she butted in. 'Those tears dried up pretty quick when you thought you were being accused of something, Louise.'

Maggie shot Kat an angry look.

Louise bolted from her seat, waving her arms furiously. 'That's it. Try to fucking help you pigs and *this* is how I get treated? I'm fucking grieving you know! Get out. *Get out!*'

Furious with Kat, Maggie tried to calm the situation. 'Louise, I can only apologize for the way my colleague spoke to you. We really do appreciate your help. Can we carry on this conversation if I ask Kat to wait outside?'

'But …' Kat wasn't pleased at her colleague's decision.

'Kat, could you do me a favour and wait in the car until we're finished here?'

If looks could kill, Maggie would have been arrested at that very moment. She momentarily felt bad for being so harsh, as Kat stomped out of the house like a petulant child.

'Like I said, Louise. I'm really sorry about that. Kat is new to this team and I think the whole case is getting the best of everyone.' Maggie hoped that her pitiful excuse would help calm Louise down. She'd deal with Kat later.

Taking her seat again, and another handful of tissues, Louise agreed to answer the rest of Maggie's questions. 'OK then. So, can you tell me who you normally meet up with at the pub?'

'I don't have that many friends. Robert made sure of that. Mainly Shell Baker. She's a great support and knows what I've been through. She let me rant, get it all out of my system – it helped.'

'And does Shell know Robert?'

'Of course. Shell and I are cousins. I don't hide anything from her.'

Maggie noted this down and circled 'cousins'.

'Can you think of anyone else? You mentioned Sharon?'

'Sharon is one of those advocacy workers. You should fucking know that, she works with you guys. I never met her at the pub; it was beforehand – you know the old magistrates' courts that were turned into a community centre? We have group sessions there, or sometimes she'd see me on my own.'

'And did she ever talk about hurting Robert?' Maggie asked.

Louise laughed. 'Not seriously. I jokingly said what I'd love to do to guys like Robert – you know, a good kicking – and she threw in her two cents' worth. The way these pricks did it to us and got away with it, it's just shocking. No wonder women like me find it hard to leave.'

Interesting. 'OK, Louise. That's great. Sorry to have taken up so much of your time. I can see myself out.'

After finishing up with Louise, Maggie returned to the car. Getting in and slamming the door, she turned to Kat. 'What the hell is wrong with you? You could have screwed up that whole thing!'

'Sorry, Maggie. It just pisses me off when people play the victim.'

'Kat, she *is* a victim. Her husband systematically abused her – physically and emotionally – for years. She just miscarried a child and now her husband has been murdered. No wonder her feelings are all over the place! You have to hold your personal views back, Kat.' Maggie did up her seat belt with a snap. Kat stared moodily out of the window.

'It just so happens, after you left I learnt that Shell Baker is Louise Millard's cousin. She never mentioned *that* when we questioned her. Also Sharon has been a bit unprofessional about her clients.'

'Maybe Shell didn't feel it was important ... and we've all said things off the cuff, Maggie. I wouldn't read too much into either of those things.' Kat twisted the key and started the engine.

'Yeah ... maybe. Shit! Look at the time. We need to get back to the station.' Maggie tapped her nose. 'We also need to speak to Sharon, and Shell Baker again at some point.'

CHAPTER FIFTY-TWO

Vicki was enjoying the new-found attention she was getting off Mick O'Dowd these last few weeks. Although she didn't really know much about him, because he'd clam up whenever she asked, people were saying that he was just out of prison for a nasty attack on his ex-girlfriend and that he'd previously assaulted his wife. But this was probably bollocks. Vicki knew he was on licence, because they often went to the probation office together, but Mick told her he'd been caught with a large amount of weed he'd been holding for a mate. She had no reason to think he was lying; he'd not so much as raised an eyebrow at her, let alone a hand, so why should she think otherwise?

Even Shell was warning Vicki to stay away from Mick. Now Vicki liked Shell, but she could be full-on when she had a bee in her bonnet. She thought back to their last conversation at the pub. Shell leaning in and shouting into her ear.

'I'm telling you, Vicki, he is bad news. He has those cold eyes and I do believe all the rumours going around about him. Don't you remember when he first met you? Think about it. He never talks about his past. He tells you some bullshit story about being on licence for cannabis ... why would they put him in a bail hostel here? Why didn't they find one in London for him? Huh!?

Just be careful, OK.' Vicki had swayed and put her drink down, promised Shell that the first sign of trouble and she'd break it off.

But now in her flat, thinking about Mick, she knew she hadn't felt so wanted in a long time. She had even cut down her drinking, with help from her probation officer and the substance misuse team, because she didn't want to be pissed every time they were together. This was the longest time she'd managed to stay out of prison and she wasn't about to throw that away.

Mick was coming around to her flat in half an hour. She had just enough time to run to the shops and get a few cans in. She'd wanted to go and see his new place, but he made some excuse about it being a mess. He'd just secured a flat of his own through the probation hostel. *He obviously wanted to make a good impression.*

Mick arrived not long after she got back from the shop, and when she opened the door, he had a single red rose in his hand.

'Aww, wow. No one has ever given me a flower, let alone a rose before.' Vicki could feel herself blushing.

'I'm surprised at that, babe. You deserve the finest.'

Vicki grabbed him by the collar and pulled him inside. Giving him a passionate kiss, she took his hands, and dragged him towards the bedroom.

A while later, she climbed happily from the bed. Grabbed Mick a cold beer, herself a cider, and joined him in the living room. Plonking herself down on the couch beside him, she took a deep breath, turned to him and asked about his time in London. 'How come you never want to talk about it? Did something bad happen?'

'Babe, I told you before, don't push me on this. I just don't want to talk about it. I'm here now. New start, new life. Why can't you just leave it at that?'

Vicki didn't like his tone. If it had been lighter in the room she might have seen the look in his eyes and she might have stopped there. But she carried on. 'I was just asking, all right. You don't have to get so fucking arsy about it. Maybe the rumours are right …' She regretted the words the moment they left her lips.

Mick turned to her and through gritted teeth replied, 'What fucking rumours?'

It was at that moment that Vicki saw the cold look that Shell had told her about. Mick's face seemed to change, an icy calm came over him, and his body locked up with rage.

'No rumours, hon. I just said that out of anger. I feel like you're shutting me out. Sorry, I shouldn't have said that.' Mick rolled his shoulders and within seconds, he'd changed back to his old self. Now that was a side of Mick she did *not* want to see again.

'Let's go back to mine in a bit, darlin'.'

'Sure thing. Anything you like.'

She snuggled into him hoping that all was forgiven.

CHAPTER FIFTY-THREE

Mick O'Dowd had now been under Lucy's supervision for a good few weeks and she was still none the wiser about his background. The transfer area hadn't sent their file across and what had been sent was vague and incomplete. Also, Mick wasn't very open about his past and, when Lucy tried to discuss his convictions, he immediately shut down the conversation.

Mick didn't know that Lucy had some suspicions about his relationship with Vicki Wilkinson, after seeing the pair leave probation together once or twice previously. On one of the occasions, they'd been holding hands, and Lucy had felt a chill run down her spine as she watched them walk away. Lucy needed to flag her concerns with Mark at the police, Sarah who was Vicki's probation officer, and Sharon, in the hope that she might be able to go out and see Vicki to discuss the risks. In fact she needed to contact Sharon and chase it up. The police were usually very good at sharing information with Lucy. However, she knew that they were under significant pressure with two murder investigations and some things accidentally slipped through the net.

Lucy wasn't convinced that Vicki would pay any heed to any information or advice from Sharon, but she needed to make sure that Vicki was aware of the risks. Lucy only wished that she'd known about Mick when he and Vicki had got together. Vicki had only let it slip when Lucy was covering for Sarah, but she'd quickly moved on and Lucy stupidly forgot to follow up at the time. Knowing Vicki, it probably wouldn't have made much difference.

Lucy had a meeting with social care in the early afternoon and made the decision to do an impromptu home visit to see Mick. She wasn't sure what she would find, but something told her she needed to do this. Home visits formed a part of licence conditions and, although they should normally be done in pairs, lack of staff within probation meant that officers sometimes had to go alone. Lucy would make sure she followed protocol and rang a designated member of her team before and after the visit. If she didn't call, the alarm would be raised.

There was something about how sneaky Mick came across in supervision that Lucy thought this was the best way to catch him off guard. Although she had forgotten to fill in a risk assessment form before leaving, she wasn't overly worried.

If anything were to happen, she could easily be facing a disciplinary meeting or worse, but other officers got away with it. She didn't want to raise any concerns unnecessarily.

The path leading to Mick's door was surrounded by grass that had not been cut for some time. Beer cans littered the yard and from where they were positioned, it looked like whoever had been drinking had just dropped them from the windows above. Lucy shook her head and hoped that no children were living here. She called the office before going any further and let the reception staff know she had arrived. Lucy confirmed she'd call again once the visit was over, anticipating at least half an hour, if not less.

Mick's previous probation hostel had been instrumental in securing this accommodation, so Lucy could safely assume that Mick was probably not the only offender living here. It was a two-storey building which had been divided into six flats. The door was propped open, so Lucy bypassed the buzzer system and walked inside. She was immediately hit with the sickly sweet smell of heroin. She tucked this information away in her head to share with her police colleagues, although she wasn't concerned about Mick – alcohol was his demon of choice. The carpet was mangy and worn, with stains everywhere. As Lucy made her way to Mick's door, she avoided touching as much as possible. Feeling slightly nervous, she took a breath, and knocked on the door. Lucy thought she heard a woman's voice inside as heavy footsteps made their way along the hallway.

The look of surprise on Mick's face soon turned to a sneer. 'What do you want? I don't remember you telling me you were doing a visit?'

'And hello to you too, Mick. You're right, I didn't tell you. But if you paid attention to your licence conditions, you'd know that I don't have to. Do you want me to continue explaining all this on your doorstep?' Mick stepped aside and let Lucy in.

It was Lucy's turn to be surprised when she found Vicki sprawled on the sofa, wrapped in a blanket and wearing only a skimpy vest top and not much else. At least now her suspicions were confirmed. She wanted to grab Vicki by her shoulders, shake her, and advise her to run as far as she could – but she couldn't due to data protection.

'Hi, Vicki. Is this the new boyfriend you mentioned?'

'Boyfriend?' Mick laughed at Lucy's comment. 'We're just friends with benefits, right Vicki?'

Vicki looked uneasy and Lucy mouthed, 'sorry'.

''Course, love. Not sure where she got that from. Never said anything. She ain't even my PO.' Lucy could hear the venom in Vicki's response.

'Right. I must be getting things confused. Sorry. Anyway, I won't be long. Vicki, do you mind if I speak with Mick alone for a few minutes?'

'Suit yourself, I'll go out for a fag.'

Vicki didn't even bother getting dressed. Lucy observed Vicki wrap the thin blanket around herself like a skirt, pick up a lighter, mobile phone, and a cigarette from the table in front of her and walk out the door.

'Do you mind if I have a seat, Mick?'

He pointed towards the chair. 'Suit yourself.'

'First, I need to remind you that one of your licence conditions is that you need to tell us if you are in an intimate relationship. Are you sure you have nothing to tell me?'

'What the fuck? Haven't we been through all this shit before? What business is it of yours?' Mick's voice raised slightly as he spoke, and Lucy saw Vicki peer through the window.

'Due to the nature of your current offence, and previous history, you need to tell me when you become involved in a relationship. Like you have just pointed out, we've been through all this before.'

Mick shrugged his shoulders. 'She isn't my girlfriend. I see her every now and again for … well … do you want the details?'

'No, I don't need the details. So, are you saying that you only occasionally see Vicki? As that's not the impression I'm getting. She looked very comfortable when I walked in.'

'Is there anything else you want to talk about, as I'm done with this conversation.'

He was clenching his fists and Lucy could hear the aggression in his voice. Pushing the matter could place her in a difficult and potentially dangerous situation. However, she also did not want Mick to think that he could intimidate her or blatantly breach the conditions of his licence without having to deal with the consequences.

Standing up, she stared evenly at him, 'OK, Mick – I can see you're upset, so I'm not going to push this matter now. However, I will record my concerns and because I feel that you *are* seeing Vicki and have not disclosed it, I'll be sending you a formal warning for breach of your licence. Two more and you can be recalled to prison. Understood?'

Lucy calmly picked up her bag and headed towards the door, but then had second thoughts. She could be putting Vicki at risk, especially considering she'd let slip that Vicki was the one who mentioned a new boyfriend in a supervision session. Lucy turned and told Mick that she was going to log a safe-and-well check to be carried out on Vicki in the next few hours.

She'd speak to Vicki outside. If Mick had been thinking of doing something, a threat of a police visit might buy Lucy and Vicki some time.

CHAPTER FIFTY-FOUR

To say that Vicki Wilkinson wasn't pleased with Lucy's interference would be an understatement. *Who the hell does she think she is?* On her way out, Lucy had just warned Vicki that her relationship with Mick could put her licence at risk. There was an underlying warning of another sort, which piqued Vicki's curiosity. *She isn't even my probation officer!* When Vicki returned to the flat, Mick had his shoes on and was about to head out the door.

'Where you off to, love?' she asked innocently.

Mick grabbed her arm roughly. 'Are you keeping track of my movements now? What the fuck has it got to do with you, and what did that bitch tell you?'

'Owww.' She pulled her arm away, giving him a dirty look. 'What are you doing that for? I was just bloody asking, but I won't bother next time. Lucy said fuck all to me. What's your problem?'

Mick squared up to Vicki and whispered through gritted teeth, 'Watch that mouth of yours, Vicki … I'd hate for something to happen to it.' He pushed her out the door roughly with a final warning, 'Now get the fuck out of my flat!'

'Heeeey! I only have this sheet on! For fuck's sake, at least let me get dressed. What about my keys?'

'Not my problem. I have plans. Now fuck off.' Mick locked the door behind him.

Vicki was mortified. In her alcohol-fuelled hazes she'd often woken up in strange places, outdoors, with less on than what she was wearing now, but she hadn't expected Mick to be so cruel. Vicki pulled the sheet tighter around her, ready to make the walk of shame home, but she didn't know how she'd get back into her flat. If the landlord was home, maybe she could convince him that she had accidently locked herself out. She'd ring Shell and ask if she'd drop the spare key round. Vicki could easily get a new one cut. Shell would be furious.

Prior to release from custody, Vicki had completed a course on healthy relationships. She knew she was no angel, especially when drink was involved, but she'd been to counselling and built up her confidence. Every now and again she'd felt herself fall back into old habits, but was working hard, and didn't want to fall prey to another abusive relationship. Didn't want that cycle to start all over again.

Nearly home, Vicki noticed the landlord walking down the path, two large black bin bags in his hands, his tracksuit bottoms falling down just enough to give Vicki a glance at the crack of his arse.

'Mr Bury! Mr Bury! I need to get into my flat!'

Vicki blushed when she saw him look her up and down with distaste, but he dropped the bags and gestured for her to follow him. Vicki could hear him mumbling under his breath and, in normal circumstances, probably would have used her own vicious tongue to come up with a smart remark. She was desperate to get into her flat, though, and couldn't afford to piss him off. He pulled a large batch of keys from his pocket and, within minutes, Vicki was in her flat and slumped on her old, lumpy couch. Then the tears started.

Vicki woke up, freezing cold. The crying had brought on sleep and cleared her thoughts, sobered her up. Looking at her watch, she realized that a few hours had passed. She needed to call Shell before Timpson's closed, otherwise she'd be trapped in her flat until tomorrow … and right now, Vicki needed a drink badly.

CHAPTER FIFTY-FIVE

Lucy shuddered as she recalled the mouthful of abuse Vicki threw at her outside Mick's flat. Lucy didn't expect anything less from Vicki and had accepted, a long time ago, that sometimes challenging a person's behaviour directly like that can make things worse. *Choose your battles wisely.* Back at the office, a group of her colleagues were huddled around the coffee maker, Sarah Hardy leading them all in a discussion.

'… so, then I overheard Andy saying that someone's husband had rang in, accusing their wife of having an inappropriate relationship with an offender! Can you imagine? Any guesses as to who it could be!?'

For a moment Lucy's heart stood still. *He wouldn't … no …* She approached the group nervously.

'Oooh, so what's the hot gossip then?'

'There you are! I've been looking all over for you!' Sarah repeated everything she'd overheard from their boss, Mr Bourne. It didn't sound like anything to do with her, and along with her colleagues, she was now curious. She did sympathize with whoever was being accused of the affair; Patrick had threatened to do it to her enough times.

'I was on a home visit. Mick O'Dowd. Found Vicki Wilkinson there when I arrived.'

'Oh shit. Now that's not going to end well, is it? Can you email me your notes and I'll book an appointment with Vicki as soon as possible? She'd really been making progress, but if this is true, I hope it wasn't all to impress Mick! From everything you've said about him, he's bad news.'

'It's certainly not going to end well. I tried to give Vicki a warning to stay away from him, but I could only say so much without breaching confidentiality. Luckily, she's on licence still, so I've warned her that it could place her liberty at risk. I probably shouldn't have said that – it may not be one hundred per cent true in her case – but she needs to be afraid of this guy.'

'Tough one. Might be wise if I talk to Andy about it.' Andy Bourne was the Regional Head of the area and in general a decent boss. His carefully styled hair, pout and intense stare, however, often reminded people of Ben Stiller's character in *Zoolander*. Lucy giggled at that thought every time someone mentioned it.

'You're right. Do what you need to in terms of Vicki. I'm more than happy to be your backup on her case. I'm just going to see how things go with Mick for a bit. Give the domestic abuse team a call and request a safe-and-well check on Vicki's flat, including a stop by Mick's.' Lucy rubbed her temples. 'Sometimes this job can really get to you. If only someone would get rid of all these abusers, life would be so much easier.'

Sarah rubbed Lucy's arm. 'I know, but we have to separate ourselves from it and focus on the things we can do – not the things we have no control over. Happy for you to call the police team, since you have to share info on Mick anyway. Just forward me their feedback, so I can update Vicki's records.'

Sarah always managed to cheer Lucy up. 'Sure thing. OK, OK. Enough of the moping. Was that the kettle I heard earlier? Think we could both use a caffeine injection!'

CHAPTER FIFTY-SIX

After calling Shell and giving her an excuse about losing her keys, Vicki was feeling desperate for a drink. It was on days like this that she most struggled with her drinking – she was angry at the way Mick had treated her, but at the same time, she didn't want him to get into trouble. Mick had been the first man in a long time to pay her attention. She just wanted the company. She'd been tempted to smooth the way with Mick via Facebook, but didn't have the courage.

Vicki didn't want to go out and leave her flat unlocked, but as Shell said she wouldn't be able to come around until later – Vicki needed something to calm her nerves.

She threw on some jeans and figured the fifteen-minute journey to the shops would be OK. She rarely had trouble in her building and, if she ran there and back, she could probably do it in ten. She kept a small stash of money in an old coffee jar in the kitchen, her emergency fund. The tenner would get her a few bottles of White Lightning and she would ration it out, so she wasn't totally off her face when Shell arrived. The hangover tomorrow would be enough to deal with, without having to listen to Shell preach about the drinking.

The trip to the shop was quick enough, the shopkeeper gave

her a look – and said he hadn't seen her for a while – but Vicki ignored him and handed over her money, tapping her foot impatiently as she waited for the change. Back home, she grabbed a pint glass, filled it to the brim with the liquid she knew would ease her anxiety and put the remainder alongside the other bottle in her fridge. Taking a big gulp, Vicky stood perfectly still and felt relief as the cider took hold. She chugged the glass back so quick she need not have put the bottle back in the fridge in the first place. Once she got a taste, it wouldn't be long before the first bottle had been consumed.

Vicki sat on the couch and turned on the cheap second-hand iPad she'd purchased at Cash Converters. Reduced drinking gave her some extra money. Vicki couldn't afford Wi-Fi, so often jumped on the neighbours' when they were foolish enough not to have a security password attached. Logging in to Facebook, Vicky scrolled through her timeline, the iPad screen already starting to shift in front of her eyes. She glimpsed an old post from Mick and decided to message him.

'I want my stiff bak. You were out of ordr tday. Can u drip it roymd pleez. Xx VICKI'

She saw that Mick had received and read the message. Another cider later and Vicki was getting angrier. Mick was being a prick and her previous worry about getting him into trouble was fading fast. She sent another message.

'Oi!! U cld at leasf andser me! Gimme my stuffff!!'

Again, no reply, despite the small picture of Mick beside her message telling her he had read and closed it. She shoved the coffee table with her foot.

Fuck this dickhead. I've had enough.

'I know uve read my msgs. Gimme my stuf or I'm calling the police. I'm sur they wold want to know all about you! I'll tell Lucy too – watch me.'

Vicki didn't even care if Mick was pissed off. The more alcohol that entered her bloodstream, the more memories from the past crept up and invaded her thoughts. Anger at all the men who had used and abused her, treated her like dirt, swirled into a ball. With a picture of Mick's fucking face smack dab on the front. If he didn't reply to this message, she knew *exactly* what she was going to do.

After downing nearly three litres of White Lightning, Vicki was struggling to see straight. Her body wasn't used to the alcohol, after having reduced so much over the last few weeks. She almost missed her Facebook Messenger ping and, with unsteady hands, clicked on the message to read it:

'I got your messages. Don't threaten me. You will get your stuff back. Anymore messages and your shit is going in the bin.'

Vicki debated whether to respond. The room swirled around her. She tried to think up a sarcastic response, but the words wouldn't come and she didn't want to make herself look like more of a twat. She slumped further into the sofa; her eyes felt heavy. Trying not to fall asleep. She managed to search YouTube for her favourite music and let the sound of Oasis take over.

CHAPTER FIFTY-SEVEN

Mick O'Dowd was pacing along the road, clenching and unclenching his fists. If Vicki screwed up his licence, or housing situation, she'd be sorry she ever met him. Mick withdrew his dole money from the bank and stopped at the shops on his way home. He used to dabble with cannabis and cocaine in the past and today felt that itch he'd managed to avoid for twenty-odd years. Not knowing who was reliable for gear, he settled on six cans of Tennent's Super and headed back towards his flat. Mick did consider stopping into probation and giving that bitch Lucy a piece of his mind, but knew that would only end up with another warning. He wasn't going to risk his freedom for any dumb bitch.

His flat was freezing when he got in. Noticing his window open a crack, he shut it and dropped the cans of lager on the coffee table to search for the small electric heater. He saw Vicki's tracksuit bottoms, keys, and jacket strewn across the chair in the corner of his bedroom. *Fucking messy bitch.* It reminded Mick of exactly why he was better off single. His blood boiled recounting the numerous women who had messed up his life in one way or another, starting with Moira. If it hadn't been for her, he'd still be seeing his kids instead of wondering if they even remembered who he was.

Cracking open a can of lager, he opened the Facebook app on

his phone and began scrolling through his newsfeed. He never understood why people put all their business online for everyone to see, but it passed the time, and he needed something mindless to calm him down.

Mick had initially been reluctant to use an actual image of himself on Facebook, in case some of his old associates or psycho ex-partners tried to get in touch. But he'd realized that if any of his children ever wanted to contact him, according to Jeremy Kyle, it would be Facebook they searched first.

The messages from Vicki earlier pissed him off. Re-reading them only made him drink faster, so he returned to his timeline and posted a funny meme:

'Irish I Was Drinking.'

Three 'likes' already. People are idiots.

Despite trying to put her to the back of his mind, her face kept reappearing in his mind: her standing outside talking to that other bitch. Her leaving her shit around his flat. Her threatening to ruin his life. He stood up and sank the rest of his can. The only way to stop her was to deal with it once and for all.

Four cans of Tennent's Super later, Mick clocked the time. He went to his room and gathered up Vicki's belongings, chucking them in a plastic bag. He was hoping that she'd be passed out when he arrived; the bad spelling in her messages meant she'd broken her drinking ban, so it was a likely possibility. He wouldn't be responsible for his actions, if she pissed him off again. He'd managed to control his anger on other occasions, but it was getting more and more difficult.

Mick exited his flat, locking his door. He suddenly noticed how quiet the building was. Eerie. Dark shadows filled the hallway. He made his way downstairs and listened to the silence. Pretty surprising for this time of the evening, when annoying youths would usually be hanging about outside. He zipped up his coat and headed in the direction of Vicki's estate.

CHAPTER FIFTY-EIGHT

A heavy knock on the door made Vicki jump. She put her iPad on the coffee table next to the fake crystal ashtray that weighed a ton. Stumbled across the room to her front door. Holding the door handle for balance, she looked through the peephole and saw a blurred vision of Mick. He had some sort of black bag in his hands. That was quick.

He banged on the door again and growled, 'Open the fucking door if you want your shit, Vicki. I don't have time for games!'

Vicki unchained the door and opened it slowly. She tried as hard as she could to look sober, but Mick's face told her she was failing miserably. ''S'bout time. I need my keeeez!' She reached out to grab the bag from Mick's hand, but he pushed her back into her flat. Losing her balance, Vicki fell to the floor.

'For fuck's sake. You been drownin' your sorrows or something? Fucking disgrace!' he spat at her.

'Fuck you! Just gimme my stuff and go!' Vicki tried to grab Mick's ankle to pull herself up, but he kicked her away and stood over her, pointing.

'Listen to me, Vicki, I'll only tell you once. Don't. Ever. Threaten. Me. Again. Got it?' His finger was so close to her face.

Before she knew it, Vicki had taken hold of it in her mouth and bitten down.

A swift punch to the face released Mick's finger and Vicki saw red. What Mick hadn't realized about Vicki was she had a fiery temper. The violence she could unleash when alcohol fanned the flames could cause significant damage. Her previous convictions could attest to that. As if possessed, Vicki pulled herself up, and launched at him with her arms flailing. She managed to smack him to the side of the head, before he grabbed her arms and pinned her down on the couch.

Mick laughed in her face and with his forehead pressed against hers he mouthed, 'Is that all you got, you little bitch?'

That was it. Vicki took the opportunity and headbutted Mick with as much force as she could muster. Her vision blurred, and it was too late for Vicki to react.

Mick grabbed her face and shouted. 'All right, all right, bitch, is this how you want to play it?'

Shoving Vicki to the floor he sat across her chest and rained blow after blow to her face. He almost admired her resilience, but not so much that he was going to let her get the best of him. Vicki continued to grab at Mick's shirt, nearly tearing it as she pulled him towards her and spat in his face. That was the last straw for Mick. He grabbed her by the hair and slammed her head against the floor.

His eyes darted around the room and he spotted the crude-looking ashtray on the coffee table. 'If you breathe a word of this to anyone, *anyone*, I will hunt you down and finish the job.' And with that, Mick smashed the ashtray in Vicki's face repeatedly until she was a pulpy mess of flesh, blood, and broken teeth.

Breathing heavily, Mick sat back across Vicki's legs, exhausted. *Feisty bitch.* But when the reality of the situation hit him, Mick was soon pacing around the room, looking for ways to avoid prison. He hadn't touched anything unusual, given the fact he'd been in a 'relationship' with Vicki, so fingerprints could easily be explained. He grabbed a pair of gloves from under the kitchen sink and began tossing the place. If it looked like a robbery, it would place him out of the frame. He was under no illusion that he'd probably be questioned or arrested, but given that robbery wasn't in his history, he reasoned that he should be released without charge while the police moved on, chasing ghosts. He happened across an old coffee jar in one of the cupboards, discovering a nice little stash of money inside. That would come in handy, but also help further the robbery scenario he'd devised in his mind. Mick pocketed it and looked around the flat. Once satisfied that it would throw the police off the trail, he washed his face and hands in the kitchen sink, and then made his way to the front door. Voices in the hallway stopped him dead. He waited, breathing heavily, until he heard a door close. Taking a chance, he looked out the door to check the coast was clear.

Mick snuck out through the empty hallway and shoved the rubber gloves in his pockets. Using the key that Vicki had left at his flat, Mick locked the door behind him. That would delay any chance of someone just randomly walking into the flat and coming across the bloody mess that lay on the floor. He used the stairs to avoid meeting anyone in the lift.

It was now dark outside, so Mick was confident that any blood on his clothes would be difficult to see by passers-by. He pulled his coat around him and, with his hands in his pockets, made the reasonably short journey back to his flat in record time.

CHAPTER FIFTY-NINE

Shell was pleased with herself. She managed to finish the job earlier than she'd told Vicki. She placed the key in the door and locked up the premises. Headed to her car and loaded her supplies into the boot. Although she was annoyed, Vicki was desperate for her keys and Shell couldn't turn away a friend. It would be a half hour drive, so Shell turned up her music and headed towards the Lockwood Estate.

She was relieved to see some light seeping out of Vicki's front window as she pulled up outside the flats. Vicki seemed pretty agitated when they spoke earlier, so Shell had been worried that she'd pass out after doing her usual: downing a bottle when she found it difficult to cope. If the lights were on, she was probably still awake and sober. Vicki tended to drink heavily in the dark, like she needed a blanket of darkness to hide her sorrow. Shell thought about how well Vicki had been doing and decided that now would be the perfect time to offer her a part-time job in her cleaning business.

Shell reached into her pocket for the spare key as she approached Vicki's door, but decided to knock first, out of politeness. After knocking three times and hearing nothing from the other side of the door, she let herself into the flat. She immediately saw Vicki's legs sticking out from behind the couch.

205

'Well, that's a sight to see. I thought you were off the drink?' Shell sighed. She shut the door behind her, mentally reconsidering the cleaning job offer. She walked towards Vicki, with the intention of helping her back on to the couch and giving her a mouthful as well.

When she got closer, however, Shell stopped. The keys fell from her hand and spiralled slowly to the floor. They landed with a thud. Bounced and then were still. A long moment passed before Shell realized her throat was raw from screaming. She stood there for what seemed like an age, staring in shock at Vicki's almost unrecognizable face. At the pool of blood on the floor. She snapped out of it and quickly dialled 999 from her mobile phone. Her hand was shaking as she requested the police and an ambulance. Shell was frantic, pacing around the flat. She could barely speak when the call handler asked her if Vicki was still alive. She didn't know what to say and couldn't bring herself to check for a pulse. She just stared at Vicki's chest and noticed with relief that it was rising and falling, albeit slowly.

'Yes, I think she is alive. But she's unconscious and her face … oh God, I can't even tell if it *is* her.'

Shell took in a deep breath and listened to the call handler's instructions. Crouched by Vicki, holding her friend's hand, she waited for the police to arrive and, when the sirens could finally be heard, without thinking, she placed Vicki's hand on the floor, hung up on the operator and ran out to the street to wave them down. A small crowd had gathered outside the building, blocking the paramedics' pathway to the flat.

'For fuck's sake, can you bastards move out of the way!' Shell shrieked. Shell followed the paramedics up the stairs to Vicki's flat and showed them inside. Her body shook uncontrollably as she watched them talk to Vicki and strap her on the gurney. The police wanted to ask her some questions, but she couldn't think straight.

'Please, officers. Can you just give me five-bloody-minutes?

I'm watching my friend be wheeled into an ambulance after someone attacked her. Leave me alone.'

'We understand, Miss?'

'Baker. My name is Shell Baker.'

'OK, Miss Baker. We need you to step out of the area. Go into the hall and have a breather. Give me a wave when you feel we can have that chat. The sooner we get what you know down on paper, the quicker we can find whoever did this to your friend.'

The tears started flowing down Shell's face. She needed the fresh air and took the officer's advice. Hoped the police found whoever did this first, because if she found them first, there would be hell to pay.

Shell dealt with the officers' questions, but couldn't offer them anything other than what she saw when she arrived. She explained that Vicki had lost her key and Shell had promised to drop the spare one round. She'd noticed the empty bottle of White Lightning in the kitchen and told officers that Vicki had reduced her drinking over the last couple of weeks. After that amount of alcohol, she would have been shit-faced.

In the past, Vicki could drink six litres or more of that stuff and it wouldn't even phase her. The police asked whether Vicki had any enemies, and Shell was forced to tell the truth: over the years Vicki had made many enemies and the drink had made her abusive and violent at times. She knew the police would be checking her out on their system, so there was no point keeping anything back. Finally, the officer asked whether Vicki had been in a relationship with anyone recently. The hairs on Shell's neck stood on end.

'Why would you ask that? Don't you think it's a robbery?' Shell looked past the officer into the flat at the torn-apart room – open drawers and cupboards, items strewn about. 'There are a lot of druggies in this area. Though why they would think Vicki had any money, is any one's guess.'

'We just need to explore all options and speak with anyone who may have seen her.'

'I don't know for sure, but I think she was hanging out with this guy named Mick. Shagging him, even though I warned her to stay away from him. I'm not sure what his last name is. He's definitely on probation though, because they sometimes go to their appointments together. Vicki's PO is Sarah something or other, but she also saw Lucy ... uh ... I think that's her name.' Shell felt herself redden and bit her lip. The less she could share about Lucy, the better, given that she was sleeping with her husband.

'There were rumours going round the pub about Mick. That he likes to beat up women. But Vicki swore he'd never laid a hand on her ... I warned her. For fuck's sake, why didn't she listen to me? If he did this, I swear I'll ...' Shell started crying again and couldn't get her words out.

'Thanks for your time, Miss Baker. Can we just get your number in case we have any follow-up questions?'

Shell gave the officer her details and showed them out. Forensics were still collecting evidence, so she left them with the spare key, so they could secure the property.

Leaves were swirling in the wind as she stumbled her way to her car. Shell was shaking as she heard the bleep of her car door unlocking and sat down. She took a moment, fighting back the tears. She dug her mobile out of her bag and dialled Patrick's number. He answered after two rings in a hushed voice.

'What the hell are you calling me for?' The line was quiet. 'Shell? Shell? Are you still there?'

Shell stared silently out at the rows of grey flats.

Patrick's voice got louder. 'Look, I'm outside now. You just caught me at a bad time. Where are you?'

'I'm ... on my way to the hospital. Vicki's been beaten pretty badly, and I don't know if she'll survive.' Gathering herself together, she carried on, 'I wanted to let you know that I won't be around for a few days, until I see that she's OK. And I tidy her flat … you know … so it's ready for when … if … she comes home.'

'Babe, I'm so sorry. Look, I might be able to sneak out. Do you want me to meet you there? I've missed you.'

'No. I need to do this myself. I have a few things to take care of. As soon as I can, I'll call you … and Patrick …'

'Yes?

'I love you.' She hung up without waiting for a response. She wasn't prepared for one, so she did what she always did and shut the conversation down.

CHAPTER SIXTY

Mick stripped out of his clothing and placed them in a plastic bag. He'd dispose of them soon. He jumped in the shower to wash any remaining blood off him, sprayed the shower with bleach and rinsed out the water. Mick was sure he'd seen something on one of those *CSI* shows: bleach would get rid of evidence. His tub was filthy anyway, so even if it didn't work, it might clean the place up a bit. Mick was surprised at how calm he felt, considering his days were numbered and that bitch, Lucy, would recall him for being in a relationship. He looked at his hands and turned them over, feeling the sting of the scrapes and cuts on his knuckles. He'd have to figure out a way to explain these to the police. He thought for a minute and then settled on an idea: maybe pick a fight when he went to the pub.

Mick grabbed a pair of jeans off his floor, put them to his nose and breathed in. They could last one more day, despite the stain on the knee. He chose a dark T-shirt and threw on his black hoodie. Put his ear to the door, listened to the silence outside. The streets were quiet for a change and Mick thought perhaps his luck was in. He might just get away with what he'd done to Vicki.

I only slapped her around. She'll have a headache and a few bruises at most. No big deal.

Mick didn't want to be seen leaving his flat; that way he could choose his reported time of arrival at the pub. It would be heaving tonight, and he could get lost in the crowd. Darts nights always drew the crowds. He'd usually avoid them, but tonight it would give him the perfect opportunity to create an alibi.

He put Vicki's money and spare key in his pocket, making sure everything else was removed from the clothing he'd worn earlier. He was planning on dumping them in a large rubbish bin that sat near the entrance to the underpass, where some local homeless people had set up camp.

Mick took a chance and peered cautiously out of the door. Satisfied, he sprinted along the pathway and headed down Browning Street towards the underpass. At this time of night, most of the homeless people would be too drunk, or fast asleep, to remember him. It was just his luck that as he approached the waste bin, one of them headed towards him.

'Spare change, mate?'

Normally Mick would have told the drunk man to fuck off, but tonight he didn't want any trouble. He pulled out some loose change from his pocket. The man swiped it out of his hand before, Mick could say anything, and then headed in the direction of the shops.

No one saw him dump his sweater and tracksuit bottoms in the bin. Mick stared into the underpass, lost in his thoughts about what had just happened.

'Oi. You! What are you doing there?' shouted one of the homeless men. A few others sat up on their cardboard beds and eyed Mick.

'Nothing, mate, just getting rid of some rubbish. That all right with you?' Mick gave him a hard stare. The man lay back down and turned over, grumbling incoherently. Mick carried on through the underpass, without looking at the folk who called this place their home. *Fucking saddos.*

When Mick arrived at the pub, he looked through the grotty window, satisfied that he'd easily blend in. As he pushed through the door, he looked at the bar to make sure that Kevin had not spotted him. Kevin had a memory like an elephant and if he saw Mick now, he'd clock the time, and any chance he had of pulling off an alibi would be scuppered.

He headed towards a group of men he'd chatted with before. Although he'd never class these guys as his mates, he often enjoyed banter with them over a few pints. 'Mind if I join you, lads? I was over the other side of the room and those wankers are just talking shite.' Mick laughed. He had picked up a half-empty pint glass off one of the tables, on his way across the room, to make his story believable.

'Hey, Mick! Good to see ya, mate! Don't normally see you here on a Thursday,' Billy noted. 'Jesus. What's happened to your hands?'

'I pop in on a Thursday now and again, but only stay for a pint or two because of all the noise. I ain't no spring chicken you know!' He looked at his hands. 'I had a bit of work on a building site. Let's just say, manual labour and I don't mix.'

Billy laughed and raised his glass. 'Can I get you a pint, Mick?'

Mick reached into his pocket and pulled out a tenner. 'It's on me, if you don't mind getting it? Just don't fancy standing in that bloody queue.'

'Sure thing ... and thanks!' Billy took the £10 note and patted Mick on the shoulder.

While he waited, Mick put the half-filled glass down and mixed in with the other men around the table. He hated small talk, but knew he needed to shore up his alibi. Best to spend Vicki's money, too. He offered to buy a round. The men at his table soon took him into their conversation, and he smiled to himself.

Can I really get away with this?

Billy arrived back at the table with the pints. 'Kevin was asking when you arrived,' Billy said casually.

'Oh yeah? And what did you tell him?' Mick's voice was loud and he felt his hand shaking.

'Calm down, mate. Not sure what's got your knickers in a twist, but I told him you've been here ages.'

Wondering why Kevin was so curious, Mick looked over to the bar and raised his glass. He gave Kevin a nod and got one in return. Probably just being paranoid.

CHAPTER SIXTY-ONE

Mark took the information he gained from Lucy to DS Hooper.

'She confirmed that Vicki Wilkinson was in a relationship with Mick O'Dowd? Why the hell didn't she tell us this before?'

'To be fair, guv, I think she only just found out. It was just an assumption initially, but seeing them at O'Dowd's flat confirmed it. I just picked up the email.'

'Mark, I don't know why you feel the need to defend Lucy – and to be honest, I don't want to know. But let's face facts here. She fucked up. The minute she suspected anything, we should have been informed.'

Mark knew that no amount of explanation would change his boss's mind. Once Hooper had his jaws locked onto something, there was no letting go. 'So ... what do we do now, guv?'

'Are you serious, Mark? We need to speak to Mick O'Dowd. Grab PC Reynolds and go pick him up!'

Mark blushed. 'Yes, guv. On it.'

He headed back to the unit and looked around for PC Reynolds. The newbie was nowhere to be seen. 'For fuck's sake. Has anyone seen Reynolds?'

Maggie looked up from her computer and shook her head.

Mark turned to Kat. 'Kat, do you know where Reynolds is?'

Mark didn't like the sly look on Kat's face, as if she was ready to wind him up. Frankly he wasn't in the mood.

'Reynolds is at the photocopier. I asked him to copy some shit.'

'Well, now you can take over. I need him to come with me. Hooper wants us to pick up Mick O'Dowd and bring him in for questioning.'

'Uh … since when did you become my boss?' Kat swivelled her chair casually.

Mark was grateful when he caught Maggie raising her eyebrows at Kat, 'Just do what he says.'

'This is fudonkulous.' Kat grabbed her coffee and slouched her way to the copier.

Huh? Mark and Maggie looked at each other quizzically. Maggie shrugged.

'No clue. She is always making up words. I'm guessing there's a fuck in there somewhere …'

Within minutes, Reynolds was back in the office, looking like Kat had put *him* through the photocopier. 'So, where are we off to then?'

'Just grab your coat, Reynolds, I'll tell you on the way.'

'Can I grab a quick cuppa? I'm parched.'

'No … no chance. Now get your coat and let's go!'

Mark heard a faint laugh from the office as PC Reynolds stumbled his way out after him.

Mark and PC Reynolds arrived at Mick's flat, hoping he wasn't involved in the assault on Vicki. They already had enough pressure, following the Millard and Talbot murders, without adding a serious assault to their caseload.

The path up to the flats was littered with cans of beer and rubbish that the council must have given up on collecting. They buzzed the door and a woman answered. She had obviously had a rough night and, by the sound of her raspy voice, was probably a heavy smoker.

'Yeah, who is it?'

'Police, ma'am. Can you buzz us in please?'

'Why should I? Who are you here to see?'

'I'm afraid I can't discuss that. If you won't buzz us in, I'll just contact your landlord.'

'Ha!' The officers heard a loud, hacking cough from the upper level. 'Good luck with that.' The door buzzed and then clicked open. They walked towards Mick's flat and heard footsteps above them. Clearly the female occupant wanted to know who the police were coming to visit. Mark looked at the dilapidated flat entry, paint peeling off the walls and rubbish strewn along the unkempt walkway. He raised his hand and knocked on Mick's door.

'What a shithole.' PC Reynolds verbalized what Mark was thinking. Mark punched him in the arm and pointed upstairs.

'Keep it closed, Reynolds. We have company.'

'Yeah, Reynolds. You prick!' They could see the woman looking over from the walkway above. Clearly she wasn't impressed with Reynolds's observation of the property. They heard a door slam above and knocked once more on Mick's door.

'Don't think he's here, Mark.'

'Really? What gave you that impression? Your detective skills are on fire today, Reynolds.' Mark radioed in to the station as they left.

'Maggie, do we have any details of known associates or hangouts for one Michael Edward O'Dowd? Also known as Mick. No one at his property.'

'Standby. I'll find out.'

Mark and Reynolds were getting back into the car when the radio buzzed and Maggie's voice cut through the cold night air.

'Mark, the guv says to call it a night for now. You can pick up where you left off in the morning and I'll get Kat to put a list

together for you. I've logged what you've told me and if Mick is seen, he'll be picked up by the field teams on patrol.'

'Thanks, Maggie. OK, Reynolds. You heard the lady. Time to head back, clock out, and go home!'

As Mark and Reynolds drove back to the station, a call out came over the radio.

'Officers required at The Smith's Forge. Two men fighting. No weapons reported.'

'Looks like we're not going home after all.' Mark sighed as Reynolds actioned the siren.

A crowd had gathered outside, blocking the entrance to the pub, and Mark noticed one of the panes of glass from the front window had been smashed.

'Criminal damage will be one of the charges then.' Reynolds nodded.

The officers pushed their way through the crowd and found two men shouting at each other. Being held apart at opposite ends of the pub.

'About time you arrived!'

Mark assumed this was the landlord of the pub. 'And you are, sir?'

'Kevin. I run this place. Look at the bloody mess this pair have created.'

'OK, Kevin. Can you tell us what happened?' Mark wanted to calm the situation down to avoid any further conflict arising.

'These two ... gentlemen ... and I use the term loosely, started rowing with each other. I looked away for one second and the next thing I knew, that guy over there threw a punch and this guy, Patrick, retaliated.' Kevin pointed angrily at the two individuals being held apart.

'Thanks, Kevin. We'll take it from here. Reynolds, can you speak to Patrick and I'll have a word with the instigator.'

There wasn't actually that much damage to the inside of the room. The floors would need a good cleaning, the furniture would have to be picked up, and the glass swept, but nothing that couldn't be fixed if Kevin paid his cleaner a bit extra.

Mark walked over to the man who was seated with his hands over his face. 'Can I get your name please?'

When the man looked up, Mark smiled.

'Well, hello, Mr O'Dowd. I've been looking for you. Mick O'Dowd – I'm arresting you for the charge of criminal damage and assault. Stand up please.' Mark placed the cuffs on Mick's wrists while continuing to read him his rights.

As they passed the other man talking to PC Reynolds, Mick shouted, 'This ain't over!'

Mark placed O'Dowd in the back of the police car and requested another car to the scene. Ensuring his car was secure, he radioed Reynolds, who gave him Patrick's version of events: he had attended the pub for a quiet drink after dropping off his daughter at her grandparents for the night. He had only consumed one pint of lager, but was in the middle of getting his second, when he saw a few people he recognized. Reynolds continued, 'He was making his way through the crowd when he felt someone grab his shoulder. He confronted the man – Mick O'Dowd – and said a few choice words. Someone in O'Dowd's company had mentioned Patrick's wife; Mick made a few further derogatory comments about Patrick's wife. They argued and, when Mick punched him, Mr Quinn alleges he defended himself.'

'OK. I've called for another car which I think I see coming now. Caution him and bring him out here.'

Following Mark's instruction, Reynolds directed Patrick towards the assisting car and placed him in the back. They stood for a moment next to their vehicles and watched the crowd dispersing from outside the pub. 'Looks like it won't be an early night after all, Mark.'

Both cars headed back to the police station to process their arrests. Mick wouldn't be interviewed until the morning. He smelled so strongly of booze that Mark and Reynolds feared they would end up drunk off the fumes alone. Mick was processed and placed in a cell for the evening by the custody sergeant. Patrick was still waiting to be processed and would more than likely be released pending further investigation. He was shouting that he wanted to call his wife, when Mark approached him.

'Sir, you need to calm down. Once the custody sergeant processes you, you will either be bailed, or you can call your wife then. If you carry on shouting, this could end up being a long night for you … erm … sorry, what was your name again?'

'Patrick. Look, I just want to get this over with. My wife is going to be pissed off and to be honest with you, after tonight, I just don't need the fucking hassle.'

'I get that, Patrick. But ranting isn't going to get you anywhere quicker, is it?'

Patrick looked up at the police officer. At first Mark thought he may have a situation on his hands, as he noticed Patrick squeeze his hands together tightly, but a few deep breaths later, the man obviously thought better and played the game. The custody sergeant called Patrick forward and Mark left Reynolds to deal with the arrest. Tomorrow was definitely going to be a long day.

CHAPTER SIXTY-TWO

Lucy was surprised there were no lights on in the house when she arrived home. Using the side entrance, she unlocked the door, and walked into complete silence. 'Hello? Patrick? Anyone home?'

No answer.

What's he playing at? Lucy slammed the door angrily. After the big deal he'd made of her being late home that evening. *Where's Siobhan?* She turned on the lights and looked around the counters for a note.

None.

Panic set in. *What if something's happened?*

She felt the buzz of her mobile in her pocket and checked the screen to see who was calling.

Private Number.

'Hello?'

'Hi, Lucy. How are you?' It was Maria, Siobhan's grandmother.

'Hi, Maria. This is … um … a nice surprise. How are you? I'm afraid Siobhan and Patrick are out.' Lucy knew Maria wouldn't be calling to speak with her.

'I know. Siobhan is here with us. Didn't you know?' Maria laughed.

'Oh … yes, of course! Sorry, I just got in from work – it was a busy one – and my head's still a bit foggy. What can I do for you?'

'Patrick said it was OK if Siobhan stayed the night. I was just checking whether he'd be picking her up for school in the morning or if he wants us to drop her off? She has all her school stuff with her. I tried Patrick's mobile, but he's not answering.'

'Would you mind taking her? Patrick's out now and I'm not sure when he'll be back. It might be too late to call you.'

'That's fine, love. You have a good night. Bye.'

'Bye, Maria. Give Siobhan a kiss from me.'

Lucy was even more curious now. And upset. Patrick knew he'd be out when she'd texted him earlier. She wondered why he was starting his games again. For the last few days though, things were OK – she actually thought she'd have a few weeks of normality, if you could call it that. The thought that maybe he was having an affair had crossed her mind a few times, but deep down she didn't believe he'd do that to her. There were times when Lucy almost wished he was. It would be an easy way out for her, and then she wouldn't have to explain any of the abuse she'd endured. She could just get on with her life. That is, if Patrick would let her.

She shook the thoughts out of her head. Didn't want to waste the peace and quiet. She dropped her work bag on the dining room table, went upstairs, and ran the bath.

She hadn't been feeling well lately.

It would be her irritable bowel syndrome playing up with all the stress. Lucy grabbed her Kindle, slipped into the hot bath and sank down. *Just what the doctor ordered.*

CHAPTER SIXTY-THREE

Patrick calmed down after the few hours in the cells, and read over the paperwork he was handed from the custody sergeant. He checked the conditions of his bail, which included staying away from Mick O'Dowd. *Who the hell did that O'Dowd fella think he was? If he thinks this is over, he has another thing coming!* There had been some discussion about an evening curfew, but luckily the duty solicitor had convinced the police that this could affect Patrick's chances of employment. The police tried to raise the call-outs to his property relating to domestic incidents. He overheard one of the officers say that, because there had been no charges, they didn't want to risk placing his wife at further risk by forcing him to stay on the premises. *What a fucking joke!*

Patrick glanced at his watch, and guessed that Lucy would be furious with him. He wasn't in the mood to deal with her shit, considering he'd been defending her honour. *Ungrateful bitch!* He hadn't bothered calling anyone when he was finally offered the opportunity to do so, but now he noted three missed calls on his mobile.

He had thought about ringing Shell, but given her friend was in hospital it was doubtful she'd come to the police station to pick him up. The duty solicitor was certain that under the circumstances, the charges against Patrick would be dropped – because witness statements taken from others clearly showed that Mick had been the instigator. Patrick wasn't sure what made him angrier – the fact that this prick made lewd comments about his wife in a pub full of people or the fact that Patrick hadn't flattened him when he had the opportunity. He had been defending himself.

He wasn't thrilled at the idea of catching the late bus to collect his car from the pub's parking lot. It would be nearly one-thirty in the morning by the time he got home. For once, Patrick hoped that Lucy would be asleep. If she wasn't, one look at his face would tell her to leave well enough alone. Patrick pulled his cigarettes from his pocket and lit one up as he waited for the next bus to arrive.

Lucy had given up ringing Patrick at ten thirty that evening. Knowing that Siobhan was safe at her grandparents, and after a hot bath to relieve the tension, she didn't want to break her mood. Choosing a new book from her shelf, she placed the hot water bottle on her stomach and settled into bed with Craig Russell's novel, *Lennox* – a book she'd been dying to read for some time. Lucy didn't get more than two chapters in before sleep engulfed her.

She woke up with a start, what felt like only minutes later, and thought she'd heard the back door being slammed. *Was that Patrick?*

Lucy picked up her mobile phone. It was one forty in the morning. She unlocked her phone and was ready to dial 999 when she heard the fridge door and the familiar crack of a can of lager being opened.

It was Patrick; the sound of him cracking a lager always went through her, like nails on a chalkboard.

Not wanting a confrontation, she held her phone in her hand and strained her ears to listen to his mumblings, hoping she'd eventually fall back asleep. She'd deal with it tomorrow.

CHAPTER SIXTY-FOUR

Sharon had a meeting with Louise Millard, to close off the case and offer any further support she could. Even when an open case was terminated, the agency still offered the women voluntary support so that they didn't feel alone. With Robert Millard now deceased, Sharon wasn't surprised that Louise wanted to meet her at a coffee shop. Louise would try to socialize more now, to come out of the psychological and antisocial prison that Robert had kept her locked in.

Sharon ordered a coffee and reviewed the details of the case. She had known Louise for a few years now. Although these women would never treat her as a friend, she maintained a sort of bond with them, even after their cases closed. With Louise, she always feared that someone would end up dead – she just never thought it would be Robert.

Sharon spotted Louise the moment she walked in. Her head was down, her clothes dishevelled, and her shoulders hunched. Louise looked like she'd given up on life. A sadness swept over Sharon. Louise sat at the table and looked at her. It could take years for Louise to feel truly free of Robert. Statistically, it was more than likely she would end up in another abusive relationship.

Sharon clenched her fist at the thought.

'How are you holding up, love?'

Sharon could see the puffiness in Louise's eyes as she spoke.

'I'm OK. Well, I'm not OK. I just don't know what to feel, Shaz. I hated him. Really hated him. But I loved him too. He was my husband ...'

She placed a comforting hand gently over Louise's and stayed silent. Nothing she could say would help. Eventually she gave her hand a squeeze and smiled. 'I know. I'm not going to tell you it will get better in time, but I hope it does. You know that. Even though I'm closing down your case, you can still contact me – anytime – OK? Just ring the office and they'll get hold of me.'

'Thanks, Shaz. That means a lot. Have the coppers been to speak to you?'

Sharon frowned. 'Why would they do that?'

'I thought they might. They were around mine the other day and asked me questions about people I spoke with.'

'Sorry, love, still confused. Spoke with when? About what?'

'Just before Robert died. About how I wanted him dead. How I wanted to kill him. And they asked who I said this to and what was said back.' Her eyes were wide.

Sharon leaned closer and smiled nervously. 'OKaaaay. And what exactly did you tell them about me?'

'Look, I didn't mean anything by it. I thought they were joking. It was just what we talked about at the community centre. Just banter. How you said you'd happily kick the shit out of him and he didn't deserve to walk this earth. Don't worry, I said you didn't actually mean any of it.' Tears started rolling down Louise's face and Sharon took out a crumpled tissue from her bag.

Sharon's face fell. 'Ah don't worry, Louise. Like you said it was just banter. You haven't done anything wrong.' Shuffling the papers in front of her, Sharon carried on, 'Shall we just get on with signing these? You'll then have me out of your hair for good!'

Sharon wondered if the police were going to take Louise seriously. She sipped her coffee and watched Louise sign off the paperwork. Her mobile suddenly rang.

'Excuse me for a minute, Louise.' Sharon stood up and walked towards the doorway. 'Hello? Yes, Louise is here with me now. She said you may want to speak with me. OK, yeah. I can be there in about half an hour.'

Sharon said her goodbyes to Louise and left the building, heading to Markston Police Station.

CHAPTER SIXTY-FIVE

Papers were strewn across Maggie's desk. The follow-up meeting with Shell Baker shed no further light on the current investigations. Shell had admitted that she was Louise's cousin, but she said she had mentioned that during the officer's first visit. Maggie stood up and stretched her arms. There was something niggling at her about this case, but she just couldn't put her finger on what it was.

'Right then, so who wanted to speak to me about these murders?' There was no mistaking Sharon Bairden's strong, Glasgow accent.

'That would be me, thanks for coming in. Do you want a drink?' Maggie headed towards the kitchen.

'I'm not planning on staying long enough for a drink, so the sooner we get this ridiculous interview over with, the better.'

'Follow me then.' Maggie escorted Sharon to one of the free offices on the floor.

'I'm not exactly sure what you think I know, Maggie, but I can tell you one thing: you're *wasting* your time. Look at me. How the hell would I overpower two men?'

'I take that on board, but we need to explore all avenues. You never know, you might have a vital bit of information subconsciously stored away and—'

Sharon raised her hand. 'Stop right there. I don't appreciate your tone. There's no need to be condescending. I've been doing this job a lot of years and if I had any information, you … the police … would be the first to know.'

Maggie continued, 'Where were you on the night that Robert Millard was murdered?'

'At home. In my bed. Asleep … and alone.' Sharon crossed her arms and slumped back in the chair.

'So no one can account for your whereabouts?'

'You could always ask my neighbour, Jackie. Fancies herself as the neighbourhood watch. If I had gone out, she would have seen it.'

'And what about the night that Drew Talbot was murdered?'

'You're having a laugh now, aren't you? Am I seriously being considered as a suspect? Do I need a solicitor here?'

'Routine questions. That's all. We're trying to eliminate anyone who may have come into contact with, or had a reason to harm, these men. I'm going to level with you, Sharon. More than one person has commented on some of the things you have said about Millard and the other individuals we monitor.'

Sharon leaned across the desk, and Maggie sat back. 'You listen to me. I have never hidden what I think about the people managed in this unit: they are the scum of the earth. Am I upset by what happened to them? Not really. But I am also the one who has to deal with their victims on a daily basis. You'll have to forgive my unprofessionalism when I sometimes say that so-and-so deserves a good kicking. Karma is a bitch. But I would never take the law into my own hands. As shit as the criminal justice system can be,' she narrowed her eyes into slits, 'it's not my place to mete out whatever punishment is due. Now if we're done here …'

Sharon stormed off without waiting for an answer.

Returning to her office, Maggie flopped into her chair and sighed. 'I really don't need this shit.' At that moment she really just wanted to be sitting in front of the TV, sharing a pepperoni pizza with her brother. Tapping her pen on the table, she didn't want to admit that this case was getting to her. But it was. She rubbed her forehead hoping they had a break soon as she didn't know how much longer she could keep it together. She replayed the conversation in her head. Sharon had a strong dislike of domestic abusers, but Maggie put her words down to passion and not revenge-seeking. She would give it a day and then ring Sharon to apologize. She didn't want any animosity in the team and they still had a killer to catch.

CHAPTER SIXTY-SIX

Lucy woke feeling groggy and slightly nauseous. After hearing Patrick come in last night, she'd lain awake until she heard his snores. Desperate for a coffee, she crept out onto the landing and listened. Patrick was still snoring; it was at times like this she was grateful he could sleep through an earthquake.

Lucy hurried past, careful not to wake him as she brewed herself a cup of strong coffee. The kitchen was a mess, cans littered the counter and lager spilled on the floor. While waiting for the kettle to boil, Lucy grabbed a cloth, knelt down, and began wiping up the mess.

She felt his hot breath on her neck, 'I'll have a cuppa if you're making one.' He wrapped his arms around her waist and tried to kiss her. Lucy wondered wearily how she missed his approach.

'Patrick, not now. I'm not feeling too great and I have to get ready for work.'

He shoved her away. 'Always fucking work. What about me? This relationship is a fucking joke.'

Lucy could tell he was still drunk and didn't want him to kick off before she had to go to work.

'Sorry, look, I'm just tired. Didn't sleep much.' She touched his hand and noticed some cuts. 'You OK? What happened?'

'What is this? The third fucking degree? I went out. Is that a problem?'

Lucy wasn't convinced.

'I was just asking. Never mind. I'll make the coffee.'

'Fine. Can you make it quick? I need to pick up Siobhan from school.'

'Oh, I forgot to say, Maria called last night and said she'd take Siobhan to school. I didn't know what time you'd be back, so said that was OK. You weren't answering your phone.'

Lucy wasn't surprised when Patrick grunted, 'I was busy. You could've said something earlier. I would've stayed in bed.' Before she could answer, he stomped his way up the stairs.

Lucy put her questions to the back of her mind for now and got ready for work. She had enough on her plate at the moment; everything else could wait.

Lucy was barely through the door at work when Sarah rushed over, her eyes wide with excitement. 'Oh, my god! Have you heard what happened?'

'I just got here, Sarah.' Lucy laughed. 'Can you give me a minute to drop this at my desk?'

'Of course! Sorry. I just can't believe it! I thought you'd know anyway since your Patrick was involved.'

Lucy stopped dead in her tracks. She turned around slowly. 'What do you mean *my* Patrick was involved? Involved in what, Sarah?'

'You really don't know?' Sarah was no longer smiling.

Lucy could feel the colour draining from her face as Sarah pulled her into the staff room, looked around and then whispered, 'Patrick was arrested last night.'

Lucy couldn't hide her shock. 'Arrested? He was home last night, and I spoke to him this morning. How do you know all this before me?'

'An email came through for the duty officer – that's me today

– and you were copied in because Mick O'Dowd was also arrested—'

'What the hell? With Patrick?' Lucy's mind was racing.

'Yes! I'm supposed to call the police back. They want some information on Mick—'

'Leave it with me, I'll sort it. Thanks, Sarah. Does anyone else know?' Lucy cut Sarah off before she could finish.

'Not yet. Andy isn't in until later, and I'm not about to spread any office gossip about you. Is everything OK?'

Lucy nodded. 'Don't worry. This must all be a misunderstanding. I'll sort it.' Lucy was torn: she didn't know whether to contact her boss now, or wait until she heard the full story. She didn't want to be caught out. Lucy knew who could give her some answers. She picked up the phone and dialled.

CHAPTER SIXTY-SEVEN

Lucy set her palms down flat on her desk. She couldn't breathe, her chest tightened. Before she even had the chance to hear what Mark knew about Patrick's arrest, he had other news to share. She listened through the headset as Mark explained the limited details they had on the Vicki Wilkinson assault. Lucy again relayed the conversation she'd had with Mick and Vicki on the day of the attack. Mark advised Lucy that they may need to speak with her further pending enquiries.

Lucy was shaking as she hung up the telephone. Sarah must have spotted she was upset and came over.

'Hey, are you OK? You look a bit shaken up.'

In a daze, Lucy hoped that Sarah couldn't see how uneasy she felt.

'What is it, Lucy? Do you want a cuppa?'

Lucy shook her head. 'No … no, I'll be fine. I've just got some news about Vicki Wilkinson and now I'm worried that I should've seen this coming.'

'Oh, my god, has something happened to Vicki? What? Why didn't they contact me?'

'According to the police, Vicki has been attacked. Apparently, it's pretty bad – she's in a coma. I guess they let me know because I emailed them about that home visit.'

Sarah gasped and squeezed Lucy's shoulder. 'Oh no! Did they arrest anyone?'

'No, but I think Mick O'Dowd might be involved. Remember, I'd spoken to them, and I warned Vicki to be careful. I warned her. What if my threat triggered him off?'

'You can't think like that. *If* Mick was involved, he made the decision on his own. And no matter how vulnerable Vicki is, she is also capable of making her own choices. You can't blame yourself for any of this.'

Lucy knew Sarah was right. It still didn't stop her from feeling guilty. At least Sarah understood, but it was everyone else she was worried about. People outside of probation didn't get the stressful decisions they had to make. Without really knowing what the job entailed, assumptions from others often caused good officers to lose confidence in their abilities.

Lucy thanked Sarah and composed herself. She needed to update her records and then speak to her line manager. This would no doubt end up as a serious further offence investigation. *Fuck! Fuck! Fuck!*

After informing her manager of the situation and being reassured that her decisions were defensible, Lucy was desperate to call Mark again, to see if there were any further updates on the case. She hesitated, her hand above the phone. What would calling Mark achieve? He might grow suspicious and start asking questions that she was not ready or prepared to answer. She shook the idea out of her head, logged off her computer, and locked away her paperwork. When she was feeling like this, she didn't want to go home.

CHAPTER SIXTY-EIGHT

The dark circles under Mick O'Dowd's eyes told Maggie that he had barely slept a wink. He was slouched on the bed in his cell looking annoyed at the flickering fluorescent light above him. She heard from the custody sergeant that every now and again he'd shout abuse through the steel door to anyone within earshot. Significantly sober now, Maggie guessed, he would be recounting the goings on of the night before, preparing himself for questioning.

'Can I get some fucking paracetamol in here? How can you interview me if my head is pounding!?'

Maggie stood back as the officer accompanying her unlocked the cell door. The officer situated himself in front of Mick with a tray full of something that was supposed to pass for breakfast. Maggie could understand the look of distaste on Mick's face.

'I can't eat that shit. Do you have any headache tablets?'

'You'll have to wait for the doctor, I'm not—' the PC replied, looking at Maggie for some assistance.

'Forget it, I don't want to hear your procedural shit. When am I going to be interviewed?'

'Mr O'Dowd, my name is DC Maggie Jamieson. I'll be interviewing you shortly. I just wanted to see that you were sober enough to answer our questions.'

'Fuck's sake. Are you going to be long? Take that shit with you … wait … leave the coffee and the juice.'

Both Maggie and the PC ignored Mick as the door was locked behind them. Looking through the small window, Maggie watched him guzzle down the orange juice like it was the first drink he'd ever had. Maggie noted the injuries on O'Dowd's knuckles, as he held the cup of coffee to his mouth. She'd certainly be asking about them.

Before going in for the interview, Mick was allowed to see his solicitor. The tall, grey-suited man entered and took a seat in front of Mick.

'Hello, Mr O'Dowd. My name is William McCabe.' He pulled out some paperwork and laid it on the table. 'I see the police want to question you about a criminal damage, affray, as well as the more serious offence of grievous bodily harm.'

Mick pretended to be shocked.

'Whoa, whoa … whoa! I get the criminal damage and affray – and pretty much hold my hands up to them – but what the hell is the GBH charge you're talking about? No one was seriously hurt in that fight last night and no weapons were used. Just my hands.' Mick showed his solicitor the cuts on his knuckles as proof.

'I see. Well according to this,' he gestured at the paperwork, 'the GBH relates to a serious assault against someone by the name of Victoria Wilkinson. Do you know her, Mr O'Dowd?'

'Vicki? Oh, my god. What's happened to Vicki?' His acting skills were better than he hoped, because the solicitor looked genuinely concerned.

'It seems, Mr O'Dowd, that Vicki was beaten and left for dead in her flat. On the same day that you got into a fight with a Mr Patrick Quinn. The police suspect you're involved with the serious assault on Vicki, because you have a history of domestic abuse. It says here that you're currently on licence for an offence against an ex-partner. Is that correct?'

Mick nodded.

'I swear I had nothing to do with Vicki. We cooled things off after my probation officer warned me that I could be breaching my fucking licence.'

The two men discussed Mick's whereabouts during the time in question and he explained the incident in the pub as an unfortunate misunderstanding.

'Right. Well, from what I see here, the police don't seem to have much evidence to charge you in the case of the GBH at this moment in time. It seems you have an alibi, if what you're saying checks out. You'll likely be charged with the criminal damage and affray – but given the circumstances, I think we can get you out on bail.'

Mick smiled. 'Thanks, Mr McCabe. Can we get this over and done with? My head's pounding.'

The solicitor nodded. Mick knew that a lesser charge might just keep him in his nice, cosy flat, and he'd make sure nothing would affect that.

The solicitor stepped out for a moment and returned with the two officers from earlier. A digital recorder was switched on by the woman. She reminded Mick he was still under caution and explained how the questioning would go. Mick nodded his understanding. *Keep it together Mickey boy …*

CHAPTER SIXTY-NINE

Maggie tapped her pen on the table – a habit she'd had since her teenage years – and talked Mick through the preliminaries. She was sitting beside Mark in the interview, opposite Mick and his solicitor.

With all the information the police had on the affray and criminal damage, Maggie knew those would be the easier crimes to get Mick to own up to. Sure enough, he recounted the events of last night and held his hands up, stating he was 'guilty as charged'. Maggie could see that Mick had something further on his mind, though.

'Excuse me, officers, my client wants to know a few things before we proceed.'

'Go on, Mr McCabe,' Maggie responded.

'He wants to know if the other man involved in the affray has been charged, whether Mr … erm … Quinn is pressing charges, and what would happen if my client didn't want to pursue the assault charges against Mr Quinn.'

Before Maggie had the opportunity to say anything, Mark answered, 'Mr Quinn has not made any indication whether he is going to pursue the assault charges. I can't tell you anymore than that. It will be up to you, Mr McCabe, to pursue once you're finished here. As for what would happen if you didn't pursue charges … in all likelihood, the matter would be dropped. You both would still be liable for the criminal damage charges, because the owner of the pub whose window you smashed is pressing charges. The CPS will make the decision on how to take that further. Does that answer your question, Mr O'Dowd?'

Mick nodded.

Mark sighed. 'For the benefit of the tape, Mr O'Dowd has just nodded his agreement to understanding.'

'So, Mr O'Dowd, what caused the physical altercation with Mr Quinn?' Maggie stared, maintaining eye contact and hoping to make him slip up.

'Like I just told you. Someone pointed out that his wife was a fit bird.' Mick slid his tongue over his nicotine-stained teeth and Maggie cringed. 'Maybe she doesn't like to be associated with an arsehole, which is why I've never seen her with him. Anyway, I said a few choice words about his missus and what I'd gladly do to her if he couldn't satisfy her needs … that's all. He said something back that I didn't particularly like, some bullshit rumour.' Mick puffed his chest out and leaned back in his chair. 'So I thought I would teach him a lesson. Seems he didn't like that much either!'

Maggie rolled her eyes and, much to his displeasure, interrupted him. 'But there's a reason for that, isn't there, Mr O'Dowd?'

'Yeah. There may well be. But that has nothing to do with what I'm here for, lady. I did my time, so why don't you move along.'

Mick's solicitor nudged him. 'DC Jamieson, can we just stick to the facts of the current matters, please?'

The look of contempt Maggie fired at him did not go unnoticed by the others in the room, but she didn't care. 'Mr McCabe, I'm trying to establish the facts, and in terms of Vicki Wilkinson, the facts are: (a) she was severely beaten to within an inch of her life (b) she was in a relationship with Mick O'Dowd (c) Mick O'Dowd has a history of domestic abuse. And he's currently on licence for an assault against a previous partner ... so what part don't you understand as factual?'

Mick's solicitor wouldn't meet her gaze and, instead, directed his answer to her colleague.

'I understand the points raised. However, unless you have *evidence* that places my client with the victim at the time of the assault, all this is irrelevant.' He smiled at Mark. 'What he's previously done, and what he's on licence for, has nothing to do with these matters.'

'I'm over here, Mr McCabe.' Maggie waved her hands about. 'Speaking to my colleague rather than me won't change my line of questioning. Can we get on with this now? And in future – look at me when you have something to say. I'm the lead detective in this case ... OK?'

CHAPTER SEVENTY

Shell contacted the hospital to check on Vicki. The nurse who answered the phone sounded sympathetic, but told Shell that she could only share information with family members. She must have heard the distress in Shell's voice, because she whispered into the phone that, if Shell were to turn up at the hospital, she'd find her friend in a stable condition. Shell breathed a sigh of relief and thanked the nurse for her understanding.

Shell had made a copy of Vicki's spare key a while back; Vicki was always prone to losing things when she was under the influence, so it had seemed like a good idea. Given that the assault on her friend happened a few days ago, Shell was fairly certain that the police would have cleared out by now and she didn't want her friend coming home to a bomb sight.

She packed her car with cleaning supplies and headed over to the estate. Letting herself into Vicki's flat she surveyed the mess and shook her head. She couldn't tell whether the chaos had been caused by the police, or by whoever had trashed the place. Fingerprint dust covered various points in the room and clothes were strewn all over the floor. Starting with the kitchen, Shell began what was likely to be an all-day task.

Hours later, Shell found herself in Vicki's bedroom. The room had barely been touched, because the majority of the crime had taken place in the living room and kitchen. Shell wanted the whole place to feel cosy, so Vicki didn't struggle coming back … and she'd be back. Shell wasn't ready to accept the possibility that her friend might not wake up. That would be too much to bear. Shell gripped the mop tightly and tried to control her anger.

Shell cleaned faster, removing the bedsheets and searching Vicki's closet for some fresh ones. Finding some in a plastic bag at the back of the closet, Shell started to make the bed. Her hand touched something on the left side of the double bed. A notebook. Shell debated whether to look inside and was surprised that the police hadn't found it. *Maybe they looked inside and found nothing of interest.*

Curiosity soon got the better of her. The inside pages looked like they'd been written by a child. Hearts adorned various pages and **VICKI + M** was littered about the surface. Shell scanned the notebook until she got to the last few weeks before Vicki's assault. Open-mouthed, she read as Vicki described feelings of desperation. 'M' shoving her, shouting at her, and at one point punching her so hard in the arm it left a bruise.

Reading on she noticed that Vicki was making excuses for M's behaviour. and alarm bells began to ring. Shell pocketed the notebook. She needed to prove who 'M' was, before taking this to the police. And Shell knew exactly who might be able to give her the information she needed.

CHAPTER SEVENTY-ONE

Maggie smiled as she continued her probing line of questioning; she had Mick O'Dowd bang to rights. 'Mr O'Dowd, where were you between the hours of four o'clock and eight o'clock last night?'

Maggie waited as Mick looked at his solicitor who nodded. 'I was at The Smith's Forge. I'm not sure what time I arrived, but it wasn't long after I picked up my dole money. That would have been about three that afternoon. You can check my bank statement.'

'No need for that right now. Do you always go to The Smith's Forge on a Thursday?' Maggie leaned forward.

'No, not always. It's a busy night, darts club, and normally I just like a quiet drink.'

She lifted the pen she was holding to her mouth. 'So how come you decided on this particular day to go to a pub that you usually avoid on a Thursday?'

Before Mick could answer, his solicitor interrupted. 'What are you implying, DC Jamieson?'

'I'm not implying anything, Mr McCabe. It is a legitimate question. I just find it odd that Mr O'Dowd happens to go to a pub, on a busy night that he generally avoids, on the exact same night that his girlfriend gets seriously assaulted. Don't you think that's odd, Mr McCabe? A pretty big coincidence?'

Maggie could see Mick's knuckles whitening on the edge of the table. Mick leaned over to his brief and she thought she heard him whisper, 'Do I have to answer these questions? I'm getting pissed off now.'

'Sorry? What was that Mr O'Dowd?' A hint of a smile grew on Maggie's face. 'Could you speak up?'

Mick fidgeted in his seat. The solicitor answered for him. 'I'm instructing my client to answer no comment. You're on a fishing expedition and going in circles. Do you have any evidence to support what you're insinuating, DC Jamieson?'

'I'm not insinuating anything. I'm being thorough. Asking questions. Doing my job. Are you saying that Mr O'Dowd is now refusing to answer any further questions?' Maggie looked across at Mark. 'Seems like Mr O'Dowd is trying to hide something, would you agree?'

Mark nodded.

Mick suddenly slammed the table with the palms of his hands. 'Fuck this shit. How many fucking times do I have to say this? She wasn't my girlfriend! Either charge me or let me go! I'm not answering anymore of your stupid questions!'

Maggie and Mark knew they didn't have enough to charge Mick in relation to the assault on Vicki Wilkinson yet. Instead, he was charged with affray and criminal damage and released on bail with a GPS tagging condition. At least they could track his movements. Maggie and Mark escorted the pair to the custody suite, where bail would be sorted out, and then they made their way back to the office.

'There's something just not right about his story, Mark. I'm not liking this one bit! His fingerprints were all over Vicki's place. He had cuts on his knuckles. Hopefully we'll find some of Vicki's DNA when the lab results come back. In the meantime, we need to search the area around his property. He may have dumped something on his way to the pub.'

'Officers are on that already. They'll update us if they find anything. I can't be sure, but these current charges may be enough to get him recalled. I'll give Lucy a call and find out.'

'Good plan. I don't want this prick to get away with this.'

CHAPTER SEVENTY-TWO

After learning of Vicki's assault and Patrick's arrest, Lucy's head was a mess. She didn't know whether to call Patrick first and hear his side of the story, or call the DAHU and speak to Mark. She didn't want to be blindsided if any questions were asked. No doubt the police would be looking for a recall on Mick, but that would depend on the charges and whether the police had remanded him in custody. Lucy knew if Mick O'Dowd was charged with the assault on Vicki, however, that could lead to a serious further offence investigation and awkward questions might be asked, given that Mick had been arrested after starting a fight with her husband. *Fuck! How the hell did Patrick end up in all this?*

Patrick would still be in bed at this time and, not wanting to deal with him, she contacted the police station. If she appeared vague and didn't offer any information, they might not immediately realize that Patrick was her husband.

'*Domestic Abuse and Homicide Unit, DC Maggie Jamieson speaking, how can I help?*'

'Hi, Maggie, it's Lucy. Is Mark about? I have a message to call your team.'

'*Oh, hi! Good timing. No need to speak with Mark – I can*

246

tell you what you need to know and hopefully you can help us out.'

Damn. Lucy's friendship with Mark meant that he'd sometimes share additional information. 'Sure thing, Maggie. I heard that Mick O'Dowd has been arrested.'

'Yes, he was, but he has been bailed with GPS tagging. We've charged him with criminal damage and affray, but it's unlikely the affray will stick as both Mick and the other injured party don't want to press charges. We're still waiting for further evidence to connect him to the assault on Vicki Wilkinson, but what we really wanted to know is whether he can be recalled?'

'Erm … tough one. Given that you have him tagged and based on the information you have just shared with me, I'm not convinced the Parole Board would feel he is enough of a risk. They'll view that the tag will keep him indoors and he'll be monitored by the police. I trust there are conditions to keep away from the victim of the affray? Is it a female? Sorry for all the questions, I need to get as much information as I possibly can, so I can discuss it with my line manager.' Lucy realized her hand was shaking. 'In all honestly, with prison overcrowding, it's unlikely my boss will agree on this one.'

'Well what about the serious assault on Vicki Wilkinson? Who manages Vicki's case?'

'Sarah Hardy, but I'd still be responsible for Mick's recall. Has he been charged with anything in relation to that?' Lucy was getting worried now; if two people who she worked with on her caseload were involved in serious matters, it meant more stress. Once they learnt that her husband was involved in the affray, they may want to investigate further. Lucy wasn't ready to disclose what had been happening at home.

'Not yet. There's not enough evidence, but the investigation is ongoing.'

'Same situation then, I'm afraid, Maggie. Can you account for his whereabouts?'

'He says he was at The Smith's Forge during the time of the assault. We're speaking to witnesses to corroborate that information. He also said he and Vicki saw you earlier in the day. We'll need to discuss that.'

'Of course. I did send the home visit information over to the police group email and spoke briefly to Mark about that.' Lucy closed her eyes and hoped Maggie couldn't hear the tension in her voice.

'Ah, OK. Crossed wires, I guess. I'll have a look and come back to you if I need anything else. Are you OK, Lucy? Only, you sound a bit funny.'

'Uh, no … I'm fine.' Wanting to change the subject Lucy asked, 'So what was the affray about? Do you know any details?'

'I'll scan over the charge sheet, you can have a read. In fact, can we drop by at some point to have a chat about O'Dowd and Wilkinson? My gut is telling me he was involved; I just don't have anything on him and it's frustrating the hell out of me. You might be able to help. One of us will call you to confirm.'

Lucy checked her diary, her hand still shaking. She had a meeting she couldn't reschedule easily. She fiddled with her earring. This whole situation was a nightmare.

'My diary is clear in the afternoons for the next few weeks, just let me know when you are coming in case I have to move something about. Is that OK?'

'That's great. We'll be sure to let you know when we're coming. See you soon.'

Lucy hung up the phone and dropped it onto her desk. She needed to speak to Patrick, and to her boss. It felt like her two worlds were coming together and the collision would be disastrous.

CHAPTER SEVENTY-THREE

With her Saturday morning jobs finished, Shell wasted no time heading to The Smith's Forge to speak to Kevin Pearson. Shell knew that if anyone could confirm that Vicki was seriously involved with Mick, it would be Kevin.

The pub had the usual weekend faces dotted about, but thankfully wasn't too busy. Shell didn't want anyone to tip off Mick that she was asking questions. 'Hey, Kevin. How's things?'

'Well look who it is!? Been a bit on the quiet side without you here lately! All loved-up, are you?' Kevin let out a burst of laughter and Shell couldn't help but join in.

'Yeah, I've been otherwise occupied.' Shell winked.

'Right ... I knew it! Anyone I know?'

'Maybe ... maybe not. But I'm actually hoping you could help me out a bit.'

'I can try. What are you needing?'

'Have you heard that our Vicki was attacked a few nights ago?'

'I did. Sorry, I should've asked how she is.'

'Thanks. Not too good, Kevin. Her face was mashed to a pulp, and she was barely breathing when I found her—'

'Whoa! *You* found her? Shit, that must have been horrible.'

'It was. She's still not out of the woods though. She's stable, but in a coma.'

'Do the police have any idea who did it?'

'They suspect it was a robbery gone wrong. Her place was torn to pieces, ransacked. But they won't tell me anything more than that.' She didn't mention Mick – the less people know, the better.

'Sounds like it could have been more than one person. Maybe one beat her while the other trashed the place.'

Shell shuddered at the thought. 'Don't know, Kevin. Guess we won't know until they arrest someone, or until Vicki wakes up.'

'Well if you do go and see her, will you tell her I was thinking of her?'

'Of course, Kevin. When was the last time you saw her?'

'Hmmm … well since she cut down the booze and hooked up with that fella of hers, it's been a while. Couldn't say for sure though. Might be days, could be a week or more.'

'Did you know the fella she was with?'

'Yeah. I do.' Kevin leaned in closer. 'He could be a right prick. New to the area. I think you had words with him one night. That rough-looking fella – thin, pointy nose. Only been here a few months – from London …'

'Do you have a name?' Shell shifted on the stool.

'Oh right.' Kev laughed. 'I think it was Nick … or Mick … hang on … gimme a minute.'

Shell tapped her foot impatiently as Kevin walked up and down the bar, trying to remember. She knew that kicking off wasn't going to make him any faster.

Kevin suddenly smiled. '*Mick*. It was definitely Mick. Not sure of the last name though, but he comes in here often, mainly on Tuesdays and Fridays. He sometimes pops round during the day. I don't think he works … He was arrested here the other night.'

'Really? What for?'

'He kicked off with that Patrick fella – that guy you know. Tallish, good-looking – dark hair.'

Shell's heart was racing.

'Anything else?'

'The police arrested both of them and took my statement. They haven't been in touch with me since, so I can't really add anything else. What I will say is that I didn't notice Mick was here until later on in the evening. It was unusual to see him—'

'Wait. Why unusual?'

'Like I told you, he mainly comes in on a Tuesday or Friday. Thursday is darts night and we're generally packed. Probably why I missed him arriving.'

'And he was fighting with Patrick? Patrick Quinn?'

'Is that his last name? The fella I've seen you chatting to a few times.'

'Do you know what the fight was about?'

'Well, that Mick fella had said some nasty words about Patrick's missus.' He looked around nervously and lowered his voice. 'He grabbed Patrick by the shoulder and said he'd show her what a real man could do, or something like that. Patrick didn't seem to like that and spouted something back.' Clearly enjoying spilling the gossip, he smiled. 'They fought, broke the front window, knocked over a few tables and chairs and I called the police.'

'Thanks. That's helpful. If you think of anything else, call me. Doesn't matter what time it is. OK?' Shell wrote down her number on a napkin and handed it to him.

Making her way to her car, Shell found it hard to breathe. Fumbling with her keys, her hands shook as she unlocked the car door. She needed to sit down and catch her breath.

Why the hell was Patrick defending Lucy? Had she been played for a fool all this time?

CHAPTER SEVENTY-FOUR

Mick had spent the day drinking in his flat. The tag meant he couldn't leave after 6 p.m., so he went out early, grabbed some lager and settled on his couch watching TV. He felt a breeze on the back of his neck and looked over his shoulder to the open window behind him. He pulled up the collar on his shirt. Couldn't be arsed with getting up and closing it. Put his feet up on the table and cracked a can, flicked through the channels. Eventually sleep took over.

The crash on the floor woke him. *What the fuck was that?* Mick looked around but it was pitch-black. He had to wait as his eyes adjusted to the darkness. He saw the ashtray from the windowsill smashed on the floor. The window was wide open and it was freezing cold. Mick got up to have a closer look and stepped carefully over the broken ashtray. He thought he heard a creaking floorboard, and turned towards the kitchen. Nothing. Probably just his neighbours. He closed the window and bent to pick up the larger pieces of glass. Something plunged into his neck.

He tried to scream but a gloved hand clamped his mouth shut from behind. Mick struggled to reach his neck, but his hand was too heavy. As the liquid surged through his veins, he felt his

252

body crumple and he landed like a piece of lead on the floor, facedown.

'Well we can't have that, now, can we, Mick?' He didn't recognize the voice. 'I need to see that pretty face of yours.'

The figure grunted as they turned him over. The shadowy figure was padded out in a black bomber jacket, black hoodie, a mask and combat boots. Mick felt sick to his stomach. He was afraid that if he puked, he would choke on his own vomit. He couldn't move a single muscle, but could feel everything. His eyes darted around the room, afraid that if he lost sight of the person, they would land another kick in his side. His chest tightened with fear.

'Think I'll have a look around your flat, Mick. You don't mind, do you?' The hooded figure laughed.

The shadow stepped over him, and Mick strained his eyes to watch them head towards his kitchen. He knew it was filthy, but now wasn't the time to worry or care. His attacker didn't stay in there long, before they went in the direction of the bedroom. He could feel a tingle in his foot.

A small yelp escaped his lips when the figure returned. They placed the lighter fluid from his dresser into their pocket. Then he noticed the wooden truncheon in their other hand. They began smacking their hand with the truncheon and Mick could see the glint of pleasure in their eye as they said, 'Mick! You ready? I think we're about to have some fun.'

His vision blurred as he thought about his children and how they would never know how much he missed them.

CHAPTER SEVENTY-FIVE

Maggie ended the call and raced into Calleja's office. A nervous sweat glistened on her brow under the glow of the police station's artificial lighting.

'I don't like the look on your face, Jamieson.' Calleja looked up and frowned.

'You shouldn't. There's been another body found. Mick O'Dowd.'

Calleja pulled up the list of nominals from the police database. 'For fuck's sake! He's that transfer in from London. What the hell is going on here?'

'Police are already at the property, but from what I gather, there are definitely similarities to the Millard and Talbot cases. It's not looking good; the media will soon be all over this with their serial killer theories. We need to catch this guy soon.'

'Have you told the rest of the team?'

'Briefly. Thought you'd want to speak with everyone.'

'OK. Let me think.' The DI stood up and began to pace the room. Maggie watched him move back and forth.

'I'll get in touch with probation. See what information they have. We can match that up with anything we have on our system and identify any patterns between the three crimes. Kate has also been working on her profile and we can look at any associates. That sort of thing.'

'Yes, you or Mark do that. Do we know anything more about the body?'

'Beaten pretty badly. No defence wounds. Seems a Taser and another weapon was used. His throat was cut just like Talbot's and Millard's. Oh … and his face, hands, and genitals were set alight.'

'What the hell? Who found him?'

'A resident was on their way back home and cut through his garden. He noticed the side door slightly ajar and, when he looked through, smelled what turned out to be burning flesh. Said he thought someone was having a barbecue inside the house. He called the emergency services right away.'

Calleja ran his hand through his hair. 'We'd better gather everyone together, see if we can make sense of any of this.'

'Good idea.' Maggie headed towards the open-plan office.

The briefing didn't last long. Her colleagues listened and thrashed out ideas, listing possible persons of interest they would need to talk to, but there was a sense that the investigation was running away from them.

Everyone was assigned a task and asked to report back as soon as possible. Calleja looked in shock, his hair ruffled and his tie in disarray, as he stood at the front of the room and addressed the group. The team was at breaking point: Mark's shoulders sagged. Pete rubbed his temples and Kat's swearing had reached the verge of her being mistaken for someone with Tourette's. Maggie jiggled her foot uncontrollably as Calleja told them that he feared that the DAHU would be disbanded soon if he didn't have answers for the PCC. Maggie could tell he was not looking forward to preparing his report, his statement for the media or the response he was likely to receive. They needed to catch the killer – or killers – soon or they wouldn't have any nominals left for the team to manage.

CHAPTER SEVENTY-SIX

It had been a long day. Maggie looked at the information on her desk and resigned herself to the thought that she still had a few more hours' work before she could get home. She rubbed her forehead wearily and noticed a shadow over her. Dr Moloney peered down at the papers on her desk.

'How's things, Kate?' Maggie sat up straight and tried to smooth down her hair, hoping she didn't look as rough as she felt.

'Fine. Just wondered how you are? You're all looking pretty stressed lately.' Kindness glowed in her eyes and Maggie's heart fluttered.

Turning her attention back to work, Maggie forced a smile. 'Actually, I'm glad you're here. I've been through these papers and have a few thoughts I'd like to run by you.' She paused and took a deep breath. 'Maybe we can grab a bite to eat afterwards … my treat?'

'How can I say no to that?' Kate pulled up a chair. 'Right, so tell me what you have.'

Maggie gave Kate a brief rundown of the evidence so far. The way Kate creased her forehead when she was thinking made Maggie smile. She couldn't help staring at the doctor. Kate suddenly looked up.

'What? Is there something on my face?' Kate wiped her chin self-consciously.

'No. Sorry, I was just watching you process the information. Do you have any thoughts?' Maggie couldn't believe she was caught out … again.

She moved the papers on her desk and showed Dr Moloney her notepad. 'I think I've found some similarities between these cases, and I'd like to recap what we have so far and then run my thoughts by you, if that's OK?'

Dr Moloney smiled. 'Sounds perfect. Let's hear what you've got.'

'Well, none of these men put up a fight. There were no defence wounds. Talbot was hit over the head and a needle was found stuck in his neck. Robert Millard also has a needle mark on the right side of his neck. Mick O'Dowd may have one too, but his face and neck were burned, so we're waiting for the pathologist to confirm. All three men were severely beaten with some sort of blunt object – probably a bat or wooden pole, but it could even have been fists.'

'Yep. What else?'

'All three men had their throats slit and bled out.' Maggie pointed at the photographs on her desk. 'And they seem to have been lying down, facing their killer.'

'I noticed that too. Why the difference in kill methods? Why didn't they fight back? Do you have the toxicology reports?'

Maggie smiled as it was almost like she was talking to herself. Dr Moloney reached into her bag, pulled out a notebook and jotted something down.

'Talbot's and Millard's tests showed no drugs in their system at the time of discovery, but any drug used could have left their system, especially in Millard's case, given the time he spent lying on his floor before being discovered.'

Maggie took a sip of water.

'As for Mick O'Dowd, he was set alight with lighter fluid. That's

257

what alerted the neighbour so quickly. The killer wasn't trying to dispose of the evidence – as the whole body wasn't covered in fluid – but O'Dowd suffered serious burns to the face, neck, hands and genitals. We don't know how long the attack lasted before his throat was cut—'

Kate interrupted. 'Surely the autopsy report should be able to shed more light on that? It will be able to at least tell us whether the attack happened before, at the time of, or after the throat was cut.'

Maggie watched Dr Moloney writing in her notebook again.

Seeing Maggie's curiosity, Dr Moloney held up the notebook. 'Sorry, when something niggles me, I have to write it down. It prompts me to revisit the information. The needle marks and the throat cutting have gone in the book.'

Maggie understood, she often did the same thing.

Revenge? Anger? Was there more than one killer? Were the murders all connected or just a strange coincidence?

'The cut to the throat suggests a connection, but that had been reported in the news. Anyone could have heard what happened and copied the crime.'

'I definitely think it's one killer though.'

Maggie looked at Dr Moloney.

She was tugging at her ear, her tell that a thought was brewing, and she was ready to share. 'I agree … *but* I'm struggling to determine whether the killer is male or female. Given the beating, the assumption by you guys is that we're looking for a male suspect. However, if a weapon was used, couldn't the killer be a woman?' Dr Moloney flicked her hair back and continued. 'Would a beating with fists or kicks rule out a woman? Especially if the victim was incapacitated somehow.' She glanced up at the ceiling. 'There are two possible profile types in my opinion. The killer could be targeting these men because they witnessed someone important in their life – like their mother – being abused. They're angry and seeing the abuser as someone personal to them – a father or stepfather. Hence the viciousness of the attacks. The killings won't stop until they feel they have sated their anger.' A line etched between Kate's brows. 'The other is a vigilante. These men are known to them. Has either hurt them or someone close to them. Once their revenge has been exacted, the killings will stop.' The notebook was out again. Dr Moloney finished writing and looked at the clock on the wall.

Noting the time herself, Maggie wrapped things up. 'Thanks so much for this. I think we should bring our ideas to the team tomorrow. How about we go and grab that bite to eat now? I don't know about you, but a glass of wine might help me wash the meal down perfectly!'

Maggie was pleased that Dr Moloney was still up for it. She enjoyed her company, her intelligence, and the way she put people at ease.

She's your colleague, Maggie … focus on the job.

CHAPTER SEVENTY-SEVEN

Hooper rubbed at his face vigorously, as if he could wipe away the anxiety before anyone noticed. Three bodies. Similar circumstances. It wouldn't be long before the press started with the 'serial killer on the loose' headline and then he would have all the high-ups on his back. And he'd just been given a piece of information from the Custody Sergeant that changed everything. Hooper headed to the briefing room.

He walked inside, trying to look confident, dreading what he was about to have to tell the team. 'Right, folks, what have you got?'

Dr Moloney followed him into the room and took a seat. Hooper looked around. A room full of blank faces. This did not bode well.

'C'mon! I have to brief the DI in an hour. You must have something! Or maybe you'd like me to start? We now believe there is enough evidence to presume that Mick O'Dowd was responsible for the attack on Vicki. Bloodied clothes were found, not far from his property, which contain traces of Vicki's blood and Mick's DNA. At least that is one case we can close down, unless Vicki Wilkinson tells us something different when she wakes up. Over to you.'

Hooper paced the room, his mood darkening as the silence grew.

Mark was the first to speak. 'Well, we have the connection to our team. All three men were domestic abuse perps. Do you think it could be revenge killings?'

'I would say that was fucking obvious, Mark.' Kat smirked. She wasn't one to mince her words.

Without taking any notice of Kat, Mark continued, 'They were also under one kind of probation supervision or another. Do we know who their PO's are, guv?'

Hooper rubbed his temples before responding.

'Both the recent victims are – were – supervised by Lucy Sherwood. Turns out, Lucy also has another connection to Mick O'Dowd. The fight he was arrested for … it was with her husband.' A stunned silence filled the room, and Hooper ran a shaking hand through his hair. 'The records also indicate that Lucy warned Mick off Vicki Wilkinson hours before she was attacked.' DS Hooper relayed the information to his team with a sadness in his voice. He didn't like to assume, but the link to Lucy Sherwood was undeniable.

'Whoa! Are you saying Lucy is somehow involved in this? No fucking way! Each of us knew those men one way or another. What possible motive would Lucy have?' Mark's voice was defensive and, before Hooper had a chance to address it, Maggie joined the conversation.

'Calm down, Mark. I don't think anyone was implying that. But you have to look at the facts: Lucy is connected to all three men, more than any of us, and she will need to be questioned further. Why didn't she tell us that Patrick Quinn was her husband?'

Mark had gone pale, but he shrugged his shoulders in defeat and offered to interview Lucy himself.

'No way is that going to happen. I think you need to take a step back from this one,' Maggie said firmly.

Mark turned to Hooper and began to protest, but Hooper interjected. 'I'm afraid I'll have to agree with Maggie. You're too close to Lucy.' Mark had gone bright red and Hooper raised his eyebrow. 'I meant in the sense that you both run the domestic abuse group, but looks like it's more than that by the colour of your face ... care to share?'

Knowing that this would only bring more unwanted attention, Mark shook his head.

Hooper looked at Dr Moloney. 'Anything to offer, Dr Moloney?'

Dr Moloney opened her folder and looked over her notes. 'Well, DS Hooper, after hashing out ideas with Maggie last night, I can tell you that the perpetrator is familiar with their victims. There's no forced entry or defence wounds present on any of the bodies. I can't say for sure whether the killer is male or female at this time. It could be a vigilante, an angry family member of their previous victims, or a female seeking revenge of some sort. I do—'

'Sorry to cut you off, Dr Moloney. After our conversation last night, I thought about everything a little bit more and I'm still not sure what I believe. Do you really think a female could commit this type of offence and if so why would they be targeting these particular men? Maybe you can go over it again for everyone?' Maggie interjected.

'I was just getting to that. I now know that a syringe, filled with succinylcholine or SUX, was used to incapacitate the victims. I had suspected this after speaking with Maggie last night. This drug, once in the system, effectively paralyzes the victim, but they remain able to see and feel, to a certain extent, what is happening to them. Now this drug wouldn't show up in the system, unless specific tests were asked for. I had put in the request through DS Hooper. Toxicology rushed through the request and dropped the information off just before I came in. It doesn't appear to be the case that Talbot had this – or any drug – in his system. Although he was a known heroin user, the syringe found in his neck was

262

clean. Perhaps the killer was still perfecting their MO. However ... Millard and O'Dowd did have SUX in their system.'

Hooper looked a little affronted. 'Why didn't they leave it with me, or even DI Calleja; it would have been helpful to know that before I came in here.' He looked at Dr Moloney with eyes that said – *You better have a good answer for me.*

'You were already in here and they caught me on the way. I guess because you requested the tests on my behalf, they figured I'd want to know. Does it really matter? I had a brief look before coming in. I know about this drug from the books I read on serial killers.' All eyes seemed transfixed on Dr Moloney after her last statement and Hooper covered his mouth to hide the smile forming.

'Whaaaat? I'm a criminal psychologist ... do you think I read books about fairies and leprechauns? As I was saying, Martin Steventon, an American serial killer also known as The Somerville Stalker, used this drug on several of his victims. I don't know how someone in the UK got hold of it ... but they did.' Kate sat back down. Scanning the room.

Mark looked gobsmacked. 'Jesus Christ! Two of the three victims were injected with this drug? All three were managed in the DAHU? Did the victims know each other in any capacity – outside of probation that is?'

Kat rolled her eyes. 'Have you not been bloody listening, Mark? We know all that already! They must have run into each other at the pub more than once – they drank at The Smith's Forge. Most of our cohort hang out there.' Kat seemed to be getting more agitated by the minute. 'Look, I'll happily go interview Lucy; do we need to speak with her boss or anything, guv?'

'I would say negative on the boss front for the time being as this is really just to see if Lucy has any further information to add. I don't have any reason to suspect her of any crime. OK, folks, are we done here?'

Hooper wrapped up the meeting, tasking individuals before

they left the room. 'Mark, can I see you in my office before you head out?'

'Sure thing. Give me five minutes.'

When Mark arrived, Hooper was sitting waiting for him, a stern look on his face. He said bluntly, 'I hate to do this, Mark, but I do need you to be honest with me. Is there anything going on between you and Lucy Sherwood?'

Mark blushed again. He didn't know how to answer that, but thought the truth would be a good start. He sat down and told Hooper about the past few months, leaving nothing out.

After Mark left his office, assuring him that nothing was going on with Lucy but disclosing he 'may' have a soft spot for her, Hooper clasped his hands together. What the hell was going on with his team? And with the investigation? The victims, in his mind, were not victims at all – although this wasn't a view he could share openly with anyone. He knew that he should be putting all effort into finding the killer, but a part of him just wanted to shake the person's hand. But he had a duty to perform and he didn't want another murder on his patch, so all efforts had to be made to resolve these crimes as swiftly as possible.

The team needed to pull together the common themes and try to narrow the suspects down.

The stress was overwhelming.

Hooper spread the information across the conference room table, in the hope that something might leap out at him. One thing was certain, all these individuals were linked to Lucy Sherwood. Hooper hadn't told the team but Lucy had disclosed on her police vetting form some domestic abuse between her and her husband. When PNC checks were undertaken, it was noted that there had been a few police call-outs relating to assaults on Lucy and criminal damage from heated arguments in the early days of their marriage. Apparently, her husband had agreed to undertake a domestic abuse course at the local RELATE charity and no charges were brought against him. Hooper took out his notepad and jotted down: '*Check whether P Quinn completed the course.*' It could be nothing, but his gut told him to pursue it. Could Lucy Sherwood, her husband, or both, be their killer?

CHAPTER SEVENTY-EIGHT

Looking up from her emails, Lucy noticed PC Kat Everett and DC Maggie Jamieson in the reception area. The glass on the doors and windows in probation were one way: staff could see out, but members of the public couldn't see in.

What the hell? They never confirmed they were coming today. Lucy glanced through her diary to see if she'd just forgotten, but when nothing was noted, her brain went into overdrive. *Maybe they're here to talk to Sarah or someone else. Please let that be the case.* She nearly jumped out of her chair when her phone buzzed. It was reception, apparently the officers wanted to speak with her. *Oh fuck. What do they know?* Without thinking, Lucy picked up her bag and headed to the reception area.

Worry gnawed at her. Naturally with three people on her caseload recently murdered the police would, of course, want to speak with her. When she saw the look on their faces as they stood in reception, she knew for sure that something bad had happened. This didn't bode well.

'Hi, Lucy, how are you? Is there somewhere we can talk privately?' Maggie asked her softly.

'Sure, we can go into one of the interview rooms.'

Maggie nodded, and Lucy turned to the receptionist to advise her of where she'd be. Still hoping this was about collecting more information on the murdered men and nothing to do with Patrick, Lucy's curiosity overrode her nerves momentarily.

'Is this about those murders? Do you need to look at my records or something?'

The police officers looked at each other warily.

'Well, sort of. But it's best we wait until we have some privacy, OK?'

Lucy thought it was unusual for Kat to be so polite.

They entered the room, and the officers placed themselves directly across from her. Lucy laughed nervously. 'Why do I feel like I'm about to be interrogated? So, uh … what is this all about?'

'We're going to be upfront with you. We have been asked to have an informal conversation with you about Drew Talbot, Robert Millard and Mick O'Dowd. Are you OK with that?'

'Well, I guess so, Kat. I have nothing to hide.'

'Right, so I'll ask the questions and Maggie will jump in if she feels I've missed something. Do you understand?'

'Yes. Am I under arrest or something? Am I under caution?'

'You're not under arrest or caution, we just want to have a conversation. You're free to go at any time. However you should be aware that if you do leave, we may have to ask you to come into the station.'

Lucy began to shake. *Why is this happening?* Having nothing to hide, she knew that the best course of action would be to just answer the officer's questions. 'I understand. Ask away.'

'We know that all three of the murdered men were known to you on probation. Did any of them express concerns about being harassed or followed?'

'Any conversations where risks are raised are shared with Mark. Off the top of my head, I never met Drew, he was coming in so I could prepare a report for court. Neither of the other two men discussed any concerns they had about people after them. You would need to check the records if you're looking for absolute certainty.'

'Were you contacted by anyone who felt at risk from Mr Talbot, Mr Millard or Mr O'Dowd?'

'Louise Millard never contacted me directly. I generally liaised with Sharon when it came to the victims, because it's not appropriate for me to speak with them. As you know I did have concerns about Mick's relationship with Vicki Wilkinson.'

'So, no one threatened these men?'

'No. Don't you think I would have said something?'

'Normally, we would.' Maggie jumped into the conversation. 'However, you failed to let us know when your *husband* …' Maggie looked down at her notes 'Patrick Quinn, was involved in an altercation with Mr O'Dowd … and we also learnt from our enquiries, that someone overheard Robert Millard tell your husband that he thought you were having an affair with a police officer.'

Lucy could feel the colour draining from her face. The room swirled before her eyes and she felt breathless. *Why the hell would Robert say that to Patrick?*

'Are you OK, Lucy? Kat, go get some water.' Maggie reached out and touched Lucy's hand, but she snatched it away. 'Calm down, Lucy. It looks like you're having a panic attack. Breathe in and out, OK? I've just sent Kat to go and get you some water.' Lucy bent over and put her head between her knees while Maggie rubbed her back. 'Deep breaths, Lucy. That's it. Deep breaths …'

Fifteen minutes had passed, and Lucy felt calmer. She had been given water and eventually managed to control her breathing. Now she was back at the table and the officers were about to continue. 'Everything OK to carry on, Lucy?'

'Uh, yes. Sorry, I don't know what came over me then. You're right. My husband did get into a fight with Mick O'Dowd. I didn't think to speak to you about it because … well, I guess I figured you knew the story and if you had any questions, you'd come ask me.' She couldn't meet their eye. 'Looking back, I suppose I should have said something. As for the other thing. I had no idea that Patrick knew or spoke to Robert Millard. I don't talk to my husband about work stuff, I don't frequent pubs in the evenings and there is no way I'm having an affair with a police officer … my god, my husband would—' Lucy stopped short.

She was too ashamed to continue.

'Your husband would what, Lucy?' Maggie leaned forward.

Lucy gripped her hands together and tried to stay calm. 'My husband would have told me about a conversation like that. He never did, so I can only assume he figured Robert was lying. But that's only a guess. I suppose you'd have to speak to him.'

'Yes, I suppose we might have to do that. All right, sorry to have had to put you through this. Are you sure you're OK?' Maggie frowned.

Lucy nodded. She felt sick and needed some fresh air. 'Are we finished? Only I have a few cases booked in and if I need to organize cover, I'll have to do it now.'

'We're done. If we have anymore questions for you – we'll let you know. Thanks for your time.'

Lucy showed the officers out of the building and ran to the toilets barely making it into the cubicle before she threw up. She hadn't been feeling well lately and speaking with the officers had not helped. But she also feared it could be something else. Reaching into her bag, she pulled out the pregnancy test she'd picked up at the chemist earlier.

She needed to know.

Oh God. Is Patrick involved in any of this? Why did Robert Millard say I was having an affair with a police officer? Why didn't Patrick say anything to me?

Lucy recalled a night that Patrick had come home from the pub fuming. His anger was unleashed full force.

She traced the scar above her eyebrow slowly. Another reminder of his so-called love.

She was broken.

She felt broken.

Physically, financially, but most of all … emotionally. He turned her from a confident, carefree, intelligent woman, into a shell. She felt like nothing. Like she was in someone else's body, skin, mindset. She leaned her head against the cubicle wall and her thoughts wandered.

I actually preferred the beatings. I knew what to expect. Bruises fade or could be covered up. But emotional scars stay. Eat away at my very existence. Until I believe I am nothing, too.

I gained weight in the hopes that this would turn him off sexually. Leggings, PJ bottoms, and oversized jumpers to make myself less attractive. I even stopped wearing make-up unless I absolutely had to.

'Look at you, you ugly, fat, bitch!'

'Fucking slag.'

'Stupid bitch!'

The words and phrases I'm greeted with on a daily basis.

When Patrick first started with his insults, not long after we were married, I argued back.

'Don't call me that!'

This just encouraged him more. The twisted grin and empty, drunken stare.

'Who do you think you're talking to, bitch!?' I could feel the tension rise in the room as he approached and towered over me. His forehead pushing against mine and if I tried to turn away – he'd push harder. Teeth clenched and that sneer mocking me.

'Why do you make me do this? Why do you have to piss me off?'

If I answered, I got a slap, or a shove. If I didn't answer, I got a slap, or a punch. So instead, I cried, and Patrick laughed. I wish I had the courage to stop him.

Lucy snapped back into reality and looked at the pregnancy test she held in her hand.

It was positive.

CHAPTER SEVENTY-NINE

Lucy wasn't sure how she managed to make it home, but she did. Sitting in the living room, she was trying to work up the courage to tell Patrick about the baby. He already had two kids from two different mothers, but Lucy was never quite sure how he'd feel if they were to have a child. Or even if she wanted to have a baby, especially when the sex was forced. *How could I let this happen?*

Patrick often made Lucy feel it was her fault that he was involved in years of court battles with Siobhan's mother. But it had been Lucy who spent hours typing up the paperwork, paying the solicitors and barristers, and taking days off work to sit outside the family court room while Patrick was trying to get custody of Siobhan.

Her phone pinged. A text from Patrick. He was on his way home and wanted Lucy to go to the shop to get some beers on her way home from work. She told him she'd been unwell, so was already home. Instead of showing any concern, his reply was:

Can you get the beers or what?

Charming.

Not wanting to get into an argument, Lucy grabbed her coat. She thought that the fresh air might infuse her with courage to tell Patrick the baby news. She was so confused. Lucy grabbed an extra can of beer from the shop to put him in a good mood.

Turning the corner onto the cul-de-sac where they lived, Lucy saw Patrick's car in the drive; he was obviously closer to home than she thought. She took a deep breath and pasted a smile on her face to open the front door.

'Hello? Patrick? Where are you?'

'In the kitchen. Have you been to the shop yet?'

Lucy placed the bag on the counter, trying to gauge his mood. He seemed OK.

Patrick reached in and pulled out the cans.

'Eight? What have you done?'

'Wh-what do you mean?'

He laughed in her face. 'Why so nervous? Have you actually *done* something? I was just surprised to see eight cans; you're normally the beer fucking Nazi.'

'Oh ...' she joined in the laughter, hoping her nerves didn't give her away. 'I just thought with you looking for work and all the pressure we're under, you deserved a treat.' She could feel herself gagging as the words left her lips.

'Thanks, babe.' He pulled her in for a kiss. Lucy felt like turning away but that would only enrage him – the feel of his lips on hers made her cringe.

Lucy gently pushed Patrick away. 'I do have something to tell you but ...' she could see his face change. 'It's not bad, Patrick – why are you looking at me like that?'

'Well ... what is it then?'

Lucy reached into her pocket and pulled out the positive pregnancy test. Patrick's eyes widened. He looked happy, but she couldn't be sure.

273

'Is that what I think it is? Are you pregnant, babe?'

'Yes.'

Patrick came towards her quickly and her natural reflex made Lucy pull her arms up to protect herself.

'Why are you doing that? I just want to hug you … this is the best news ever!'

Lucy felt foolish then, but this is what her life had become. Not knowing how to react. 'So, you're happy?'

'Of course! I'm going to be a dad again. You and I are going to have a baby together! Why wouldn't I be happy?' Patrick pulled her closer.

She felt like she was suffocating, and the reality soon set it. Of course, he was happy – she was tied to him, for life – and no matter what her future held, Patrick would always have a connection. *Maybe he won't hurt me anymore …*

'Time to celebrate! Well me, anyway, as you can't drink while you're pregnant!' He cracked open the lager. 'This really is the best news! Can you put those cans in the fridge, Lucy – you know how I hate warm beer,' he strolled into the living room.

What have I done?

After telling Patrick the news about the baby, Lucy went upstairs and called Sarah. She forgot to call her boss when she got in earlier, but hoped Sarah would've covered for her. Sarah knew that Lucy hadn't been feeling well lately. Sarah was silent on the other end of the phone as Lucy told her.

'Are you still there, Sarah?'

'Yes. I'm just worried about you, Lucy. Having a baby is not going to solve your problems. It could make it worse! We both know that the risk of domestic abuse is greater for women who are pregnant. Oh, Lucy, I don't mean to preach, but how did you let this happen?'

Lucy began to cry. 'I know, Sarah, I know. What have I done?'

'OK, hun. Calm down. Don't start stressing yourself out. Maybe this is just the opportunity you need, OK. You can come stay with me and Justin until you figure things out. We can speak to Andy at work and see if he can help—'

'I can't tell anyone at work. And Patrick would *kill* me if I left …' Lucy whispered. It was then that she looked up and saw him standing in the door. Lucy gasped.

'I have to go now, Sarah,' Lucy said coldly. She saw the look in Patrick's eyes and ended the call. The phone slipped from her hand and the screen smashed into pieces on the floor.

Three hours later, her lip was split and swollen. Blood dripped onto the floor of the bathroom. She looked in the mirror and gasped at her reflection.

Her right eye was swollen shut. Her stomach and back ached where Patrick had repeatedly pummelled her with his fists. She could still see the glazed look in his eyes and the rage seeping out of him with each punch as he shouted, 'You think you're going to leave me?!'

She needed to lie down and winced as she made her way to the bedroom. Lucy was scared. Remembering her phone call with Sarah, the horror in her friend's voice at the mention of her pregnancy. Lucy felt ashamed. If Patrick found out, he'd kill her … he really would. He prided himself on the persona he put out there and if that was shattered, he'd snap. Not to mention if Claire Knight ever found out. The weekly check-ins would start again, and Lucy would have no choice but to disclose to her line manager about the abuse she was enduring at the hands of her husband.

Oh God, what have I done?

The pain in her belly felt like period cramps. But she was pregnant, it couldn't be. Her face glistened with sweat as she struggled to get off the bed. Using the wall to brace herself, Lucy forced herself to get to the bathroom. She saw the blood. There would be no baby. Calling the NHS helpline from the landline, they told her there wasn't much they could do, but if the bleeding persisted, she should get herself into A&E. She didn't bother telling Patrick then. She would only get the blame. She left him downstairs and returned to her room. She hugged the pillow and lay down.

Her sleep was restless that night. Waking up every hour, drenched in sweat, feeling confused, and clutching her stomach in the hopes that her unborn child was still thriving in her womb. The pain still unbearable.

That was when it hit her. The feeling of emptiness enveloped her – she knew the baby was gone, and the depression set in, shrouding her in complete darkness.

CHAPTER EIGHTY

Lucy had taken compassionate leave from work for the remainder of the week, explaining to her line manager as much about the situation as she could – she left out the violence and hoped that Sarah would keep her promise. Andy was very understanding and for that Lucy was grateful. She spent most of the week sleeping and fighting off the depression that threatened to take hold. When she'd texted Sarah the news, Sarah had immediately tried to call her, but Lucy couldn't handle speaking to anyone.

On her way back from the GP surgery, where she picked up a sick note, Lucy got a text message. It was from Rory. She opened up the message and began to read.

I shouldn't tell you this. My dad is having an affair. With someone named Shell. I'm sorry.

Lucy stopped in her tracks in the middle of the pavement. It had started to rain but she stood dead still and let the water wash away her tears. *An affair? Shell? Who the hell?*

The tears streamed down her face and she ran the rest of the way home. She burst through the front door. Running up the stairs and into the bedroom, she checked for signs of Patrick. She rummaged through all his pockets, looking for something to prove he was having an affair with this Shell woman. *Is this where he went when he said he was going to look for work? Was Shell the mysterious Steve that Patrick was always meeting up with?* She could have kicked herself for being so naive.

Lucy didn't have any time to waste, she went to the wardrobe, grabbed her overnight bag, and began stuffing it with anything that would fit inside. She'd call Sarah and ask if she could stay with her while she worked out what she would do next. Siobhan was being picked up by her grandparents from school and staying the weekend. Lucy would have to figure out a way to explain. She'd also contact the social worker. There was no way she'd allow Siobhan to be left alone with her father.

Rory hadn't been in contact since he'd witnessed Patrick and Lucy fighting the last weekend he had stayed. Lucy had seen the pain in his eyes and had messaged him to apologize, but Rory was angry at his father. Angrier than Lucy had ever seen him, but she didn't tell Rory that Patrick blamed her for that. He was just a child and didn't need to know.

After putting up with the shame, humiliation, and fear for years – this was the last straw. Lucy laughed. An almost hysterical sounding laugh, but then again – she felt crazy. *What the fuck was I thinking? Years of abuse … YEARS … in the time they'd been together, and a miscarriage. But when Patrick crossed the line it was by cheating with another woman. The ultimate betrayal. That was the straw that broke the camel's back!*

Lucy was in shock. She frantically threw some final pieces of clothing into her suitcase and looked around the room. It was a bomb sight, clothes strewn everywhere, but she didn't care anymore. She was getting out. Deep down, she'd always had a suspicion that he'd been cheating throughout the whole marriage, but there was never any evidence. She'd ignored the niggling thoughts. Buried them. Even if she had confronted him, he'd have done what he always did: deny and make her feel like she was being paranoid, stupid, ridiculous.

Lucy looked at her watch. Patrick could be home at any minute. She needed to find her documents: bank book, passport, and the small amount of cash she had hidden away for emergencies. As she rummaged in a wardrobe, she heard a creak on the landing. She froze. It was probably nothing, but her heart was racing. She started searching through the cupboards again, tossing stuff out onto the floor. A cold voice behind her stopped her dead.

'And just where do you think you're going, bitch?'

Lucy could smell the alcohol before she even saw him. Had he been in the house the whole time? She could have kicked herself for not checking all the rooms first.

'You're even more stupid than I thought. You not going to answer me? Nothing to say? You really think I'm going to let you leave?'

Those were the last words Lucy heard before Patrick's closed fist connected with the side of her face.

CHAPTER EIGHTY-ONE

The pain in her head was excruciating. Lucy tried to open her eyes, but her vision was blurred. She heard footsteps; someone outside the bedroom door. She thought it was pushed open – there was a shadow. A person? Or were her eyes playing tricks on her?

Lucy could barely move. Voices. She thought she heard voices? From the bathroom but she couldn't be sure. Was someone was running down the stairs? She never heard the front door. She must be imagining things. What had happened? She remembered flashes: Patrick's face leering closer, pain and confusion. Violence. But she couldn't make her mind settle and only flickering images of the previous hours remained.

Lucy raised herself up off the floor, using the bed as leverage. She felt so dizzy and was afraid she'd pass out again. She needed to see what he'd done this time. Her body ached. It took her forever to reach the bathroom. The dizzy spells were overwhelming, the whole building rocked under her feet, and she had to stop every few seconds.

Pushing open the door, the mirror directly ahead, Lucy stifled a scream. This was too much. She hardly recognized herself. Enough was enough, she was going to call the police and press charges this time. Lucy was struggling to remember exactly what had happened, but the damage to her face told enough of a story. Turning to leave, Lucy noticed someone was in the bath. It was Patrick. A knife stuck out of his chest, his eyes wide open, and milky. Blood pooled around and sloshed all over the tub. He was dead.

Lucy couldn't remember what had happened. Someone had killed Patrick and her greatest fear was that she was that someone.

CHAPTER EIGHTY-TWO

DC Maggie Jamieson was getting ready to go home when the call came in. She threw her coat on and ran out of the door. She knew Lucy and, despite the discussions with Hooper and the team, she never really believed Lucy could murder anyone. Then again, although she had some suspicions, she'd not been sure of the domestic abuse in Lucy's life. Lucy always appeared to be focused and together. She chaired the Domestic Abuse Forum meetings and was the probation Lead for Domestic Abuse. Maggie shook her head in dismay. *You just never knew what people were capable of and what others might be hiding.*

Maggie headed down to the custody suite first to see how Lucy was, but also to try to figure out what the hell was going on. When the cell door opened, Maggie felt saddened. Huddled on the bed, rocking herself, sat Lucy. Her face battered, and she had dried blood in her hair.

'How are you doing, Lucy? Do you need anything?'

Lucy raised her head to see who had walked in and attempted to smile but looked completely bewildered and still in a lot of pain.

'Oh, Maggie! What have I done? What have I done?' The anguish and confusion in Lucy's voice tugged at Maggie's heart, but she knew she had to maintain her professionalism.

'Look, Lucy, you're still under caution. Anything you say to me won't be kept between us, OK? I need you to know that. When I heard the news that you were here, I just had to see if you were OK.'

'Does Mark know?'

Maggie's eyes dropped to the floor. 'I don't know, Lucy, I can find out for you.'

Everyone in the team knew that Mark and Lucy's friendship had grown since they'd been working so closely together. Maggie remembered Mark's embarrassment in a recent briefing when Hooper had hinted at his fondness for Lucy. It was another question she'd have to ask though. A question she wasn't looking forward to, because Mark may need to be questioned in relation to Patrick Quinn's death.

Lucy began rocking again. 'I don't know what happened.' She moved back and forth, staring blankly at the wall. 'I can't remember anything. He was just there … in the tub … with the kni … and the blood, all the blood …' Lucy was shaking, could barely finish the sentence. 'Is he dead?' She suddenly stared straight at Maggie. 'He's dead, isn't he? Did I do this? No … no … no …' She leaned her head back against the wall, and Maggie took hold of her hand.

'Hey, breathe, Lucy. By the look of your face, it looks like you took quite a beating. Have you seen the doctor yet?'

'Doctor? No, not yet. I don't need a doctor. I think I fainted when I got here. Everything went blank. I feel like I'm losing my mind! Why is this happening? Am I going to go to prison?'

'I can't answer that right now. I'm concerned about you. I'm going to find out when the doctor will be in to see you, OK? Are you sure you don't want some water?'

'Water would be great.' Lucy seemed to be calming down. 'If it's no bother, of course. I don't want to cause any trouble.'

Maggie squeezed Lucy's hand. She looked at the battered woman before her. This wasn't the Lucy Sherwood she knew. 'It's

283

no bother at all. Hang tight and I'll be back when I have some answers. PC Knightsbridge will bring you some water.'

Maggie left the cell and headed to the custody desk. 'Any idea when the doctor will be in to see Lucy Sherwood?'

'Sherwood? We have her down as Quinn. Regardless, DC Jamieson, the doc is making his rounds now and believe it or not – there are others worse off than that poor lass. Do you want me to let you know when she's been seen?'

'That would be great. I'm really concerned about her mental well-being. Make sure that someone checks on her regularly until the doctor has been to see her. He may have some ideas of what else we can be doing.'

'Will do.'

Maggie needed to speak to DS Hooper and then Mark. She had never been faced with a colleague who was under arrest and knew that she'd need to tread carefully. Everyone was going to be on edge.

In her gut, she still didn't believe Lucy had killed her husband, or any of the other men for that matter. If asked right now, she couldn't explain why, but something didn't feel right. She also didn't believe Mark was capable of hurting Patrick, but she knew his views on men that beat women and about his friendship with Lucy. You never know what people can be capable of when pushed.

Although most solicitors these days don't encourage a 'no comment' interview, Lucy's solicitor had advised her to go 'no comment' throughout the police interview. Maggie guessed it had to do with the unanswered questions that still remained. Despite this, Lucy kept saying she must have killed her husband and deserved to be punished.

With Lucy's lack of recall in terms of the assault on herself and the murder of her husband, she was returned to the cells and would appear in magistrates' court at the earliest opportunity.

Maggie found it a very difficult interview. When she raised

the deaths of the other men, Lucy looked blank, as if she had no idea what Maggie was asking or why. The team didn't know what to think but Maggie was determined to find out the truth.

CHAPTER EIGHTY-THREE

Lucy was remanded in custody, her case committed to Crown Court. She'd have to wait for more details from her solicitor, but accepted the decision without any fight. So many emotions clouded her thoughts. Patrick was really dead. Pain gripped her chest as she thought about Siobhan and Rory. Would they ever forgive her? Would she ever forgive herself?

She was still in a daze. Followed the women in the line as they were inducted into the prison. Slamming doors and the echo of footsteps invaded her ears. A strange smell of bleach and mould hung in the air. She couldn't believe she'd ended up here.

When she was asked for a list of people who she wanted on her visiting order, her heart sank. She didn't know who would still want to be associated with her. Rory's name was one of the first she did include, because they had grown close. Rory might not want to see her, but their brief telephone conversation made her think otherwise. She also listed her parents and sister. At court she couldn't bear to see the pain on her parents' faces. When she had spoken to her father in the cells at the court, she told him she'd understand if they couldn't visit. It was the first time she saw him cry.

There was a TV blaring in the cell next to her. She looked at the empty bed across from her, dreading the time when another inmate would be joining her. For now, she was alone with her thoughts. Lucy had not pleaded guilty in court. She would have done, but her solicitor convinced her otherwise. Wrapping her hands around her knees, she rocked back and forth on the hard bed she would now be sleeping in. She didn't want to keep everything bottled up inside anymore. Maggie and Mark, along with her solicitor, had encouraged Lucy to speak with Dr Moloney. After a little persuasion, Lucy had agreed.

The doctor who had seen her, following her arrest, believed that the head injury sustained during the assault, as well as the systematic abuse she'd suffered over the years, could have caused selective memory loss. It wasn't uncommon for trauma of this nature to induce a psychological barrier, so the doctor suggested that Lucy speak with a psychologist while she underwent some further tests.

Lucy was awaiting the results of the MRI. She had sporadic flashbacks of the evening. Wasn't sure whether her fantasies of Patrick's death had crossed over into reality and, somehow, she was remembering things she wished had happened rather than what actually happened.

The guard came to collect her, unlocking the cell door and stepping inside, and Lucy followed behind with her head down. The coldness of the prison gave her permanent goose bumps, and she hated the green walls closing in on her each day she had to remain inside. Her solicitor was attempting to get her bail, but this would take time, if it was even possible, so she had to do what was asked until they had an answer from the judge. The female prison guard was one of the friendlier ones. She used to listen to her female offenders complain about their treatment in custody. The name-calling from guards, the shoving, abuse, and derogatory behaviour – Lucy was now experiencing all of this. What made it worse was the fact that the guards knew she was a probation officer. This placed Lucy in a vulnerable position with the guards themselves, but also with other prisoners. She had managed to keep it secret so far, but it was only a matter of time before one of the prison officers let it slip. Most prisons were privately owned now, with inexperienced staff for whom confidentiality was a word they failed to adhere to. Especially if it meant a few extra pounds to take home at the end of the month. Lucy used to have three prison officers on her caseload for this very thing.

Lucy was led to one of the legal visit rooms. It was small but at least out of earshot of others. She sat quietly waiting for Dr Moloney to arrive. The room had two separate entrances, one where prisoners were brought through and the other where visitors entered. The large table in the middle of the room took up the majority of the space and two chairs were bolted to the floors on each side. Plastic windows surrounded the room like a fishbowl.

Lucy was reminded that she was one of *them*. Not long ago, she would have been arriving through the other door. She watched as another prison officer escorted the young, goth-looking woman down the hall. She seemed familiar. On entering the room, the woman held out her hand. 'Lucy Sherwood? Or would you prefer I use your married name? I understand you only used your maiden name for work?'

'Sherwood is fine.'

'OK, so – hello, Lucy. I'm Dr Kate Moloney. I'm not sure if you remember me? We've only met briefly on a few occasions.'

Lucy stood up and shook her hand. She remembered the soft Irish accent and kind face.

'Hello, Dr Moloney. I knew you looked familiar, but unfortunately my memory isn't so great at the moment.'

'That's OK. Have a seat, Lucy. We don't have much time today, I'm afraid. Have they told you why I'm here?'

'Yes. My solicitor said you were going to assess me? Ask questions about the night I mur … I mean Patrick was murdered … to see what I can remember.'

'Yes. You're partially right. I will be assessing your state of mind at the time of the offence. I also want to walk you through exactly what happened. The police may have done this, when they first interviewed you, but given the trauma you suffered – I've seen the photos of your injuries – it's unlikely that you'd have been able to give them any specific details of that night. How does that sound?'

'Yes, that's fine. That day … I mean, that afternoon, or whenever it was … it's still not clear to me. I have these flashbacks sometimes. But I'm not sure if they're things I wished would happen, or if they actually happened. Does that make sense?'

'It does. You have to remember that you have been through a great trauma yourself, so your brain has gone into protective mode.'

'I've heard of people who have blocked out whole events. What I'm worried about is when all that information surfaces. How will I be able to cope?'

Lucy shifted in her seat and rubbed her forehead. Her breathing quickened, and her face had flushed slightly. A bead of sweat had formed where her hairline and forehead met.

'Take your time, Lucy. We don't have to finish everything today. I have a few visits pre-booked with the prison. Look at me and take a few deep breaths. You can start wherever you feel comfortable, all right?'

Lucy nodded. Taking a few deep breaths, she closed her eyes. Began to recount the details as they flickered through her mind. 'I remember being upset, although I'm not exactly sure why. I felt betrayed about something. I remember Patrick's face, he was in my face … shouting. Close up. He was always angry with me. I think he punched me. I hit my head on something hard. I don't specifically remember waking up.' Lucy wrung her hands together repeatedly. She felt as if she were somewhere else, in a different body looking down on the interview room from above.

'You're doing great, Lucy. Can you remember anything else?'

Lucy rubbed her face in frustration. 'I can't ... I just can't ... well, except ... I thought I saw someone.'

Dr Moloney sat up in her seat.

'You *think* you saw someone? Or you *did* see someone?'

'Arrrghhhhh ... I don't know!' Lucy twisted uncomfortably in her seat, her eyes wild. 'Maybe it was Patrick. I just don't know!' Guilt tormented her.

'OK, breathe, Lucy. It's OK. Don't push yourself. I want you to do something for me.'

Lucy looked at the small notebook Dr Moloney placed in front of her. She swallowed and glanced nervously out of the window at the guard.

'It's OK. I cleared this with the Governor.'

Lucy skimmed through the notebook. 'What do I have to do?'

'Well, sometimes this helps people in similar situations. Whenever you have one of your flashbacks, write down what you remember. No matter what it is. Whether you believe it to be real or not. Do you think you can do that?'

'Yes. What about my nightmares?' Lucy's hand was shaking as she picked up the book.

'Anything and everything. I've left my telephone details in the front. Add me to your list of calls and then if you need to speak before we next meet, you can call me. It doesn't matter what time.'

Lucy looked at Dr Moloney blankly. 'Why? Why are you trying to help me?' Her hands were shaking. 'You work for the police. So how can I trust you?'

'I'm not a police officer. I'm a consultant in a civilian capacity. If you feel uncomfortable or don't want to do it, that's fine. I just want to help you unscramble the flashbacks. However, it may also prove your innocence. OK?'

Lucy got a sense that Dr Moloney wasn't trying to trick her. 'OK. I'm not saying I will do this. But I'll think about it.' Dr Moloney gave Lucy a reassuring smile. The sound of keys jangling and doors being unlocked made them both turn towards the doors. A prison officer shouted, 'Time's up!' and stood out of the way so Lucy could get by.

Lucy turned to look at Dr Moloney over her shoulder. 'Thank you,' she whispered.

'You're welcome, Lucy. I'll see you next week.'

As Lucy was escorted back to her cell, looking like a lost child in prison uniform, Dr Moloney busily scribbled notes. Something told Kate that Patrick's murder wasn't as straightforward as they all believed. *What was Lucy Sherwood hiding? Or more importantly, who was she protecting?*

CHAPTER EIGHTY-FOUR

Later that night, Lucy picked up the journal for what felt like the hundredth time. There was something about writing down her feelings that made the remand in custody a bit more bearable. Dr Moloney was right. Lucy knew that she had to get the thoughts out of her head, but she had to be careful. Telling the truth would have consequences that she was not ready to deal with yet. Instead, she wrote about what it was like to live with Patrick on a daily basis. Maybe someone would understand why she did what she did. Lucy didn't give any of the entries a date or title, she just wrote what came to mind, letting the words tell the story …

Every day in that house with Patrick was becoming more and more of a struggle. I'm not sure people could or would ever understand how I felt … still feel … and how I could go about living a lie. Inside the bricks and mortar, which were no longer a home, I felt exactly the same way as I do now – imprisoned. It was like living with Dr Jekyll and Mr Hyde at times. Never knowing which of the two I would be dealing with – yes, dealing – and negotiating my own feelings, to keep Patrick happy. Now that's a joke! I'm not sure Patrick was ever, or could ever, be happy. A deep-rooted anger took hold of him some years ago, before he ever met me, and he never let it go.

Work was my only escape. Somewhere I could be something else … someone else completely. I suppose that was also part of the reason I used my maiden name at work: I told people it was to protect my identity on social media – but that wasn't the truth at all. Being Lucy Sherwood meant I could be assertive, in control of my life, confident. The 'Lucy' I used to know. I could laugh, tell totally inappropriate jokes, be fun.

Even more ironic was the fact that I work with … specialized in … domestic abuse cases. The abusers, not the victims. I hate that word – victim – though at times it was exactly what I felt like. I'm a survivor, but that still doesn't feel right as I stare out of the bars on the window in my cramped cell. The only thing that each of the men and women I worked with had in common: the absolute desire for complete power and control over another person or people.

Why didn't I just leave? Oh, if it was only that easy! Being made to feel like you'd be hunted down, never be able to live your life free of the threats, constantly looking over your shoulder – those are some of the reasons I didn't leave. I was afraid if I left, Siobhan, and Rory would have no positive role models, no one to teach them what they should or shouldn't accept, even if that wasn't actually true. I thought that by giving up my own happiness, I could somehow secure theirs. I know, that really doesn't make sense. But when you're in a situation like the one I was in, crazy thoughts become normal, logical thoughts.

I also feared Patrick would turn his anger towards them. He loved his kids, but I have seen it happen. The loss of power over the partner and that anger needs to be redirected. The bullying starts, the child becomes the target – easy to manipulate, degrade, and better yet, too afraid to ask for help. There was no way I was going to let that happen.

CHAPTER EIGHTY-FIVE

Maggie looked over Patrick Quinn's toxicology report. Lucy had virtually confessed to the murder, but the dots didn't match up. The report noted that he had a large amount of duloxetine and alcohol in his system. According to his medical records, Patrick had a nerve disorder, but his prescribed dosage of duloxetine didn't match what was found in his system. *Had someone drugged his drink?*

The CPS believed it was an open-and-shut case. Lucy's fingerprints were on the knife that caused the fatal wound; but she lived in the house. Lucy admitted to stabbing Patrick, even though she didn't recall significant or key events. She had been a victim of domestic abuse for years at the hands of Patrick and so logic dictated, according to the CPS, that she'd finally snapped. Maggie wasn't buying it, nor was Dr Moloney. The state of Lucy's face when arrested, the dizzy spells, and inability to stand for long periods, at least four hours after it was estimated that Patrick was killed. Lucy couldn't have plunged the knife into Patrick, let alone get downstairs, grab the knife, and then make her way back upstairs to the bathroom.

Maggie was looking forward to meeting up with Dr Moloney to compare notes in the hope something obvious would come to light. She also planned to revisit the Talbot, Millard and O'Dowd cases: the only evidence that linked Lucy to these men was her work, but her phone records and computer were being interrogated and even the smallest thing could open a whole new Pandora's box.

As part of the ongoing investigation, Maggie was a regular visitor to the prison. Trying to jog Lucy's memory of that fateful night. Dr Moloney believed Lucy was hiding something. Maggie couldn't understand why though. *Why would Lucy risk spending the next ten years, to life, in prison? Did she want to punish herself?* It was pure luck that her solicitor had convinced Lucy to plead not guilty and opt for a trial, on the basis that there were miti-gating circumstances. Lucy would have been suffering diminished capacity, due to the years of abuse she suffered and the serious assault she had endured.

As a defence witness, Dr Moloney could put forth a convincing argument that it was all the years of abuse and the severe beating on the night in question that caused Lucy to snap. Maggie didn't want that; it was a last resort.

She gathered the case files to look over them one more time. Maggie was determined to find the missing link and prove Lucy's innocence, while also trying to uncover the real killer. Maggie would never be able to live with herself if the wrong person was convicted. Only one question remained: *If Lucy didn't kill him, then … who did?*

295

CHAPTER EIGHTY-SIX

The police station seemed to be busier than usual when Dr Moloney arrived. She headed straight to her office, greeted those who acknowledged her presence, but kept her head down. Working in the police environment was strange at times, and she still felt she was an outsider. Many of the police staff outside of the DAHU wouldn't accept the work she did; she often heard them muttering about psychology. Or her favourite: 'head quacks can't solve crimes'. She laughed.

DS Hooper was waiting in Kate's office when she walked in.

'Hello there!' She waved. 'To what do I owe this pleasure? … Oh, and not to sound rude, but can you get out of my chair, please? This may be a police station, but this is still my office last time I looked.' Dr Moloney pointed at her nameplate on the door.

Kate tapped her foot and glared at the DS until he got out of her chair. She placed her files on the desk, and asked Hooper if he wanted a coffee.

'Only if you're making one for yourself, I don't want you to think I expect it.'

Kate laughed. 'Calm down. I was offering. How do you take it?'

'Black with one sugar, please.'

Kate left the room and when she returned, Hooper had moved closer to her desk to nose through her files.

'I don't think you'll find anything of interest to you in there.' She slammed the door and a crimson colour rushed up his neck.

'I … uh … sorry. I can't help myself.' He smiled and moved his chair back. 'I'm just curious about how your appointment with Lucy Quinn or Sherwood, whatever she's calling herself now, went the other day.'

'I thought you were against us working with her? I'm not about to feed you information, you know.' Although Kate knew that Hooper was keen on ensuring the right person was convicted for the crime, she was still wary of his motives. She also wasn't obligated in a professional capacity to share any information unless it placed Lucy, a child, or a member of the public at risk of serious harm.

'Look, you're absolutely right. I'm not sure I understand why we're working with her. For me, it's a clear-cut case … and the prosecution agrees. She practically admitted to killing her husband, even though she claims she can't recall the details. She confessed.' He waved his arms in the air and leaned back in his chair. 'Unless you're trying to link Lucy to the other murders, I mean, *that* is understandable. Let's say she didn't have the courage to kill her own abuser, so she took it out on the other men. Maybe she saw Patrick in their mannerisms, killed them and then blacked out?'

'I don't think she did it.'

Hooper looked shocked. 'And how did you work that one out?' He crossed his arms and sighed.

'I don't have all the answers yet. It's just a gut feeling. The police are always going on about trusting their gut, and I believe mine. Lucy admits that she wanted to kill her husband on a near-daily basis. A normal reaction for women trapped in abusive relationships. However, she never once acted on or expressed any thoughts of killing her husband.'

'Whoa. You just said she had feelings, aren't they the same as having thoughts about it?'

'Forgive me. What I mean is, there never was any *intention* to carry out those feelings. Had there been, Patrick Quinn would have been dead long ago. Lucy's morals, her ability to lead two lives, and I actually believe her job as a probation officer, played a huge part in stopping her from acting.'

Hooper shook his head. 'Like you said, this woman was systematically abused for years. How do you know for sure that she didn't just lose the plot?'

'I don't. Circumstantial evidence is stacked against Lucy. But I genuinely think we're missing something.' Kate got up and began to pace the room. 'She can't recall specific details about the actual murder – I would have thought some of them would have come back to her by now. Also, physically she couldn't have gone downstairs, grabbed a knife, and plunged it with significant force into her husband's chest. When she arrived at the police station, she fainted. She could barely move. I know she's suffering from some sort of traumatic amnesia at the moment, but she keeps saying she *saw* someone. What if she did? What if someone else came into the house, saw Lucy unconscious on the floor and murdered Patrick?' Kate stopped pacing.

'Let's say I buy your theory … why would she admit to it? And more importantly, who has a motive to kill Patrick … other than Lucy?'

'Feelings of guilt?' Kate swept her hair back and stared evenly at Hooper. 'A belief that she must have done it because she'd wanted to? Protecting someone? Could be a number of reasons. Patrick Quinn wasn't well liked in his area. Your door-to-door enquiries proved that. Neighbours said he was a "loud-mouthed prick", drunk 24/7, and had on occasion heard the way he spoke to Lucy. I bet they were glad to see the back of him, yet none of them have been questioned further. Can we really sit back and let a potentially innocent woman go to prison for a crime she

298

may have not even committed? All because it was easier than finding the real killer?'

'All right, all right.' Hooper sighed in defeat. 'No need to go on anymore. Let's go speak with DI Calleja and see what he thinks.'

Kate grabbed her notes, and left the room with a smile on her face. She was beginning to feel like her work mattered and only hoped that her instincts proved correct.

CHAPTER EIGHTY-SEVEN

It had been over a week since Dr Moloney had interviewed Lucy. She wasn't sure why the police wanted to help her, or whether she trusted them. Following the assault, she was still struggling with how she felt about the situation she found herself in. She looked at the journal that Dr Moloney had given to her. She was fighting to write down the details she did recall, in case it helped her remember. Dr Moloney seemed genuine in wanting to help, but Lucy would still plead guilty. Her solicitor convinced her to plead not guilty, and Lucy complied, but she wanted everything over with now. It was too much.

Lucy had disclosed everything to her solicitor. Though the physical scars had long since healed, she wondered if she would ever get over the mental ones. Her solicitor had spoken to her colleagues, friends, and family. Although she had a strong case, Lucy's behaviour outside of work had masked a lot of what she had experienced at home. The jury may find it difficult to believe or even empathize. Sarah Hardy would be a key character witness. It was Sarah who had raised the alarm when Lucy was initially arrested. She knew about the abuse, although not to the level the police had advised, and had been there for Lucy, pestering the police to dig deeper. During one of her visits, Sarah made it clear that she believed Lucy was hiding something. Lucy didn't know whether to hug her or shout at her. She looked at the journal again, picked up a pencil, and began writing.

I find it hard to write down and share my feelings. I've always felt this way. It's hard for me to explain what I mean, but I've always felt I should've known better. I did know better. But I thought I was strong enough to handle it. Given the situation I now find myself in, I guess I wasn't. Do I feel remorse? I feel something, but I'm not sure it can be called remorse. I worry about Siobhan. I know she's with her grandparents now, but I took away her father. She must hate me. I regret that. And Rory. He's older, so understands more – he remembered what Patrick did to his mother. He witnessed what Patrick did to me.

What's worse is that I feel it's my fault. Rory was so happy to meet his dad again, and I burst that bubble by making Patrick angry when his kids were around. I know it's wrong to believe that, but it's how I felt. How I feel – it's how Patrick made me feel. It's all your fault, Lucy. You made Patrick do this. Keep your mouth shut. Don't answer back. Don't fight back. Just don't …

I've sent Rory a visiting order, in the hope that he will want to visit. I need to explain why I did what I did. He's still so young. I need to make him understand. Rory has his whole life ahead of him. I only hope that he stays in contact with his sister and explains everything – well, not everything, but most things – to Siobhan in the future. I stayed with Patrick because I really believed it meant the kids would have a safe environment. Wouldn't have to grow up with a parent who was an alcoholic. Would understand that they needed to find someone who let them be themselves with no fear of repercussions. They need to believe that love is not meant to hurt. I only wished I could have shown them that.

Dr Moloney read the journal entry twice and then looked up at Lucy. She had lost weight, her hair was now cut short and there were dark shadows under her eyes. Kate leaned back in her chair. Although it hadn't been long since their last visit, she had to admit she'd been hoping for more. There were some things here that needed more exploration. Lucy's next court appearance was in three months; they were running out of time. If they had enough information to cause the prosecution to question the charge, Lucy could well be released on bail. Even with conditions attached, bail would be better than seeing Lucy waste away on remand. She was a shadow of her former self. *What is she hiding?*

'Was it difficult to write that entry, Lucy? You looked pained as I read it.'

'I know it wasn't what you wanted. I'm sorry.' A tear rolled down Lucy's cheek. She didn't bother to wipe it away.

Maybe she'd cried so many tears she didn't even know they were falling?

'Why would you say sorry? You did what I asked. More even. This is as much for you, Lucy, as it is for us.' Dr Moloney reached out to put her hand over Lucy's, but Lucy flinched away.

'Sorry. I don't like being touched. I'm not worth all this effort. I told you, Patrick is dead, and I'm glad. Serving a life sentence inside these walls is better than the life I had outside.'

'Will you continue with the journal? It doesn't have to be every day. This is brilliant, but I would like you to consider writing down your flashbacks. What you remember. What you dream, or even your nightmares. Anything and everything.' She pushed the journal towards Lucy.

'OK. But don't expect much.' The sadness in Lucy's voice was heartbreaking. Kate really wanted to help her, but Lucy needed to help herself first.

CHAPTER EIGHTY-EIGHT

'Where are we at with the Talbot, Millard and O'Dowd investigations?' Calleja queried.

'Well you know that Dr Moloney has her own theories about this case. Maggie and Mark are still pulling together the evidence, while Kat and PC Reynolds are trying to tie all the loose ends together, guv.' Hooper hoped he didn't sound too unsure in his presentation of the investigation so far.

'Hooper, what kind of feedback is that? Some theories? Getting the evidence together? Tying up loose ends? What the hell? We need answers and we needed them yesterday! I have the DCI harassing me every bloody day about this. If one more body shows up, the media are going to be hounding us daily – I don't want that to happen.'

'I know, gov. We have a briefing in an hour and I'll make sure we have some solid leads.'

Hooper left his DI's office in a fluster. His chest tightened and he noticed the way it was affecting the team – the dark circles under their eyes, constant pacing of the room – he hated how this was affecting them. In all honesty, they didn't seem any further ahead – there was still nothing definitive. Lucy Sherwood was their probation officer, but they really didn't know who or what else tied these men together. And where did Patrick Quinn fit in, if at all? Dr Moloney still believed a vigilante was responsible, and she was adamant that the killer was female. Even with the drug, though, how could a woman inflict that much damage? According to Lucy Sherwood, none of the men were intravenous drug users, although Talbot did have a history of sporadic heroin and crack misuse.

With the briefing about to start, Hooper poured himself a coffee and waited for his team to assemble. Kat arrived with PC Reynolds in tow – 'Morning, guv,' they said in unison and Hooper nodded in acknowledgement. Once everyone was seated, Hooper called order.

'OK, everyone, DI Calleja is breathing down my neck, because our DCI is breathing down his … where are we at with these cases? We're at risk of having to hand everything over. There's even talk of this team being disbanded on the basis that we're causing more harm than good. Come on! We need this resolved.'

There were some murmurs in the room. Dr Moloney stood up.

'May I, sir?' she said as she pointed to the investigation board.

'Be my guest.' DS Hooper stood out of the way and she took centre stage.

'I'm not going to go over everything we have so far, as I assume we all know the facts. I'm still convinced that we're searching for a female perpetrator. These murders are personal. As I've always said – the victims were incapacitated – and I think this was so that *she* could commit the offences without any risk of being attacked. There's clearly an underlying anger here, as shown by the wounds to the victim's throats. Is this the killer's way of silencing the offender? According to the pathology report, this is the last thing that's done. We know that she – or he – beats the victims. A Taser was also used in the case of Mick O'Dowd. Maybe because the killer either didn't have the opportunity to get close enough to inject him a second time or perhaps the effects didn't last as long. It does not appear that Talbot was injected with the same drug as the other two, but instead, was initially attacked from behind and then an empty syringe stuck in the neck. Another statement perhaps? Mick O'Dowd was also set alight – his face, part of his neck, his hands, and his genitals.' They all looked at the board.

It was filled with names and lines linking individuals to the victims.

Kate continued walking back and forth in front of the board. 'Lucy had a connection with all of the men. A victim of domestic abuse herself, she certainly had motive. Shell Baker knew two of the men. Her close friend was now in hospital after being assaulted by Mick O'Dowd. Her cousin suffered years of abuse at the hands of Robert Millard, but there is no evidence to connect her to Talbot at the moment. The team had recently discounted Kevin, the barman, as he didn't seem to have any grudges to bear. Patrick Quinn's murder does not appear to be connected to the three murders at this stage – though the police are still unwilling to rule anything out.'

'The team have questioned whether any of Mick's children had returned to seek revenge, but there were no links to Robert Millard or Drew Talbot and no evidence to suggest they'd been in contact.'

Maggie spoke up. 'I agree with a lot of what you're saying. Every one of the people mentioned has reason to want these men dead. We need that one connection. Where would someone get the drug? Surely that has to be what will solve this for us – at least with Millard and O'Dowd. Though what if Talbot *is* known to the killer, and he or she didn't have access to the drug when the opportunity to kill him came around?'

'I like your thinking, Maggie.' Kate smiled. 'Succinylcholine is hard to get a hold of. Hospitals and Vets may have it – so we'd need to see if any reports of drugs stolen have been made in the weeks leading up to the murders.'

Maggie stared at the crime scene photos on the board in front of her. Piece by piece everything began to fall into place. The witness statements, evidence, and photos flickering and flashing in her mind. She was suddenly back at the crime scenes, seeing them take place in real time. The images cleared in her mind and the killer was revealed. The face clear. Maggie smacked her hands on the table.

'Oh, my god.' She stood up. 'It was right under our noses all along. We do know someone who has links to hospitals and a vet's surgery.'

CHAPTER EIGHTY-NINE

The team knew that they needed to be one hundred per cent certain, before rushing out to make an arrest. Maggie joined heads with Dr Moloney. Together they looked over previous interviews, notes taken, and the links to the victims, until they agreed that this was their killer. The pieces of the puzzle were finally coming together. The alleged suspect grew up in a house filled with domestic abuse, had a mother who suffered systematic abuse, who'd turned to alcohol and drank herself to death. Leaving the child to be taken into care. No previous convictions, although they had been cautioned for a public order offence in their teens. *How did they not see it?*

Maggie and Mark headed to the address. Kat was waiting for the search warrant to be signed off and would let them know as soon as it was available.

Given the nature of this individual's job, they knew that the working hours could be early mornings and late nights but were pleased to see a car out front when they arrived.

It was still fairly dark, and the streets were quiet. Maggie signalled for Mark to go around the back and make sure there were no access points for escape. Maggie knocked on the door – three fast, hard knocks.

She waited.

Nothing.

Just as she was about to knock again, the hall light came on. The occupant opened the door with a look of surprise, but also relief.

'I wondered how long it would take you to figure things out.'

'Shell Baker, I'm arresting you on suspicion of the murder of Robert Millard and Michael O'Dowd—'

Maggie was so busy cautioning Shell she failed to see her reach into her pocket and pull out the Stanley knife. Shell backed away from the door and into the hallway, holding out her wrist.

'Ms. Baker … Shell … put the knife down. It's over. You don't want to hurt yourself.' Maggie stepped after her down the hallway, her hands raised, palms up. 'Don't give those men the satisfaction—'

'I did what I had to do. I don't need to do it anymore.' Shell backed into the living room. 'It really is over – over for me.'

Maggie stood across the living room from her, her hands still raised, and continued to try and talk her down. Shell's eyes danced around the room as she held the knife against her wrist. Maggie edged closer and just when it looked like Maggie had turned the situation around and Shell was about to hand the knife over, Shell sliced her wrist deeply with a sudden movement and screamed. Blood filled the room and Maggie ran forward. Shell collapsed to the floor.

'Oh, my god.' Maggie raised Shell's arm above her head to try and stem the flow of blood. It was everywhere. 'Mark! MARK! Call an ambulance, quickly.'

Mark raced into the room and immediately called for assistance.

Maggie could see Shell's lips moving and bent down. Shell whispered in Maggie's ear, 'Everything you'll be wanting – what I used – it's in my bedroom under the floorboards. In my closet. Please don't trash my place.'

'OK Shell, we'll do our best. Now stay with me. Don't close your eyes … I've got you.'

Shell was quiet as the ambulance took her away. She would have to be interviewed by the police and knew she'd be arrested and charged. But with Patrick gone, Vicki recovering, her cousin Louise safe, and Drew not able to hurt another woman again – her anger had dissipated. She was done.

There wouldn't be a long trial. Shell would answer their questions and spend her remaining years at Her Majesty's Pleasure. That thought didn't scare her. She closed her eyes and smiled as she was driven to the hospital.

CHAPTER NINETY

After two days in the hospital Shell was released into police custody. She refused a solicitor. Sitting across from her in the interview room, Maggie shrugged and reminded Shell that if at any point she wished to stop the questioning and request the services of one, she could.

'I understand. I just want to get this over with.'

Maggie could see relief in Shell's eyes and almost felt sorry for her. *What would make someone commit such brutal acts of violence and ultimately face a life sentence?*

'Shall we start?'

'The sooner the better.'

'Present in the room are Ms Shell Baker, PC Mark Fielding, and myself – DC Maggie Jamieson. Ms Baker, can you just verbally confirm once again that you declined a solicitor?'

'Yes, I declined.'

'Ms Baker, can you also confirm that you told my colleague and myself, on arrest, that you committed the offences for which you are being questioned about now?'

'Yes.'

'Yes, what, Ms Baker?'

'Yes, I confessed to murdering Drew, Robert and Mick.' She almost spat their names out.

Maggie and Fielding looked at each other. 'Sorry, did you say Drew?'

'Yes. Didn't you know about Drew?'

'We were going to ask you about him, but now that you have cleared that up, can you tell us the circumstances surrounding each murder, please?'

Shell Baker spent eight gruelling hours recounting the details. She grew up in a house where violence was the norm, had watched her father beat her mother, and taken her fair share of beatings. She was home, hiding under the bed when her father beat her mother and then left her for dead. Her father was evil. Shell detailed her time in care homes where the abuse didn't stop. Although it didn't happen in every home, it seemed social care liked pairing her up with families that used abuse to put the fear of God in children. She'd have been better off living on the streets, but refused to let him win. Then she met Drew and thought he was her knight in shining armour. That is, until he beat her up and she packed her bags and left. She then moved away. But it seemed he followed. After hearing from Wendy what he did to his girlfriend, and not wanting him to do the same thing to others, Shell made sure he would never do it again.

Shell's annoyance flared as she explained to the officers how her anger remained deeply hidden, suppressed because she wanted to make something of herself. She didn't want her past to control her but when people she cared about – her family, close friends – fell into the same trap of violence, something inside her snapped.

She looked at Maggie. 'Someone had to do something.' The coldness in her eyes sent a tingle down Maggie's spine.

'What did you use to incapacitate the victims, Ms Baker?'

Maggie wanted to be sure that Shell wasn't covering for someone else.

'Victims? *Victims?* That's a fucking joke! The only victims were Heather, Louise and Vicki. Someone needed to protect them.'

'Ms Baker, can you tell us what you injected Robert Millard and Mick O'Dowd with? And why not Talbot?'

Shell sighed. 'My uncle's a vet. I clean his clinic and have keys to all the cabinets, including the safe. When I was younger, I used to help him. I saw him inject something into the animals to relax them before surgery. I asked him about it. He told me the name, and what it did, and I'm not sure why, but I never forgot it.'

'What was it, Ms Baker?'

'Succinylcholine.'

'And what did you do with it?'

Shell told them she'd stolen the succinylcholine and syringes from the clinic. Maggie nodded. The items including the drugs were exactly where Shell had told her they would be: under her floorboards, including the notebook from Vicki's flat which officers had failed to find. Heads would no doubt roll.

Shell had googled how much would be required to make someone collapse without killing them, but the drug would only last ten to fifteen minutes and was difficult to trace. She always had a spare syringe but, once her anger had been released, the men had died before it was required. Shell smiled when she learnt the men had actually drowned in their own blood. Shell didn't have the succinylcholine when she found out what Talbot had done to Wendy's daughter; she crept up behind him and knocked him over the head. She found the empty syringe inside his pockets and thought that if she injected air into his veins, he would die instantly. When he didn't, she slit his throat and slashed the top of his legs. She had read somewhere that there was a big vein in that part of the leg that, when cut, could cause someone to bleed out quickly. She then bashed his hands to a pulp. 'Fucking prick deserved it.'

She recounted the look on the other two men's faces as she rained kicks and punches down on them, a manic look in her eyes. With Mick the drug was wearing off so she tasered him.

'They could feel everything.' Maggie started to feel sick as she watched Shell continue to talk. 'They were helpless and knew they were going to die. And you know what?' Shell looked at both officers. 'I laughed. I fucking laughed my arse off. Those fuckers finally knew what it must have felt like for Heather, Louise and Vicki. Those pricks deserved to die.'

When asked about Patrick Quinn, Shell admitted her affair but was adamant that she didn't kill him. However, when they told her about what had happened to his wife, she stopped telling her story and went pale. After a moment, she recovered herself and stated that he probably would have ended up like the others. After her father and then Drew, she'd never allow a man to lay a finger on her again. She gripped the edge of the table, her knuckles turning white. She couldn't believe she hadn't seen through Patrick. She should have listened to what others had said, but Patrick was so charming. He blindsided her. Maggie thought Shell actually looked ashamed for the first time in the long confession – not by the murders she had committed, but by the abusive man she had almost let into her life

As Maggie was recounting the interview with Shell to the team, she noticed Mark returning to the office.

Hooper and Calleja congratulated everyone on their good work in this case and agreed that the CPS would have no issue in taking it before the court. Shell could probably get a lighter sentence, if the judge felt there were mitigating circumstances. Regardless, she'd be looking at a considerable amount of time behind bars.

Maggie listened as Hooper reminded everyone that with the Talbot, Millard and O'Dowd case closed, they couldn't be complacent. Patrick Quinn's murder remained unsolved, and they needed to tie this up quickly. Even with Shell admitting to her affair with

Patrick Quinn, the MO was different – no needle mark, no evidence that placed her at the scene. They were confident that had Shell committed the crime, she would have confessed. She had nothing more to lose. Following a brief update from her, the team agreed to meet back in the morning and go through the evidence in more detail.

CHAPTER NINETY-ONE

Lucy stared at the grey walls before her, the weeks spent in prison were taking their toll. She started rocking absentmindedly back and forth on the bed. A coping mechanism she'd developed as a child, one that carried on into her adult years whenever she was anxious or upset. The tears that were flowing confused her. She wasn't sure if she was crying for herself or grieving Patrick's death. Her emotions were all over the place and she was bottling them up. People wouldn't understand how she could cry and grieve for a man who had stolen years of her life. Lucy had been guilty of those thoughts about other abused women, so why wouldn't people think the same about her?

Patrick had been a master manipulator and even now she felt her feelings weren't within her control. Looking back, she realized that he'd been subtle initially. Isolating her from her friends and family. The more Lucy would defend them, the more Patrick would go out of his way to make her question things – were they genuine? Did they love her? Why did they act that way? More thoughts, reminders of the emotional abuse flooded her thoughts, and she picked up her journal and wrote them down.

If your parents are so great, how come they wouldn't help us when we were struggling to pay the mortgage?

That's not fair, Patrick, they didn't have the money and you know it.

Didn't they? I thought I saw them on Facebook – a holiday – only a week later. Face it, they don't give a toss about you, us, or the kids.

I thought about what Patrick was saying. You know they'd saved for that holiday for ages. It was pre-booked …

Patrick smacked his palms on the table, making me jump. I remember it so vividly. Raising his voice, he'd said, like fuck they had. Wake up, Lucy. Are you stupid? Are you really that stupid!

Lucy knew exactly why her parents didn't visit. The last time they had, Patrick had got drunk and been disrespectful, not only to Lucy but to her sister and parents. Lucy's father had warned her to be careful after that final dinner they'd attended, the one where Mel was flirting with Patrick. But Lucy didn't listen. The next day, her father had called her and warned her again. Lucy had made excuses for Patrick, but her father made it clear they wouldn't be visiting again. He had sounded so sad. Almost like he was saying goodbye forever. Patrick made her believe they were better off alone.

The grey walls were closing in on her. Lucy carried on rocking. She used to believe that if he was dead, she'd be free. The reality was different, and she now wondered if she'd ever be free. *Even in death he controlled her.*

Lucy sighed. The days in prison seemed to drag, like when you're in a hospital, and every time you look at a clock it doesn't seem to have moved at all. She did have one thing to look forward to though: seeing Rory and meeting his girlfriend. Lucy smiled and stopped rocking for a moment. They would be arriving any minute now. She had become close to Rory since the murder; they wrote to each other weekly. She felt this overwhelming need to still protect him, as if she was all he had left.

When it was time, the guard escorted her into the visiting area to wait. Lucy chose a seat as far away from the others as possible. She couldn't get used to associating herself with the other prisoners. It wasn't that Lucy felt she was better than them, she just couldn't face any questions which might lead to her getting her face smashed in. No one had discovered she was a probation officer yet, but it was only a matter of time.

Visitors were arriving, and Lucy eagerly sat up in her seat. There he was, Rory was growing up to be a handsome young man, and his girlfriend looked happy and content. She waited for them to come over to the table and for Rory to make the introductions. She hugged Rory.

'I miss you, Lucy,' Rory said shyly.

'You too, little man, or not so little anymore.' Lucy stood back and looked at him. He looked so much like his father, Lucy was taken aback momentarily. 'And who's this then?' she turned to the young woman who clung to Rory's hand.

'Lucy – this is Emma. Emma Shand.' He let go of her hand and Lucy went over to hug her. Lucy didn't know if she was imagining things, but she thought she heard the young girl wince. Lucy stepped back.

'Are you OK?' Emma looked up at Rory and Lucy thought she saw a familiar glint in Rory's eye.

Turning back to Lucy, Emma replied, 'Oh yeah. I just slipped over the other day. A little sore still.' She smiled weakly. 'Really nice to meet you. Rory has told me all about you and what happened.' Lucy looked at Rory who just shrugged his shoulders.

'We don't have much time and I want to hear all about what you've been up to. Please, sit down.' Lucy pointed to the chairs across from her.

There was a strange vibe in the air. After a slightly uncomfortable conversation, Lucy noticed that the hour was coming to an end. She asked Rory to tell her all about his plans. He talked about attending college, moving into his own flat when he could, and how he was using the money that Lucy set up with her wages to help him. Despite the charge, she had only been suspended pending investigation, so she ensured that her wages, once the bills and mortgage had been paid, would go to Siobhan and Rory. She smiled.

'I'm so proud of you, Rory. Do you see much of Siobhan?' Lucy worried about Siobhan every day. Once she was sentenced for Patrick's murder, the special guardianship would be officially revoked, and the social worker informed her that Siobhan's grandparents would be granted a residency order for her. Lucy felt a tear escape her eye.

'Hey, don't cry. Siobhan's doing great! I still see her as much as I can. She is still slightly angry with you, but I tell her every time I see her that what happened wasn't your fault. She just doesn't understand. Not yet. But she will.'

Lucy squeezed Rory's hand.

'Thank you.'

'After everything you've done for me, it's the least I can do.'

Lucy's eyes widened. Looking at Emma, she whispered, 'Rory, you can't say *anything*. Never. Do you understand?'

Rory had a funny look on his face. He didn't respond, but instead turned to Emma and then back to Lucy. 'Just going to get something from the vending machine. Long journey back. Two secs.'

That's odd.

Lucy reached out to touch Emma's arm to thank her for coming, but Emma snatched it back.

'What's wrong? Do you need to go to the doctor and have your arm checked? Maybe you fractured something when you fell?'

Emma turned red and shook her head. She looked over her shoulder and appeared to shrink into her seat. Suddenly things became clear to Lucy.

'No … no … No!'

Rory was making his way back to the table.

318

'You can't stay with him, Emma. You need to leave. Please, tell me you will, or all this will have been for nothing!'

Fear overcame Emma and she whispered hurriedly, 'I can't. He'll kill me …'

Rory arrived at the table and Lucy grabbed his arm. 'Please, Rory: tell me it's not true. Please!'

He looked at Emma sternly.

'Time to go. Lucy, let go of me.'

Lucy held his arm. He stared straight at her. She definitely recognized that look. It was Patrick's.

'We have to go now, Lucy. Let go of my arm.' He pulled away sharply.

Lucy staggered. She put her hands over her eyes and fell to her knees. She was shaking uncontrollably, and felt a shiver down her spine.

Lucy heard him say as he walked away, '… like father, like son I guess …'

CHAPTER NINETY-TWO

Outside, Rory gave Emma a nervous smile. He wasn't sure why he said that to Lucy. Even if she did change her mind, he doubted anyone would believe that he killed his own father.

A tinge of guilt coursed through him and his smile faded. On the surface of it, he had no reason to kill him; he hadn't known his father long, almost a year. What motive could he possibly have? He began to feel a bit more confident. *It'll be OK.*

Rory knew he was nothing like his father. He'd listened to Patrick belittle Lucy. Had flashbacks to his childhood, hearing those same things said to his own mother. No four-year-old should hear that. He must have pushed the memories into his subconscious, but meeting his father made him relive them all on a daily basis. He should've spoken to someone.

After seeing Lucy limp up the stairs, he knew he couldn't let his dad get away with it. His mother never deserved what happened to her and Lucy didn't either. He wouldn't let his sister fall into the hands of abusive men, and he'd be damned if he'd let Patrick scare his sister any longer. Lucy thought she was hiding it from Rory and Siobhan, but they knew … they always knew.

He looked over at Emma and squeezed her hand. She smiled

at him warily and that's when it dawned on him. 'I'm not like him you know …'

'Who?'

'My dad. I'm not like him.'

Emma couldn't meet his eye.

'What happened, your arm – that was an accident. I didn't mean it. You know I love you, right?'

'I know.' She looked away again.

Rory stopped walking and turned Emma to face him. 'Look me in the eyes. Please?' She did. It was then that Rory saw it: the fear. She was scared of him. *What have I done? What am I becoming?*

'I'm sorry … I'm so, sorry.'

She remained quiet. And in the silence, Rory knew he needed to get help. He thought that once his dad was gone, everything would be OK. It wasn't though. He couldn't let Lucy take the blame for his actions. It would mean his life would be over – but maybe he'd save someone else from suffering the way his mother did.

The way Lucy did.

He couldn't believe he'd even let it get this far.

'I need to do something, Emma. You'll see.'

CHAPTER NINETY-THREE

When Maggie was called down to the front office, she wasn't expecting to see Rory standing there. He nibbled at his bottom lip as he shifted nervously from one foot to the other.

'Hi, Rory. It's been awhile. How are you?'

'DC Jamieson, I need to speak with you.'

'I'm kind of busy. Is it about Lucy? I can meet you at the café across the road around oneish, if that helps?'

'No. I have to speak to you *now*. I need to get this off my chest. Lucy can't go to prison for something she didn't do.'

That got Maggie's attention. 'What do you mean, Rory? Are you saying Lucy didn't kill Patrick? How do you know this? Did you see who did?'

'Yes. I know who killed him.' Rory stared at his hands.

'Right, let's go somewhere more private, OK?'

Rory followed Maggie to an interview room. He sat down and placed his hands on the table. Before Maggie could say anything, Rory blurted out, 'It was me. Lucy didn't kill my dad, I did. She was protecting me. That's why she's saying she doesn't remember. She knows it was me.'

Maggie shook her head in disbelief. 'Hang on, Rory. Are you confessing to the murder of your father?' For once, Maggie was at a loss for words. 'Rory, you do realize that you've confessed to murdering your father, right?'

Rory's hands covered his face, preventing Maggie from hearing what he mumbled. Gently moving his hands away, she repeated the question.

'Yes. I did it.'

'OK, Rory. I'm going to have to stop you there and speak to my boss, OK?' Maggie cautioned Rory and called in one of her colleagues to sit with him while she went to speak to DS Hooper.

She ran into his room and slammed the door behind her. He looked up in surprise.

'Holy shit, guv. You are not going to believe what has just happened.' Maggie relayed her conversation with Rory to her boss as he stared at her in disbelief.

'What the hell? Has he been cautioned? How old is he? Shit, we have the wrong person in prison.'

'Hang on, guv. This is not on us. Lucy practically confessed. It was the CPS's decision to follow through. Lucy was obviously protecting Rory. Maybe she doesn't even know; she was beaten pretty badly that day and still can't recollect a lot of the information from that night. I've cautioned Rory, but he'd already confessed. We'll need to call his mother, he might want her as his appropriate adult. Otherwise I'll contact the Youth Offending Team and see if they can send someone over. Seems Dr Moloney was right all along.'

'What was I right about?' Dr Moloney stood in the doorway waiting for her colleagues to answer.

Hooper and Maggie looked at one another and then at Dr Moloney. Maggie waited.

The room remained quiet.

'Well? Is either one of you going to share the information, or do I need to call in a psychic detective to solve this mystery?'

DS Hooper looked at Maggie, shrugged his shoulders, and

turned away. She was surprised he was going to allow her to share the news.

'Lucy didn't kill Patrick Quinn after all—'

'I bloody knew it!' Dr Moloney grinned and slapped her hand on the door. She came in and sat down. Maggie smiled too, and shared the rest of the details.

'Rory Quinn has come in and confessed to murdering Patrick.'

'Oh, my god, no … He's only a child! What's he said?'

'We haven't questioned him properly yet. He basically told me he killed Patrick, but this was before he was cautioned. I couldn't stop him, it just came pouring out. I needed to tell the guv first and we need to call his mother. He's only fourteen or fifteen.'

'I can be the appropriate adult. I've done the training.'

'Sorry, Kate. In these circumstances, you can't. Not only are you involved in this investigation, you're employed by the police.'

'Ah, OK. I'd not realized that.'

'Kate, can you do me a favour though and go and check on him? Tell him we're contacting his mother and the duty solicitor. I left him in Interview Room Three with an officer.'

'Will do. Anything else?'

Hooper butted in, 'No, that will be all for now. You should've been a police officer; you knew it wasn't Lucy all along.'

Dr Moloney did a small fist pump in the air and walked out of the room. Maggie could tell Kate had mixed feelings though – a fifteen-year-old boy was now facing the possibility of a life sentence. Maggie sighed.

She dreaded having to call Rory's mother.

'Do you want me to do it?'

'Thanks for the offer, guv – but I'd like to follow this through.'

'Fine. I'll get PC Reynolds to contact the appropriate adult and inform the duty solicitor.'

'Thanks.'

Maggie left Hooper in his office. She went back to her desk

and picked up the phone; she dialled the number Rory had given her when he first came in.

'Hello?'

'Hello. Is that Amy Swift?'

'Yes. Who's this?'

'This is DC Maggie Jamieson. I'm calling from Markston Police Station. We have your son here—'

'Rory? You have Rory? Oh, my god, is everything OK? Has something happened to him?'

Rory's mother's voice broke. Maggie took a deep breath. 'Rory is here at the station. He's not physically hurt. I'd rather you get here as soon as possible, as I can't really discuss anything over the phone.'

Maggie heard the dial tone. *Guess she's on her way.* Walking back into the open-plan office, she bumped into Kat.

'Maggie. Is it true? Has a bloody kid just confessed to killing Patrick Quinn?' Kat's face was lit up and she was clutching a cigarette in one hand and a lighter in the other.

'Yes, sadly it's true, Kat. Patrick's son is currently awaiting to be interviewed downstairs. Go and have your fag. I'll fill you in later.'

'Poor kid. His life is over. Not that I'm condoning what he did, but his father was a dick—'

'That's enough, Kat.' Maggie paused. 'Before you go, can you contact social services and see if Rory is known to them? I'm going to head back down to the custody suite and see if the duty solicitor or appropriate adult has arrived yet.'

'Sure thing, Maggie.'

This was the part of her job that Maggie didn't enjoy so much. Rory was probably just a messed-up kid. From what she remembered about the case, he'd only been in contact with his dad within the last year. She shook her head in dismay and stared out of the grubby window into the drizzly streets below. Taking a deep breath, she headed down to start the process of interviewing a child for murder.

CHAPTER NINETY-FOUR

Maggie returned to Interview Room Three with a heavy heart. Looking around at the faces before her, a sadness could be felt. She plonked herself down with a sigh in the chair opposite Rory, his mother, and Dr Moloney.

Maggie took Rory through the preliminaries; he looked on the verge of tears and was struggling to get his words out. Maggie glanced at his mother. She'd been crying, her eyes red-rimmed, and her nose raw from blowing into the wet, shrivelled tissue that lay limply on the interview room table. Rory was formally cautioned and the task of taking his statement began. Maggie asked Rory to start from the beginning and he leant back in his chair and began to talk.

'How far back do you want me to start from?'

'The day of the murder. What were you feeling that day?'

'I was OK to start off with. I'd made plans to go and see my dad as I knew that Siobhan was going to her grandparents.'

'Who's Siobhan?'

'My stepsister.' Rory looked at his mother to see if that was the correct term.

'Siobhan's his half-sister, actually. Patrick is ... was, her father too.'

326

'OK, Rory. Go on.'

'Lucy had given me a key to the house. Told me it was my home too, so when I got there, I let myself in. No one was downstairs.' A shadow fell over Rory's face as he talked and his hands fidgeted constantly on his lap. 'I shouted from the landing but there was no answer.'

'What did you do?'

'I took off my muddy shoes, didn't want to dirty the floors. I was going to sit in the living room and wait. Dad's car was outside in the drive, so I thought maybe he'd just walked up to the shops.' Rory swallowed. 'Then I heard a weird noise upstairs.'

'What kind of noise?'

'It sounded like water dripping, and then a thump. Like someone had slipped in the bath.' His mother sobbed but Rory carried on. 'I listened a bit, but it was quiet again. About ten minutes later, dad still wasn't back, so I went upstairs. Maybe he was asleep. He sometimes was.' A gloomy look crept over Rory's face again, and Maggie glanced over at Dr Moloney.

'What happened when you went upstairs?' Maggie could feel her heart racing. Normally she didn't prompt people she was interviewing, but she could see that Rory was struggling.

'When I got to the landing, I heard this weird, low groan from my dad's bedroom. I tiptoed to the door and pushed it open. Lucy was on the floor. I could hardly … oh it was awful … her face was bloody.' Rory ran a hand across his face. 'I didn't know what to do. I didn't want to touch her in case I hurt her or in case she was … dying or something.' Rory began to cry, and his mother rubbed his back as tears flowed down her face. She nodded as if she knew exactly what Rory was talking about.

'I went to the bathroom and saw my dad in the tub. There was an open can of beer spilled on the floor and he was passed out … drunk … again.' He choked back his anger. 'I saw the cuts on his knuckles. I got mad, I just felt so … so … pissed off.' He spat the words out. 'Lucy was always kind to me. Mum left my dad because he did bad things.' He glanced at his mum. 'I didn't believe her at first. But when I saw Lucy crumpled on the floor, the blood ... so much blood ... I thought of my mum ... and I just snapped.'

'Do you want to take a moment?'

Rory sniffed. 'I'm OK.' A strange cold glint appeared in his eyes. 'It was like I was a robot or something. I went down to the kitchen and put on the rubber gloves that Lucy had left near the sink. I grabbed a knife from the wooden block on the counter and went back upstairs. Deep down I guess I always knew my dad was an arsehole.'

'What do you mean by that, Rory?'

'I saw him with another woman. They kissed. I also checked his phone once when he was passed out drunk. He'd obviously forgot to delete a message from someone named "Steve". It said they loved him, but it was signed "Shell", with a kiss by the name. I knew he was cheating on Lucy and I didn't say anything at first. Another woman for him to beat I guess.' He suppressed a shudder. 'But then I knew I had to tell Lucy. It wasn't fair, and I thought maybe then, if she knew, she'd leave him. My dad made me so angry sometimes. But I was afraid I was turning into him ... and that made me even angrier.'

'What happened in the bathroom?'

'I stood over him with the knife in my hand. Wasn't sure what I was going to do. I wanted to scare him. He was still passed out, so I nudged him. He didn't move. I kicked his arm and he sort of woke up. This weird glazed look in his eyes.' Rory stared at the wall as if he was watching the scene again. 'He saw the knife in my hand. He asked me what I was doing. Or at least I think that's what he said; his words were slurred. I told him he had to stop hurting Lucy. And do you know what he did?' Rory shut his eyes and paused. 'He laughed at me. I lost it then. I stabbed him right in the chest.' Rory put his hands over his eyes, and his mother gasped.

'You're doing great, Rory. We're nearly finished here. Did you get him another drink before you stabbed him?' Maggie asked Rory if he'd given his father anymore of the medication.

Rory shook his head. 'Lucy was always warning him to be careful with his medication. He sometimes forgot if he'd taken them and double dosed. I don't think you're supposed to mix them with alcohol either.'

Maggie nodded. She'd have to speak with the pathologist and see whether the high levels could be down to Patrick accidently overdosing. Not that it mattered. Cause of death was the knife wound to the chest.

'Can you tell me what you did after you stabbed your father?'

He sniffed and reached for a tissue, wiping his nose. 'I stared at him for a bit. He didn't move. I thought he might try to grab me or something. But he just lay there. I think it hit me then. What I'd done. I stared at the knife in his chest and then I went and looked in on Lucy, still lying on the floor. She raised her head, and I thought I saw her eyes flutter … I closed the door and left. Dumped the gloves in the bin by the shops and went home. Never thought Lucy would end up in prison. I mean, she didn't do it.'

'Why do you think Lucy confessed, Rory?'

'I dunno. I think at first she thought she did it … I told her it was me, though.'

'You did?' Maggie's eyes widened.

'When we first spoke on the phone, not long after she was put in prison. She said she didn't want to see me ruin my life. Said she would have probably killed him or ended up dead herself anyway – she made me promise to keep it a secret.'

'OK. If Lucy was going to take the blame, why are you here now?'

'I did something bad.'

'Yes, we know. You murdered your father.'

'No. Something else. I hurt my girlfriend.' Rory looked broken

329

as he wiped a tear from his eyes. 'I was afraid I was turning into my father and I don't want to. I took my girlfriend with me to visit Lucy, and she knew. Lucy knew. And do you know what I said as I left?' Rory began to cry uncontrollably.

'What did you say?'

'I looked at Lucy …' Rory struggled to get his words out. He gulped, '"like father, like son".' The last words were said through gritted teeth.

'Oh God. Rory … no …' his mother turned away.

'I'm sorry. I need help. I don't want to hurt the people I love. That's why I knew I had to confess.'

Rory was charged with the murder of his father and the interview ended. Maggie left the room with Dr Moloney, while Rory stayed and spoke to his solicitor. He grabbed his mother in a tight hug, sobbing goodbye. He'd be remanded into custody later that day.

Dr Moloney stopped just outside the door. 'How do you do it, Maggie?'

'Do what?'

'How do you deal with a child coming in and saying all that? My heart was breaking.'

'Mine too … But it's all part of the job. Hopefully Rory will get the help he needs. But even if he doesn't that's one less woman … for the time being … who will not be a victim.'

The prospect of returning to her old team was already on Maggie's mind; this case had played havoc with her emotions. All murders were difficult, but there was something about domestic abuse cases that just got to her. So many people affected. So many hurt. Maybe Rutherford knew that when she suggested the secondment. She had wanted her to forget about the last case she worked on. Now she wished that she could go back. This case, working so close with Dr Moloney and the feelings that brought about. Her brother coming to live with her. She rubbed her temples to relive the pressure she was feeling. Then she remembered why she agreed to the secondment – Raven, and she shook her head.

Be careful what you wish for, Maggie.

CHAPTER NINETY-FIVE

Lucy closed her eyes and took in the sound of the birds singing outside the cell window. If she shut the world out, she almost forgot where she was. Almost. A key turned in the lock and brought her back to reality.

'Gather your things, Lucy – looks like you're being released today.' The guard smiled.

'What?' Lucy thought she must be dreaming. She pinched herself just to make sure.

'This is no dream, Lucy. CPS have dropped the charges. Someone else has been arrested. Get your stuff.'

She didn't have to be asked twice. In a daze, she quickly gathered up what she could, the rest she left for anyone who wanted it. The less she took, the less she'd be reminded of the experience. The prison officer directed her to the reception, where an offender manager explained that she was being released. *Someone else has confessed to the crime.* Lucy's mind was in overdrive, a million questions, but she signed papers without reading them. All she wanted was to be on the other side of those prison gates.

As she approached them, she saw Maggie and Kat. Both gave

her a little wave. She had to stand and wait while the prison officer unlocked the gated door to her freedom. Maggie greeted her, 'Hi, Lucy. I bet you're confused.'

'Yes,' she said meekly, still stunned. She wanted to be happy, but couldn't take in what had happened. Expected it to be all taken away. The realization that Rory had probably confessed weighed heavily on her mind, and wiped away any of the happiness that freedom brought with it.

'We're here to take you to the station.'

'What?' Lucy looked at the door behind her. 'Why did they let me go if you're just going to arrest me again?' Fear crossed her face.

'Whoa, Lucy. Calm down. Let Maggie finish,' Kat interjected.

'Get in the car, Lucy, and we'll explain everything.'

Lucy reluctantly entered the police car. She fidgeted with her shirt as she listened to Maggie explain what had happened: although Rory had confessed to the murder, Lucy was being bailed and may be charged with perverting the course of justice.

Maggie probably should have cautioned Lucy first and not explained anything until they arrived at the station, but she could see the fear in Lucy's eyes and thought that she'd suffered enough. Her now short hair accentuated her thin frame. She was not the same woman they had known. Prison changed Lucy, physically and mentally.

'Why are you telling me all this?' Maggie had momentarily forgotten they were dealing with someone who had a criminal justice background. All she saw was a vulnerable woman who needed to be reassured that everything was going to be all right. Lucy had been a victim long enough.

'You're right, I shouldn't be telling you any of this – but you deserve to know. We just want you to know that you're safe.'

Lucy started to cry, tears falling onto her lap in the car. She cried for herself. She cried even more for Rory and what he'd now be facing. Her shoulders shook uncontrollably.

It was then that they heard a muffled sentence from Lucy's lips ... 'Thank you ...' and all concerns were gone.

EPILOGUE

Lucy stood before the crowd of men and women, mentally preparing herself. Eight months had gone by since her release, in which time she'd started a new job. Part-time work with probation via an agency. She'd changed back to her maiden name permanently, and was in the process of selling the house that she'd shared with Patrick and his daughter. In order to move on with her future, she had to let go of the past.

Rory had been arrested and charged with Patrick's murder. He was still on remand, but his confession would go in his favour in terms of reducing his sentence – mitigating circumstances, his solicitor had said. The judge would look favourably on this. Her heart broke for Rory; it's easy to learn behaviour, a lot harder to unlearn it. Her hope was that he'd get the help he needed. He was still young enough to change, deal with his anger – Patrick had not been. The cycle of abuse wasn't one she wished to be passed on.

Lucy had been facing charges of perverting the course of justice, but in the end, with all the media attention her case had brought following her release, the CPS decided that the time served on remand was enough. Despite knowing about the affair, Lucy had visited Shell, who had been convicted of the three murders, in prison after her own release. Shell was remorseful about the affair, but Lucy could understand how easily she too had fallen under Patrick's spell. Lucy forgave her, but they would never be friends.

Siobhan was placed in the custody of her maternal grandparents. Her mother, Becky, was still unfit to care for her. Alcohol remained a crutch and a string of bad relationships would place the child at continued risk. Lucy felt a sadness for Becky and hoped that one day she'd find the strength to deal with her issues; Siobhan would need her. Every child needs their mother. With the time spent in prison, Lucy had lost contact with Siobhan and wondered if she ever thought about her. Whether she could ever forgive her. No matter what Patrick had done, Lucy understood that Siobhan loved him.

Lucy walked along the row of seats, scanning the faces. She saw Sarah's face in the crowd. Next to her sat Mark – he still worked in the DAHU – but was helping her set up the women's refuge. She waved. She suspected that Mark fancied her, but wasn't ready to let another man into her life.

As she took the podium, the room erupted in applause and her face reddened. She still struggled, after years of being called useless, to accept a compliment.

'Ladies and gentlemen, thank you all for joining us here today. We're thrilled to have Lucy Sherwood with us to talk about her experience, to share with you her journey, and to offer her hand of support for those of you who still need it …'

Lucy listened to the applause as she approached the microphone. It was a surreal experience.

'Good morning, everyone. As Ms Reilly has said, my name is Lucy Sherwood and I'm here to talk to you about my experience and the opening of the SAFE Refuge – a home where both men and women can find Strength, Acceptance, Freedom, and Empowerment during and after their experience of domestic abuse … a place where individuals won't be judged for their choices, won't be forced into decisions they're not ready to make.

Where people like you and I can come together, support one another, and be there for when you're ready to take that step.'

Lucy spent an hour explaining about her hopes for the refuge and the domestic abuse that ended with her husband's murder being the ultimate cause of her freedom. She admitted that she couldn't say for definite whether she'd still be in that relationship had Patrick not been killed. She didn't want to lie to them. At the time of Patrick's murder, Lucy told the crowd that she believed she'd reached the point where she wanted to be free.

In prison, with encouragement from Dr Moloney, Lucy had written a journal which she later self-published. Lucy read a chapter from her novel to end the conference.

'"No one can tell you how to feel, what to do, or when it's time to leave. As a survivor of domestic abuse, I lived in a world where I had to be two people: strong, assertive, confident – the professional – when deep inside I was ashamed, scared and depressed. I believed that I was staying for the right reasons. To protect Patrick's daughter and son from their dad – and in Siobhan's case, her mother too. I wanted to show them a positive role model, to guide them through life, to build them up.

'"What I showed them was that it was not OK to hurt someone you love – to belittle them, to break down their self-worth, and to make them feel unwanted."'

Lucy went on to explain she was under no illusion that she was still on her journey of survival. There was no time limit and healing would come as and when she felt in control of her life again.

She chose to believe that one day she'd trust a man, have a positive, healthy, loving relationship that didn't revolve around persistent and systematic power and control over her.

Without even knowing it, her hand reached up and touched the scar over her eyebrow. She winced. Not because of any physical pain. Just because of what that scar symbolized.

Lucy knew that many of the faces before her would leave

337

their abusive partners only to find themselves in the arms of another abuser. It's what happens. Love isn't meant to hurt – but for some, abuse is a small sacrifice to avoid loneliness, to fill a need, to ensure financial security, to save them from what they deem is something worse. Judging a person for a decision they make is not going to make them understand. The person must want to get out of that situation themselves, to feel safe. They have to know someone understands their decisions – Lucy would be that someone. She lived it. She survived it.

Maggie smiled as she listened to Lucy's talk. It wasn't very often she was witness to something good coming out of something so horrible. Her phone vibrated and she pulled it out. DI Rutherford. Maggie figured she'd call back or leave a message, so she hit reject. Within seconds a text came through and a voicemail message. Maggie read the text and swallowed. A cold feeling had settled in her stomach.

Listen to my message. Call me back immediately.

Maggie stood up and made her way out of the row, trying her best not to step on people's toes. She excused herself from the room and listened to the message from her old boss.

'*Your secondment is over at the DAHU. Raven has appealed his sentence, claimed he's innocent. Timely I'd say as there has been another murder. Either a copycat or the real killer picking up where they left off. Get your arse in here.*'

Maggie's hand began to shake, and she nearly dropped her phone. She'd thought the nightmares were over – but they may be only just beginning.

ACKNOWLEDGEMENTS

I have so many wonderful people to thank, so please forgive me if this starts sounding like an award speech, and apologies if I miss anyone out – it is not intentional, my brain is just so overwhelmed.

I'd like to thank my family and friends both near and afar, for the tremendous support they have given me since learning I was writing a book.

A massive thanks to Finn Cotton, editor extraordinaire for his patience, guidance and belief in me as a writer and to the Killer Reads team who have been fantastic since this crazy journey began.

A special thanks to the absolutely phenomenal Graham Smith and Michael J. Malone – for reading my prologue at Crime & Publishment in 2017 and giving me the encouragement, inspiration and kick up the backside to write what is now *Dead Inside*. And to the C&P writing gang who are just the most magnificent people – generous with their time and advice. And I also have to mention Karen Sullivan for the 'red card' that gave me the confidence to submit to publishers.

Another special thanks to my beta readers – WOW – you all

blew me away with your feedback. So thank you to Joseph Calleja, Sarah Hardy, Claire Knight, Shell Baker, Kate Moloney, Kat Everett, Lorraine Rugman, Vicki Wilkinson, Sharon Bairden and Abbie Rutherford for everything … particularly your names! And for the MOST part, your characters are nothing like you in real life … ha ha!

A heart-felt THANK YOU to the authors who also encouraged me to write, who read and gave me feedback/quotes – you have no idea how much it meant to me – Angela Marsons, Martina Cole, Nic Parker, Graham Smith, Mel Comley, Emma Kennedy, Casey Kelleher, Mel Sherratt, and Caroline Mitchell – a thousand #thankyous would never be enough.

To the crime writing community – do you know how SUPERB you are? I wish I could name each and every one of you – your kind words, encouragement, inspiration and overwhelming support has really touched me. Don't ever change.

To my amazing blogger friends, I want to name you all, but I can't – so if you are reading this and thinking 'is she talking about me?' the answer is – *Hell yeah, I am!* Love you all. Special mention to the #blogsquad, Kim Nash, Anne Cater, Rachel Gilbey, and JB Johnston for letting me be me, and to Emma Mitchell for editing and getting me submission-ready. You all make me smile each and every day!

A massive thanks to the Bookouture team (both the authors and my colleagues), especially Abi Fenton (who casually introduced me to my editor at Harrogate and nudged me to pitch my book – it worked!), Peta Nightingale/Oliver Rhodes for all the amazing advice and again, Kim Nash – because she is just outstanding! Adore you Batman!

Of course, I have to mention Tamworth Probation/Tamworth IOM; Stafford IOM; and all my remarkable ex-colleagues within the Police and Probation Service – both the public and private sectors. Your dedication and professionalism astound me – I may have been 'paroled' after eighteen years of service, but I think about your truly fantastic work all the time – and all the stories I now have to tell!

Finally, I just want to thank everyone who takes the time to read this book; without you, there would be no reason to write.

A NOTE FROM NOELLE

I wanted to include a brief note to explain a few things within this book. The book is set in Staffordshire; however, I have used some literary licence by making up names of towns/places to fit with the story.

Having been a senior/probation officer for eighteen years, I left in 2017. There are some references to the changes that were implemented in 2015, but I went all nostalgic and some of the work/terms refer to a time when Probation was all one service. It made things a lot less complicated. Any errors to police procedure/probation are purely my own or intentional to move the story forward.

Finally, I have extensive knowledge and experience of domestic abuse – both personally and from a professional point of view. I tried to portray this as realistically as possible, but everyone's experience will be different.

A NOTE FROM NOELLE